WITHDRAWN

Immigrant, Montana

Immigrant, Montana

Amitava Kumar

ALFRED A. KNOPF   NEW YORK   2018

Library of Congress Cataloging-in-Publication Data

Names: Kumar, Amitava, [date] author.
Title: Immigrant, Montana : a novel / Amitava Kumar.
Description: First edition. | New York : Alfred A. Knopf, 2018.
Identifiers: LCCN 2017054030 (print) | LCCN 2017050682 (ebook) |
ISBN 9780525520757 (hardcover) | ISBN 9780525520764 (ebook) |
Subjects: LCSH: East Indians—United States—Fiction. | College
students—Fiction. | Self-realization—Fiction. | Young men—Fiction. |
Immigrants—Fiction. | BISAC: FICTION / Literary. | FICTION / Coming of
Age. | FICTION / Cultural Heritage. | GSAFD: Bildungsromans.
Classification: LCC PR9499.4.K8618 (print) |
LCC PR9499.4.K8618 I47 2018 (ebook) | DDC 824/.92—dc23
LC record available at https://lccn.loc.gov/2017054030

Jacket design by Janet Hansen

Manufactured in the United States of America
First Alfred A. Knopf Edition

For Teju

The Revolution smells of sexual organs.

—BORIS PILNYAK, "Ivan and Maria"

Oh, he *loves* her: just as the English loved India and Africa and Ireland; it is the love that is the problem, people treat their lovers badly.

—ZADIE SMITH, *White Teeth*

Contents

Part I

Jennifer

Researchers found that people are attracted to people who are attracted to them. This from a clipping pasted in a notebook kept while writing this book.

I was a new immigrant, eager to shine, and if self-abuse were to be omitted from the reckoning, pure of body and heart. The letters I sent my parents in India were full of enthusiasm for the marvels of my new life. To those who welcomed me to America, I wanted to say, without even being asked, that *E.T.* ought to have won the Oscar over *Gandhi*. I had found the latter insufficiently authentic but more crucially I felt insufficiently authentic myself. Not so much fake as insubstantial. I understood that I needed a suitable narrative to present to the people I was meeting. There was only contempt in my heart for my fellow Indian students who repeated stories about trying to educate ignorant Americans in barbershops who had asked how come they spoke such good English or if they belonged to tribes or grew up among tigers. The nostalgia I had come to treasure was a hypertrophied sense of the past as a place, a place with street signs and a figure atop a staircase that I recognized. This desire had nothing to do with the kinds of claims to civilizational superiority that make men demolish places of worship or want to bomb cities into oblivion. I knew this and yet I was uncertain about my story. I lacked calm self-knowledge. If a woman spoke to me, particularly if she was attractive, I grew excited and talked too much.

I'm talking of what happened more than two decades ago; my first years here and my first loves. But the reality of my becoming who I am now, this *evolution,* as it were, goes back in time to the monkeys that surrounded me as an infant. This is my own, personal *Origin of Species.* The red-bottomed monkeys of my childhood would leave the branches of the big tamarind tree and peel the oranges left unattended on the balcony of Lotan Mamaji's house. This was in Ara, in eastern India, in the late sixties. A war with Pakistan was over and another loomed in the future. Prime Minister Nehru had been dead only a few years. In the language of the history books, *the nation was in turmoil.*

Lotan Mamaji was my mother's younger brother. A giant of a man, immense and bearded, paan tucked under one dark cheek like a secret that he didn't want to share. One winter morning, while everyone on the balcony sat listening to the radio, following the cricket commentary from Eden Gardens, a monkey stole into Mamaji's room. He climbed on the huge white bed and finding Mamaji's pistol brandished it—they say—at my cousin who was born two months after me and still in her crib. No one moved. Then, turning the pistol around, the primate mind prompting the opposable thumb to grasp the trigger, the monkey blew his brains out. He was a medium-size young male. Bits of flesh, bone, hair, and gray matter had to be cleaned from the pictures of the long-dead family patriarchs hanging on the wall.

There were so many lies repeated in the family, so many half secrets, I don't know why I never asked anyone if the monkey story was true. For a long time, it had been lodged in my mind as a baptismal tale that taught me the nature of fear, or maybe provided a lesson about fate. But then the past lost its authority and the meaning of the story changed. I had by then come out of my teen years. The main questions now were about the fiction of the past, the idea I had of myself as a person, and what it meant for me to become a writer.

For so many years, the idea of writing has meant recognizing and even addressing a division in my life: the gap between India, the land of my birth, and the United States, where I arrived as a young adult. If and when I imagine an audience for my writing, it is also a divided one. But the two places are connected, not only by those histories that cultural organizations celebrate through endlessly dull annual gatherings but by millions of individual yearnings, all those stories of consummated or thwarted desire.

Consider the monkeys in Ara, the *Rhesus macaques*. They were not just visitors to my maternal uncle's home. They have a place in my imagination because they too were unheralded immigrants in America. A few years ago, I read in a newspaper report that the problem Delhi residents were having with monkeys went back to the early years of Indian independence, when thousands from that region were sent to America for scientific purposes. As many as twenty to fifty thousand monkeys were exported each year. A newly independent India was in need of foreign exchange. The Americans needed middle-aged male monkeys for their experiments. The result of the selective trapping, according to a primatologist interviewed for the report, was the disruption of the ecological balance. The disruption took place because the family unit was broken and the monkey groups entered a process of division that the primatologist termed *chaotic fission*.

But let's take a step back from the political and enter the riskier domain of the personal. I want to focus on why monkeys came to mind when I started work on this book. I claim kinship with the monkeys of my childhood because of what I read in a magazine in 2010: *Rhesus macaques, who normally are not self-aware, will, following brain surgery, examine their genitals in a mirror. Similar evidence of self-awareness was previously limited to higher primates, dolphins, magpies, and an elephant named Happy* ("Findings," *Harper's Magazine*, December 2010, p. 84).

=====

In America, the land of the free and home of the brave, it was possible, figuratively speaking, to discuss genitalia in public.* I discovered this when I turned on the radio one Tuesday night in my university apartment in Morningside Heights and heard

* Bill Clinton on President Obama's reelection: He's luckier than a dog with two dicks.

Of course, Bill Clinton deserves a footnote in any book on love. My writing notebook also has this quote in it: *I—but you know, love can mean different things, too, Mr. Bittman. I have—there are a lot of women with whom I have never had any inappropriate conduct who are friends of mine, who will say from time to time, "I love you." And I know that they don't mean anything wrong by that.*—Bill Clinton, testimony before grand jury a woman's voice. A foreign accent, except the surprise was that she was talking about sex. She sounded like Henry Kissinger. Her name was Dr. Ruth. Unlike Kissinger, she wanted us to make love, not war.

In India, the only public mentions of sex were the advertisements painted on the walls that ran beside the railway tracks. I read the ads when I traveled from Patna to Delhi for college and was filled with anxiety about what awaited me when, at last, I would experience sex. On the brick walls near the tracks, large white letters in Hindi urged you to call a phone number if you suffered from premature ejaculation or erectile dysfunction or nightly emissions. A nation of silent sufferers! Men with worried brows holding their heads in their offices during the day and, back at home, lying miserably awake beside quiet and disappointed wives in the dark.

But not in America, where Dr. Ruth was talking to you cheerfully on the airwaves. I had no accurate idea of what *epiglottis* and *guttural* really meant, but those words vibrated in my mind when I listened to Dr. Ruth. Her voice on the small black radio in the privacy of my room offering advice to the males among her audience. Even if they themselves had already climaxed, they could help their female partners achieve orgasm.

—You can just pleasure her.

I hadn't heard that word used as a verb before. I also spoke in an accented English; I wondered if Dr. Ruth's usage was correct.

—And for women out there, a man wants an orgasm. Big deal! Give him an orgasm, it takes two minutes!

Such relief. For more than one reason.

There were details about her that I discovered later. Dr. Ruth grew up in an orphanage. Her parents perished at Auschwitz. She was very short but had fought in a war. She was once a guerrilla in the Haganah, and now, in this country, she was famous for talking about masturbation and penises and vaginas on the radio. She was on her third marriage.

Listening to Dr. Ruth on the radio that Tuesday night in upper Manhattan I was transported in my mind back to a morning in Delhi earlier that year when we were enjoying three days of spring. The year I left, 1990. My friends were in my room in the college dorm. The daughter of the warden walked past the window on her way to work, her hair still hanging damp on her yellow dupatta. She was a postdoc in history and would become a lecturer soon. And then we were running to the end of the corridor to watch the warden's daughter open the little wooden gate on her way to the bus stop. Her prepossessing calm, her very indifference to the existence of gawking others, was an incitement to collective lust. She was soon gone, and still excited but also somewhat let down, the group returned to my small room with its dirty, whitewashed walls.

—There is nothing purer than the love for your landlord's daughter, said Bheem.

—No, said Santosh, after an appropriate pause. If you are looking for innocence, the purest gangajal, you have to be in love with your teacher's wife.

As if to sort out the matter, we looked at Noni, a Sikh from Patiala. He was the only one among us who wasn't a virgin.

Noni took off his turban and his long hair fell over his shoulders.

—You bastards should stop pretending. The only true love, true first love, is the love for your maidservant.

This was duly appreciated. But Noni was not done yet.

— She has to be older than you, though not by too much, and while it's not necessary for you to have fucked her, it is important that she take your hand in hers and put it on her breast.

There was the usual silence that greets the utterance of grand truth. Three of us were sprawled next to each other on the bed, our heads pillowed against the wall. Dark, oily smudges behind us indicated where other heads had pressed in the past. Then someone started laughing.

—You are a bunch of pussies, Noni said, to dismiss the laughing. When you went back home during the winter, did any one of you get laid?

He smiled and announced his own success with another question.

—Has anyone slept with a friend's mother?

—I have, Bheem said. He had light-colored eyes. He was smiling a soft, secret smile.

—Whose mother? Noni asked.

—Yours.

Noni was my Dr. Ruth before Dr. Ruth. My naïveté was the price of admission I paid for his tutorials. Noni had discovered that the medical definition of a kiss was *the anatomical juxtaposition of two orbicularis oris muscles in a state of contraction*. This made the unfamiliar even more unfamiliar. He told me that the word *fuck* was an acronym derived from *for unlawful carnal knowledge;* this terminology was itself a rewriting, Noni said, of the medieval rule to which *fuck* owed its origins, *fornication under consent of the King.* Noni was completely wrong; at that time, however, I marveled at his knowledge of sex.

Until I met Noni in Delhi, my familiarity with sex was limited to what I had learned from the censored movies screened on Saturdays in Patna. I'd be sitting with others in the dark, the air warm, the smell of sweat around me, and somewhere a cigarette being smoked. There were probably two hundred others in the theater, almost all men and most of them older than me. In the local paper the theater advertised itself as "air-cooled," but what you breathed was the effluvia of restless groins being shifted in fixed seats that had coir stuffing poking out of torn imitation-leather covers. It was no doubt cooler in the apartment in Prague where the on-screen action was taking place. A middle-aged man had unclasped the hook on the bra that an impossibly young woman was wearing. She turned to face him, her breasts milk white, with pale pink drowsy nipples. There was a cut and a jump in the film there—the duo now in an open car on an empty road, driving under leafy trees, in bright sunlight.

But a child had started crying in the audience near me.

—*Scene dikha, baccha ro raha hai,* a man shouted from a further seat, wanting us to return to the bedroom. "Show a breast. Because if you don't, the baby will cry." The rough remark, bewildering at that time, soon lost its confusing aspect: glinting like mica in a piece of granite, it sat for a while in the nostalgic narrative about my late teenage years.

Ten years later, for the benefit of a later generation, a sex advice column in *Mumbai Mirror* had become popular in India. I made this discovery during a visit to India when my laundry came back to my hotel room wrapped in newspaper.

Q. My girlfriend kissed the tip of my penis and the next day she suffered a stomachache. Could she be pregnant? Should she take some pills?

A. She must have had dinner afterward and that probably led to the stomachache. Oral sex does not cause pregnancy and she need not take any pills.

Q. I am a twenty-five-year-old man. Please tell me if regular masturbation can increase the size of one's butt.

A. Just as your nose, fingers, and tongue will not increase in size, neither will the butt.

Q. When it comes to sex, my partner allows me to use only a finger for just a few seconds. Please tell me why. Also, when I hold my bowels for too long, my testicles swell and hurt. What could be the reason for this?

The good doctor, the Sexpert, had once again exercised a grim matter-of-factness, the humor in his eyes hidden behind the thick glasses he wore in the grainy photograph.

> A. She is probably scared by your intentions—pregnancy or an infection. Why not ask her? And, do you mean "balls"? "Bowels" refers to the intestines. Why would you want to hold them? Please explain.

In 2014, *The New York Times* ran a story on the Sexpert, introducing Dr. Mahinder Watsa to the United States. Watsa's editor said the doctor had received more than forty thousand letters seeking advice. He had tried to promote sex education but many of his own colleagues said it was pornography. Dr. Watsa was the first to use words like *penis* and *vagina* in the newspapers. A reader filed an obscenity suit against the doctor, charging that the editors fabricated letters to increase readership. In response, the editor delivered a sack of unopened letters at the judge's table. *He read them over the lunch hour and dismissed the case.* Dr. Watsa recently turned ninety-one.

The Sexpert column can now be read on the Internet. There was nothing like this when I was growing up in India. At that time, if I could have written one, which letter would have been mine? The range of problems people present to the doctor is stunning but yes, this one:

> *Q. In the last semester, I failed one subject. My parents were worried and took me to an astrologer. He asked me to remove*

Not my parents, but my forebears nonetheless. Dr. Ruth and Dr. Watsa, who ushered me into a world lit with the light of new knowledge.

my pants. He said the ejaculate after masturbation is equal to 100 ml of blood, hence my weakness. I am regretting showing him my penis. Please help.

A. The astrologer is a hoax and completely ignorant of sexual matters. Masturbation is completely normal. Visit your college counselor instead to discuss your not doing well in one subject.

═══

After arriving in New York, I would have a constant conversation in my head with a judge who was asking me questions. I had been called an impostor; I was told that what I wanted was not mine. This was my true, secret life, where I was witness to a courtroom interrogation during which another me, more articulate and unafraid, delivered long, defensive soliloquies about who I was, my reasons for being here, and why I liked what I did. The imaginary judge was white; we were in a court for those accused of false pretenses and indecent acts. Standing quietly in a dock, I recalled lines that had been spoken by others. *Sisters and Brothers of America, I thank you in the name of the mother of religions, and I thank you in the name of millions and millions of Hindu people of all classes and sects,* Swami Vivekananda had said, in Chicago in 1893, at the Parliament of the World's Religions. Unlike Vivekananda, I addressed the judge from a less exalted place but I wasn't lacking in conviction. *I am telling you all this in Immigration Court, Your Honor, because I want to assert that I knew about sex, or at least discoursed about sex, prior to my arrival on these shores. I have chosen to speak in personal terms, the most intimate terms, Your Honor, because it seems to me that it is this crucial part of humanity that is denied to the immigrant. You look at a dark immigrant in that long line at JFK, the new clothes crumpled from a long flight, a ripe smell accompanying him, his eyes haunted, and you wonder whether he can speak English. It is far from your thoughts and your assumptions to ask whether he has ever spoken soft phrases filled with yearning or what hot, dirty words he utters in his wife's ear as she laughs and embraces him in bed. You look at him and think that he wants your job and not that he just wants to get laid. I offer you the truth without shame and thank you, Your Honor, in the name of the dark hordes that have nothing to declare but their desire.*

Despite such declarations, I remained as celibate as Swami Vivekananda. But I was starting up a friendship with a woman named Jennifer.

While waiting for classes to begin, I landed a job at the university bookstore. My fellowship payment wasn't going to start till a month and a half later. I had no money and I couldn't ask my parents for anything more. After the airfare had been paid for, every additional demand for a purchase had been met with a look of panic on my poor mother's face. I had overheard my father dramatically declaring to Lotan Mamaji that because my education was important they were resigned to getting by on eating bread with salt. This wasn't entirely true, and he would never have said that in front of me, but I was aware that money was scarce. The bookstore paid very little—the job was classified as "work-study" and we didn't make minimum wage—but I liked handling books. I told Jennifer, with only the slightest trace of uncertainty in my voice, that I was a poet. Jennifer had been employed there for years and was now in charge of the humanities section. She was tall and thin and she tied her long brown hair at the back in a ponytail. I guessed she was about ten years older than me but I could be wrong. I never asked her because I had been told it would be impolite. I learned that Jennifer had suffered a nervous breakdown on the night before her master's exam and quit grad school. I was told this by our Zambian co-worker, who had also dropped out. His name was Godfrey, and everyone just called him God. He had worked in the bookstore beside Jennifer for years, and they both knew all the professors, some of whom had been their teachers long ago.

—It was very tragic, very tragic, God said about Jennifer, the vivid whites of his eyes expanding with a fine appreciation of horror.

He said Jennifer's boyfriend used to bartend at a place downtown. He was killed in a motorcycle accident on FDR Drive late one night. She was riding behind him and her lover died in her arms.

This glimpse of a tragic past gave Jennifer's life depth. But I was more immediately drawn to her clear skin and wondered what she smelled like. Jennifer dressed simply and while standing across from her on the stockroom floor I was conscious of the slope of her breasts under her pale cotton shirts. When I was alone, I imagined the white of her thighs inside her blue jeans. I had never seen a woman's naked thighs before. Everyone at the bookstore liked Jennifer because she was smart and had read more widely than any of us. She was also kind to me. When I complained to her once that I didn't want to go to the International Student social, she took me instead to a screening of Michael Moore's documentary *Roger & Me*.

Moore wanted the chief of General Motors, Roger Smith, to come back to his Michigan hometown and meet the people who were losing their jobs. The film confirmed what I was already discovering about America. Poverty or homelessness wasn't something I needed to associate only with India. *Roger & Me* explained the reality I had seen outside the university gates. Only a hundred yards from the Cathedral of St. John the Divine, where people with cameras stood in line to gain entry, I saw an old white woman walking along slowly with shit running down her swollen legs. A middle-aged woman passed me with her little girl. As she came close to the old woman, the mother covered her daughter's eyes.

The film rescued me from my passivity. It made me think about the outside world but I was thinking also of Jennifer. I would have liked to kiss her as she lay naked in my arms; I also wanted her to see me as a man with a camera. Michael Moore was honest and funny even while he seemed to embody a shambling slovenliness. I aspired to be a witty raconteur, open about wanting to seduce Jennifer with sparkling essays about ordinary people dropped in the maw of late capitalism. But that probably wasn't how Jennifer saw me. Near the checkout counter at the bookstore, there was a postcard stand and one day she picked up a card and called out to me.

—Is this you? She looked amused. She said, I recognized the hair.

I looked at the card. There was a sketch of a man sitting at a table, holding a mug, his eyes downcast. He had black curly hair. Below the sketch was a short story:

> The waitress came over and took his order for iced tea. She did so without flirting at all, something that disappointed and depressed him.
>
> —R. KEVIN MALER, "Counterfeit"

The story made me laugh, and though I was happy that I was the cause of Jennifer's amusement, I knew she was being critical. Her remark made me feel shallow. I decided I would spend more time with her. And even after classes had started, and I no longer worked at the bookstore, I stopped by each Tuesday and Thursday to eat lunch with Jennifer.

—Kailash, have you ever gone apple picking?

When Jennifer put this question to me I explained that apples in India grew in the mountains, in Kashmir, or in hill stations like Shimla. I had never been north of Delhi.

—I am from the burning plains, I said to her melodramatically, and she smiled at me then, kindly, but with enough restraint to stop me from going further.

Jennifer was one of the few people who called me by my full name. In one of my classes, a fellow graduate student had given me a nickname. Although names were shortened in America, this wasn't true in my case. My German friend Peter had begun calling me Kalashnikov instead of Kailash. It was a mouthful, but people were sufficiently amused and so he never gave up on the joke. Then someone shortened Kalashnikov to AK-47. On occasion, people called me AK or, sometimes, just 47.

On a Saturday morning, Jennifer rang the downstairs bell and called my name on the intercom. This was another thing about her; she never said her own name, even on the phone. This was a lesson to me in intimacy. You gave someone you loved a new name, or you uttered the name as if it were your own.

We left in her beaten-up blue Volvo, driving an hour or more north of the city. I had no idea that apples grew on short trees so close to the ground or that there were so many different varieties. We picked our apples and then bought cider doughnuts. I returned that evening with two paper sacks filled with fruit. When I bit into one and the sweet juice filled my mouth I immediately sat down to write a letter to my parents in Patna. I told them that my room smelled fresh and sweet. At least for the moment, I forgot my anxiety about money, forgot too the necessary practice of converting dollars into rupees, or weighing apples against the dwindling balance in the account book— *will I again be nine or ninety dollars short at the end of the month?* While I was writing the letter, my worries receded. Even my loneliness acquired a pleasant hue, the way objects appear to glow in the light of the setting sun. Earlier that day, I wrote, I had walked between the long rows of trees and I had plucked apples with my own hands. I talked about autumn and the way in which the leaves changed color in this country. I did not say anything about Jennifer.

The truth, Your Honor, is that the immigrant feels at home in guilt. How could I deny guilt and wrongdoing? I'm not talking only of the lies I had uttered when I applied for the visa, no, I'm aware at this moment only of the guilt of having abandoned my parents. A slippery slope, this. My father, my mother, my motherland, my mother tongue.

═══

Hello, USA, 212-555-5826? That is how the telephone operator from India began. Yes, I shouted, yes. It appeared that the ocean that separated us was roaring in my ear. I switched to Hindi but the operator kept speaking English and then confirmed my name. Next, my father hurriedly greeted me, and asked me how I was, before giving the phone to my mother. These calls were expensive, I knew. When my parents requested the call, they would have paid for the first four minutes at the post office. After those minutes were up, the operator would break in to ask if we wanted to continue talking. This was only the second phone conversation with my parents. The first conversation had been about my having reached New York City.

—Why have you not written? No word for so many days.

—I have, I said to my mother. I did, just last night.

—Is it very cold there?

—No, no. I went to an apple orchard yesterday.

—We took a rickshaw and came here to call you because I woke up from a dream . . .

She wouldn't tell me what she had seen in her dream, and so I told her that the only reason I hadn't written was my classes. I had been busy. I knew the cost of the call was prohibitive but felt secretly happy when my mother said, Extension, please.

They were going to visit my grandmother in the village for Diwali.

—Send her a postcard too, my mother said. You don't need to write anything much. Just write, *Mataji, I am well.* Just four words and she will be happy.

My grandmother couldn't read or write. She would have asked someone in the village, perhaps a kid walking back from school, to read my letter aloud to her. Or my cousins Deepak and Suneeta, if they weren't stealing anything at that time from her garden or her granary. About once a month, I sent my grandmother a postcard. I would sit down to write and then imagine a school-going child reading out my words. To bring to the young student a sense of wonder I would add a line or two about life in America:

> *When it is midnight in India, it is the middle of the day here.*
>
> *Even the people who collect garbage have their own truck.*
>
> *You cannot travel in a train without a ticket.*
>
> *To go from one part of the city to another, I use the train that runs underground.*
>
> *When I cook, the supply of gas is just like water. It is delivered through a pipe connected to my stove. No standing in long lines here for gas cylinders.*

═══

It was a Saturday afternoon during the early fall of 1990. Jennifer and I took the subway down to Lincoln Center. The plan was that we would walk across Central Park and emerge on the other side near Hunter College. We were going to the Asia Society to see an exhibition of photographs by Raghu Rai. As we were coming out of the subway station at Lincoln Center, Jennifer caught sight of a sign that said: GANDHI WAS A GREAT AND CHARITABLE MAN. Beneath, in smaller type, were the words HOWEVER, HE COULD HAVE USED SOME WORK ON HIS TRI-CEPS. It was an advertisement for a gym. If you joined early, you could save $150.

I said to Jennifer that the Mahatma would have found the price of the packet a bit steep. But he would have liked the thriftiness of the early-membership plan. Jennifer asked if I was offended by the ad, but I said I wasn't.

In India, Gandhi had been a face smiling from the walls of the decrepit offices in the small towns of Bihar. This use of his image for a New York City gym returned me to his different purpose, one that took the Mahatma out of the museum. This wasn't unknown in India, it was just ignored by official pieties. This was the irreverent Gandhi of the Indian marketplace. Long live Gandhi Safety Match. Long live Bapu Mark Jute Bag. Long live Mahatma Brand Mustard Oil.

A poster with the arrow pointing down to the exhibition space had a quote from Raghu Rai: *A photograph has picked up a fact of life, and that fact will live forever.* The exhibition, made up exclusively of black-and-white images, was in a long room in the basement of the building. Upon entering, our eyes fell on the photographs on the facing wall. These were pictures from the Union Carbide disaster in Bhopal from six years ago. On the other walls were images that Rai had made in Delhi and Bombay. We went up to the Bhopal pictures first. There were three of them. One was the iconic image of the unknown child being buried, its eyes wide open, a hand covering the body with ash and rubble. There was a second picture of a child's corpse. This was a girl. A piece of paper was pasted on her forehead, with her name, Leela, in Hindi, and also her father's name, Dayaram. I hadn't seen the third picture before. It showed a man on the deserted road outside the Union Carbide factory carrying a bundle on his shoulder. Jennifer took my hand in hers when I went closer to the picture to read the caption. Then I saw what she had already seen. What I had at first thought was a quilt or a heavy blanket was the man's wife. A pair of stiff, naked feet protruded from under the paisley pattern of the dead woman's sari.

The pictures from Delhi were on the wall to the right. In the center was a photograph of Indira Gandhi sitting in her office with her back to the camera. She was the prime minister at that time. A lone woman with about twenty men in white dhoti-kurtas, Nehru caps on their heads, all of them caught in poses of genuine servility. Another of a young swimmer, outlined against the sky, about to leap into the pond inside a sixteenth-century monument. In the background, in the far distance, the modern monuments, the tall skyscrapers in Connaught Place. My favorite image was one that Rai had shot from a rooftop in Old Delhi. The dome of Jama Masjid, its minarets, and the tops of other buildings formed the far horizon; dusk was creeping in, evident from the lights that had come on, and occupying the foreground but still far away, so that one didn't seem to disturb the privacy of the act, was a woman in an illuminated room. It appeared that the call for the evening namaz had just come from the mosque. The tile work and the trellis formed a delicate pattern around her, while the woman herself, or what we saw of her, was bathed in white light. She had her head covered, her hands open in front of her in prayer.

Jennifer and I walked over to the Bombay pictures. These were new to me, a different order of urbanity. Two men reading newspapers, islands of serenity, while around them were the moving, blurry bodies of commuters at the Churchgate railway station. Women arguing at a fish market; a socialite sitting in her living room in front of a giant, expensive oil painting; men in crisp white holding dark briefcases near the Jehangir Art Gallery; dabba wallahs; workers building a skyscraper in Colaba. In this air-conditioned space in New York, you didn't feel the heat in which the photos had been snapped; perhaps because Rai had made expert use of the flash, the pictures were so evenly lit, you seemed to have stepped into a land without shadows. Jennifer wasn't saying anything, but as I've said, she had taken my hand in hers. I liked this. We stood in front of an image of thin-limbed boys playing a game of marbles in a backstreet. All around them were crumbling walls, tin roofs, and dirt, but Rai had caught the fluid movement of the boys and their extended limbs.

When I was in school in Patna, I wanted to be an artist because the placid expanse of the river Ganga close to my home, and sometimes a solitary boat with a dirty sail or a red pennant, looked beautiful and somehow easy to draw. It wasn't easy, of course. But even my failures perhaps were teaching me how to see the world around me. I could be sitting in a crowded bus bringing me back from school and a voice running in my head would name the objects I saw being sold on the street, their colors, the look in the eyes of the sellers.

Jennifer and I were standing in front of a Raghu Rai photo of about a dozen buffalo feeding in a khatal (in Bihar and Bengal, *khatal* or *khataal* is the word for a cow pen) in Bombay. Hanging above the dark beasts, which were linked together by chains, and suspended from the roof of the shack were cots on which men sat or slept. Around them, from hooks and nails, dangled buckets for milk and also items of clothing. Small, cramped lives, but I was familiar from my childhood with what was shown here. I knew the smell of that khatal, the stink of animal waste and the hum and buzz of flies, and I knew I could speak the language used by those men sitting bare-chested near the buffalo. I turned to Jennifer.

—If I ever write a book, I want this picture on the cover. It will be called *Migrants*.

—It is an amazing picture, she said. There's so much happening here.

===

Jennifer brought me sandwiches made of hummus and olives. I had never eaten this food before. We crossed the university quad and sat on the stone steps of the library. Just the previous week the weather had been chilly, and one night I had seen the glitter of raindrops on my window, but this day was unseasonably warm. Bright sunlight falling on the windows of the buildings and on the faces and limbs of students sprawled on the grass. The day felt a little like those days in India when the exams were over and you could sit out in the sun peeling an orange. Jennifer took off her blue sweater. She was wearing a T-shirt with thin black horizontal stripes. I studied the freckles on her pale arm and then I took off my jacket too.

—Last year on this very day, Jennifer said to me, I returned from a three-week trip to Nicaragua.

—*Nicaragua?*

—I went there with my friend Lee. We stayed with campesinos and worked on a farm and then on a small dam near Managua.

This little detail produced a twinge of jealousy.

—Is Lee a man?

—Interesting question. Lee used to be a woman. Laura. She went to school with me. Then she decided she would prefer to be a man.

New food, new knowledge.

—Tell me something about your childhood, she said to me after a while.

I didn't have a story like the one about Lee. I found myself describing the red-bottomed monkeys outside Lotan Mamaji's home, and then told her the story of the monkey finding my uncle's gun and pointing it at my cousin in her crib. Jennifer wasn't as surprised as I had hoped she'd be.

—Kailash, what happened to your cousin, where is she now?

That was all she wanted to know.

She wouldn't have thought it a very big deal, so I didn't tell Jennifer that I couldn't even make it to my cousin's wedding. But I had felt guilty about it for years. I couldn't tell her that in a photo I saw of the ceremony years later, the sign that the painter had put up outside, with a lotus flower and a colorful pot with a coconut on it, also contained a spelling mistake: RAJESH WETS SHALINI. So, instead, I told Jennifer about the summer afternoons when we were teenagers and my cousin would listen to sad Hindi songs on her radio: songs of unrequited love during those months when we waited for rain. In the blind alley below us, a cycle-rickshaw, the sun's glare reflected off its metal rims. The rickshaw appeared defeated, skeletal, because it was now missing both a rider and a driver. With a gurgle, the water supply from the municipality would resume at three each afternoon. My cousin sighed when a favorite song of hers, from the film *Guide,* started playing. If we were lucky, there would be another sound—louder, more insistent, filled with greater yearning than any sound heard all afternoon—the call of the koel hiding in a mango tree. The heat left everyone lethargic, even stoic, but not this koel, who was unafraid to make a spectacle of his suffering. No, not just spectacle, he was making a song. Such unabashed glory, such art. Years later, in college in Delhi, I wrote a short poem about the koel and mailed it in a yellow envelope to Khushwant Singh. I was surprised when the old writer sent back a letter, praising the poem's simplicity and my art, encouragement enough for me to wax poetic when, sitting on the steps of the library, Jennifer asked me what I missed most about India. That afternoon, I was only imitating the koel.

The next day, she put a simple white card in the mailbox in my department. It had a haiku by the poet Bashō.

Even when I am in Kyoto
When I hear the call of the cuckoo
I miss Kyoto

To show my gratitude for her gift of lunch and the card, I gave Jennifer a packet of jasmine incense. It had sat unopened in the suitcase that I had brought with me from India. She put the roll up to her nose and thanked me sweetly, and then said that one day she'd have me come over to her apartment for dinner. That remark made me think that Jennifer liked me, and that maybe I ought to cook an Indian meal for her when the opportunity presented itself.

The semester's work took up my time. Once or twice, we went to campus events together. A Diwali festival organized by the South Asian students, chaat and spicy chana masala from a Bangladeshi restaurant close by, each plate costing three dollars. Pepsi and Sprite in small plastic cups for a quarter. The organizers asked everyone attending to pick rose petals from a plate and throw them at the plastic idols of Ram and Sita while they screamed "Happy Diwali." One of the women, an undergrad from Jackson Heights wearing a salwar-kameez, went around putting red tikas on our foreheads. When I thanked her, she laughed nervously and said loudly that when we went back to our apartments the other students would say that we had ketchup on our foreheads.

I talked to a couple of the Indian girls there, and I caught them looking at Jennifer while they spoke to me. During that first semester, there was at least one girl in my class whom I liked. Well, there were several I liked, but there was one in particular. I hadn't spoken to her much. I would have found the prospect of talking to her daunting, but Jennifer was easier to be with. She had slipped down the social ladder when she dropped out of school. It made her approachable. Or maybe it was because she was older and lived frugally. Is that what I thought at the time? More than once, offhandedly, Jennifer had indicated that she found me good company, and I felt pleased, as if she had recognized a hidden part of me.

One evening, we went to listen to Edward Said playing Bach piano concertos in the chapel. Jennifer had taken classes with the famous professor. I spotted two of my own professors there, including Ehsaan Ali, who had come with his wife, who was white. Western music was new to me but I saw that Jennifer was moved by it. I was in classes where Said's writings were discussed and in the weeks to follow I would start to speak of my own identity in ways that were influenced by him, but on that night, the night of his performance, Jennifer introduced me to a new idea of music that had come to her from Said. This was during dinner at my apartment after the concert. We were eating the mattar paneer and biryani I had prepared for her, and she was speaking about music in an even, clear way, telling me about polyphony and counterpoint. This kind of talk made her at once more interesting and mysterious to me. If this were a movie, I imagine a montage of scenes, like this one, that introduced me to America—a discussion about Bach, the first taste of Mexican food, the first rock concert, lectures by the teachers I came to admire. And the footage of the first snowfall. The blue of the cold afternoon, and as if someone had cut the sound from the universe, snow drifting down in the stillness. When it stopped snowing, we went sledding down a hill in a park on the other side of Morningside Drive. This was a pleasing discovery, but even as I was riding down the slope on a sled I asked myself if what I had with Jennifer was love. Every week, I spent time with my other friends, those whom I saw in my classes. I didn't discuss Jennifer with them. In the beginning at least, I wouldn't have known what to say.

But testaments to distant love were an entirely different matter, Your Honor. I was getting better and better at that. In a literature class that fall, my class presentation was about a poem that described Indian Fulbright scholars in Egypt coming across millennia-old mummies swathed in muslin from Calicut. What a surprising connection! The poem marked for me the discovery of India, and the extraordinary richness of its past. In that same class, I read about a young Sarojini Naidu, homesick and feverish with love in Cambridge, writing letter after letter to a doctor in the nizam's army who would later become her husband. I imagined writing similar letters myself—even if my lover in India was nameless and faceless. Before the semester ended, I

*sent a letter to the editor of the student newspaper describing the previ-
ous night's experience of attending a concert-performance by the tabla
player Zakir Hussain. I had never loved India as much as I did now,
when I was so far away.*

═══

The one activity that was perhaps the most stable part of my
identity that first semester was the seminar I was taking with
Ehsaan Ali. His class Colonial Encounters was held on Friday
afternoons. The seminar participants required his special permission to join. I had heard that he brought red wine each week
to his classes and you sat around discussing the day's readings
while sipping wine from small plastic cups. When the semester
began, I went to Ehsaan's office in Philosophy Hall to get his
signature. Third floor, after the set of dual radiators, next to the
notice board covered with announcements. The door was open
and I saw that he was on the phone. With his right hand, he
pointed to a chair. The tenor of the exchange suggested that he
was being interviewed. Then it became clear that the interview
was about the Iraqi invasion of Kuwait.

—Well, Bush has said that a line has been drawn in the sand.
He claims that he has no dispute with the Iraqi people. His
war is going to be against Saddam. Do you believe the ordinary
Iraqi, suffering in her home or in a hospital, is going to think our
president is being honest? No, let me explain . . .

While he was speaking on the phone, he was looking directly

at me, and I found myself nodding. The window was open behind him and on the wall to his right was a framed poster for *The Battle of Algiers*. I had watched the film, when I was in my teens, in Pragati Maidan in Delhi. The poster's background showed grainy black-and-white warren-like homes in the qasba, and leaning into the frame from the sides were the Algerian Ali La Pointe on the left, and on the right, the French military colonel Mathieu.

The film's director, Gillo Pontecorvo, had sought out Ehsaan when making the film. Pontecorvo had arrived in Algeria with his screenplay but accidentally left it on the top of a car. Parts of the screenplay soon appeared in a right-wing paper. So Pontecorvo recast the story, basing it on interviews with revolutionaries: *a fiction written under the dictatorship of facts*. Ehsaan was in Algeria then and became one of his advisers. Except that the student who told me all this, a thin, saturnine man from Gujarat, was not a credible source. He would even have put Ehsaan in the film as the main actor, a man from a scrappy background emerging, not without charisma but mainly due to the pressure of history, into the forefront of a glorious struggle. Truth be told, I wasn't too far from holding the same view myself.

Ehsaan was a man born in a village not too far from mine. He migrated to Pakistan during the bloody Partition, and later came to America on a scholarship. Awarded a doctorate at Princeton, he toured the globe and made friends with Third World leaders, especially in Africa. He had been tried for having conspired in a plot to kidnap Kissinger! How could I not look up to him? He was our hero—and thus, all heroic. He had crossed boundaries. He was a man who was without a nation, and a friend to the oppressed peoples of the world.* When Ehsaan died, in 1999, after a battle with cancer, Kofi Annan would pay tribute at his funeral. But all this was still in the future. Even the immediate deaths in Iraq were far away. Two days after the cease-fire went into effect, planes from the USS *Ranger* bombed and strafed thousands of Iraqi fighters fleeing in their vehicles. That road came to be called the Highway of Death. How did the men die? I would know the answer when a photograph was published many months later, showing an Iraqi soldier burned alive while reaching out of his truck. But on the day that I met Ehsaan for the first time, this massacre had not yet taken place. The Iraqi soldier was still sitting on a chair outside the barracks listening

---

* I wanted to title this book *The Man Without a Nation*. I applied for a grant but failed: that made me regard the title with suspicion. But the title was inappropriate for a novel. It seemed more suited to a nonfiction study about a kind of discrepant cosmopolitanism that develops as an antidote to sectarian conflicts and murderous nationalism. For a brief while I thought the book would be called *The History of Pleasure*. I had picked up the phrase in a Philip Roth novel where the narrator had this to say about himself: *But I was a fearless sort of boy back in my early twenties. More daring than most, especially for that woebegone era in the history of pleasure. I actually did what the jerk-off artists dreamed about. Back when I started out on my own in the world, I was, if I may say so, something of a sexual prodigy.* Sexual prodigy? *Your Honor, a hunger artist, more likely.* The proposed title overwhelmed me with its ironies, and so it too was abandoned.

to music or to the excited report of horses galloping around the old racetrack in Baghdad.

—You can do the math, yes? Clearly, some kids can die to make us feel safer. And the tragedy is doubled because we are not going to be safe . . . Listen, I have a student waiting to see me. I have to go. But if you have any questions about what I have said, call me back. I'll be here till four.

Without saying anything, Ehsaan reached out and took the yellow form that I was holding in my hand. He quickly signed it and then leaned back in his chair.

—Where were you born?

—India.

—That is obvious. Where in India? My guess is Uttar Pradesh.

—Next door, sir, in Bihar.

—A fellow Bihari. I was born near Bodh Gaya.

He was grinning when he said this. I smiled too but I didn't want to tell Ehsaan that I already knew a lot about him. There was a reason for my silence. I had read in an interview that as a boy Ehsaan had witnessed his father's murder. This was several years before Ehsaan left for Pakistan, traveling alone in a column of refugees. He was only five and lying in bed next to his father when his father's cousin and his sons came in with knives. Ehsaan's father knew they were going to kill him, but he covered the child's body with his own. I didn't want to acknowledge my awareness of the sadness in Ehsaan's past. I didn't know then that, as the weeks turned into months, and then into years, the details of Ehsaan's life would become a part of my life and the life of a woman I loved.

=====

One night Jennifer called me to ask if I'd go ice-skating. She said that we could rent skates at the rink. Back in Patna, I had learned to use roller skates on the smooth straight road, lined with gulmohar trees, that led to Governor House. Ice-skating required a different kind of movement and control. I held Jennifer's hand and skated around, following her instruction that we sketch a figure eight on the ice. Jennifer was wearing a woolen hat, and so was I. We wore scarves. The hands that we extended toward each other were gloved. Just then a tight group of men wearing fluorescent suits winged by like a flock of geese. I gave chase, hamming it up, and inevitably, stumbled and fell. I was laughing, and Jennifer was too, and when I was back on my feet with her help, I kissed her, first on the cheek and then, my gloved right hand cupping the back of her head, on her lips. It seemed the most natural act in the world, and yet it filled me with intolerable excitement. We skated for a while longer on the hard ice, and as we went in widening circles under the night sky surrounded by the lights of the city, I felt a euphoria that made me weightless and lifted me to the stars.

—Are you in a hurry to get home? Jennifer asked this question on the subway.

—No, no, I have nothing to do. *The effort required, Your Honor, to not sound overexcited and instead only a bit bored.*

When I tasted the scotch in Jennifer's apartment, I imagined that her mouth too would soon offer the same taste to my tongue. Yet she didn't kiss me. *Saturday Night Live* was on, with Dana Carvey imitating President Bush. I kept my eye on the television and then, weak from waiting for something to happen, I stretched out on the futon. Jennifer came closer to me and, leaning down, unbuckled my belt and smiled through sleepy eyes. Then she took me in her mouth. I hardly dared look down at her head, and even less at her parted lips and her tongue. I didn't dare to look, yes, but I did, amazed. Her eyes were closed. I stared at her open mouth and at my cock in her hand. Could she sense that I was looking? I jerked my eyes away, noticing on the side table a new book by Geoffrey Wolff that I had seen at the bookstore, and the glass of scotch beside it, and further away, beside the door, the dark stain of melted snow where Jennifer had taken off her leather boots. For weeks I had asked myself if the two of us would have sex. It had often seemed possible, at least in my fantasies, and then not. Now it really had happened—I wanted to be able to tell someone and didn't know whom. That's what I thought when I looked down at Jennifer's head again, her hair golden and shiny except for four or five, I didn't count them, gray hairs, her body close to me but also distant in my mind, removed far enough to allow me to compose an excited report from the front. And then none of these thoughts mattered.

Before I left India for America, one of my friends made me promise that as soon as I had finally fucked someone, I would send a postcard saying, *I have eaten cherry*. I had mailed the postcard after only my second week in the country, as a joke, laughing to myself. Now I wished I had waited.

Jennifer would shop at a co-op close to her house, buying half a dozen kinds of tea. Peppermint tea, green tea, and also black tea with chocolate or blood orange, the more austere Sencha, the cloying and unpalatable cinnamon spice, the smoky flavor of Lapsang souchong, which I came to prize. She would get me to try foods that she thought I would like. Pasta, baby corn with lemon juice and tarragon, roasted leg of lamb without the spices I was accustomed to, or shrimp sautéed lightly and served with chopped scallion. One afternoon, in the green plastic basket, she also added a strip of condoms. I recognized the brand; Jennifer kept a similar strip under her mattress and reached for it on days that were marked with an *X* on her wall calendar. I had never bought condoms in my life. The woman at the counter didn't even look up when she rang up the condoms, a bar of Kiss My Face soap, a candle, celery sticks, a cucumber, a bottle of tomato sauce, and a packet of ravioli. In Jennifer's apartment, I learned to enjoy tea from China and South Africa and Malaysia; I liked sitting on her rocking chair, which I would drag into a rectangle of sunlight; I spent afternoons reading books from her shelves, writers like Jean Genet and Angela Carter, whom I hadn't encountered before. She had a black cat and this was new too, stroking the cat as it lay on the wooden floor. I discovered that Jennifer had played the piano since she was a child, and gave lessons to little kids on the weekends. Young mothers, who appeared to be of Jennifer's age, brought their children to the apartment. When they saw me, they hesitated at the door, hands resting nervously on their children.

The inquiring gazes of those women at the door made me ask myself the question, Are we now *an item*? This was a phrase that I had recently acquired; the words appeared strange to me. And also the sentiment. The truth was that even at the end of the summer, although I hadn't told anyone at the bookstore that we spent time with each other, people had noticed. Often, I would be asked where Jennifer was, or what time she was coming to work. Jennifer hadn't changed her behavior with me—or she had changed it in ways that only I noticed. I was content with this; I didn't want anything more at that time. There was an imbalance in our histories. I felt she had lived a full life and I hadn't; I had only begun to experience life, which is to say, sexual life. If I were living in Patna, I'd have immediately thought of marriage, but not here. Here, just a few months into my stay in America, I was finally leading a fuller existence. I understood that this newness couldn't be shared with those I had left behind. I couldn't imagine writing and telling my friends in Delhi, those who had sat laughing and hooting in the dorm only a few months ago, that I was sleeping with Jennifer. At least I couldn't tell them anything about her that wouldn't appear a betrayal. The reverse was also true. Was there any way of introducing my friends from Delhi into my conversations with Jennifer without turning them into sex-obsessed hooligans? Twenty-year-olds who looked at women and acted like the two adolescents I was later to watch on American TV, Beavis and Butt-Head. It was easier to keep the worlds apart, even if doing so meant seeing myself as split or divided. I was already learning that I was moving away from my parents; their world now seemed so different from mine. I wrote them fewer letters. My classes, everything I was learning, made up my new reality. Except that one day I looked in the mirror and felt the sudden clutch of vertigo. I saw a future in which Jennifer and I would be married, living in a small town maybe in Ohio, where I'd find a job teaching at a college while trying to write on the weekends. During family holidays we would drive to her parents' home and each year someone would look at me and repeat the joke about Indians coming to Thanksgiving. We would return home the next day, the road winding endlessly into the future. Were there hills in Ohio? I felt I was rising and sinking with each passing breath. Then I realized that the mirror was moving. The wind made the sound a kite makes when struggling to get off the ground. When I looked outside through the grimy bathroom window I saw that the few leaves left on the branches of the trees outside were in danger of being swept away. I was safe in my apartment, and there was no immediate peril of any sort, but I was overcome by a feeling that took root then and has never left me, the feeling that in this land that was someone else's country, I did not have a place to stand.

═══

Two or even three times each week that semester, I would be at Jennifer's apartment. I preferred going to her place rather than having her come over to my cramped room. Her apartment was a two-room space, in the shape of an L, and it was located above a drugstore off 148th Street in Harlem.*

On a Friday morning, while I was there, Jennifer went downstairs to the store to buy a pregnancy-test kit. She had called me late the previous evening and said she wanted me to be with her. I didn't ask any questions. I thought perhaps her father in Ohio, who had suffered a mild stroke the previous May, had taken a turn for the worse. But when we were getting ready for bed, she said, matter-of-factly, that her period was late. I felt ashamed. Here I was, standing close to her, thinking that we were soon going to fuck. And now this news. I didn't know what to say. Then I asked whether she had seen a doctor. She shook her head and turned off the light. In the dark, I tried to work out when she could have become pregnant. I saw that during the previous week the calendar on her kitchen wall had empty black and white squares. What had gone wrong?

---

* *Orgasms of twenty years ago leave no memory,* wrote Elizabeth Hardwick in *Sleepless Nights.* Is that really true? I'm thinking now of the day only last year when I had walked past the store above which Jennifer had lived. It was a cold autumn day. The pale green paint on the wall of her apartment was still the same and looked dirty. The window where I had often sat and read books had a white fan placed in it. I wondered who lived in the apartment now. I thought I might buy something in the store. A large handwritten sign with jagged edges, orange in color, had been pasted to the front door: NO PUBLIC RESTROOM.

In the morning, I woke up first and began making coffee. Jennifer lay in bed longer than was usual, perhaps more than an hour. When she got up, she opened the front door and said she'd be back in a minute.

She appeared carrying a blue-and-white paper bag in her hand. Through the half-open bathroom door I caught sight of her sitting on the toilet bowl. After a few moments, she shut the door.

Jennifer hadn't spoken to me but I heard her on the phone saying she was calling to set up an appointment to confirm a pregnancy. Her period was late, she said, by five days. I heard her ask how long one had to wait for an abortion. Then she asked how much the operation would cost. In answer to a question by the person from the other end she mentioned the name of her insurance provider.

When she hung up, she stood at her window looking out. I went up to her and put an arm around her.

—If we split it equally, she said, it'll cost us each a hundred seventy-five. Do you have the money?

—I do, I said. I'm sorry.

Her face didn't look sad as much as blank, as if she hadn't slept at all the previous night, and who knows, she probably hadn't.

The bookstore's insurance plan provided its employees access to three abortion clinics and Jennifer chose one on Seventy-eighth Street. The doctor's name sounded Hispanic. The receptionist had told Jennifer that she could wait a few more days but Jennifer didn't want that. An appointment was made for Monday morning.

—Stay in the waiting room. I don't want you to come inside with me.

—Do they allow others to come in?

—I don't know. I haven't done this before.

I thought I should protest, just in case Jennifer was doing this to spare me. But spare me what exactly? I didn't know, but also felt that I couldn't ask. She was brittle, maybe she was angry and blamed me. I felt I ought to show that I was big enough to understand this.

A five-minute walk from the subway station and we were standing outside the clinic's beige-colored walls. The first floor had three large rectangular windows with one-way mirrors. For a minute or two, Jennifer searched in her bag and then took a card out.

We passed through a metal detector and, once inside, we waited together in silence. After maybe twenty minutes, a nurse called out her name and held the door open for her. Jennifer didn't look at me as she left. I picked up a *National Geographic* from the stack of magazines. I was skimming through the pages, looking at pictures of alligators in Australia, when I suddenly saw Jennifer's oxblood Doc Martens next to me. She had come to tell me that I could go. There was going to be a consultation and blood tests and an ultrasound. It was going to take hours.

Are you sure, et cetera.

After that, there was another wait. Was it two weeks? I

didn't keep a journal till another year had passed and I don't have any records with me now. Nevertheless, I remember the afternoon we went to watch a movie at a theater on West Fifty-eighth Street. *Cyrano de Bergerac,* with Gérard Depardieu as the lead. There was a forty-minute wait. I suggested watching *Green Card* instead. It was playing in the same theater and just about to start. Jennifer said no. She said she couldn't stand Andie MacDowell's smile. The annoyance I felt was sudden and unexpected—I frowned but then said that we ought to get a drink after we had purchased our tickets. *It goes without saying, Your Honor, that theaters are dramatic spaces. They unlock our instinct for performance. Histrionics. You look at the outsize posters showing faces presented in vivid colors and you immediately want to express yourself and, if it suits you, vent.*

Across the road was the Ulysses bar, where the white-aproned waiter, short, his hair in a ponytail, took my order for a beer. Jennifer didn't even look at the man when she said she didn't want anything.

—Why don't you have a beer too? I asked, when the waiter had gone.

—I don't want it.

—I thought that when we agreed to have a drink you were going to have one too.

—It's okay, she said. You can have your beer.

—I will but I don't think you're getting my point.

—You can tell yourself that, of course. I don't remember our discussing what each one of us wanted.

The waiter brought the beer in a frosted glass. I drank half of it in one go.

—You know, I intoned in a wet voice, after a pause during which I weighed the implication of what Jennifer had said, the medical advice against drinking doesn't apply to pregnant women getting abortions.

It was the wrong thing to say, and I regretted it the moment I had said it. A stupid, cruel remark. I had justified it by telling myself that I had not hidden what I wanted. *I had said I wanted a beer. More to the point, was it I who had remained locked in my own silence ever since finding out about the pregnancy?* But Jennifer was standing up. She unclasped her purse and took out her keys.

—I'm going home. You're such an asshole. I'm sorry I came out with you.

I didn't get up. I told myself I needed to pay for the beer. Jennifer's dismissal of me seemed so final, so complete, that I didn't think I should accompany her. I paid and crossed the street. It was dark and quiet in the lobby of the theater. I took in the silence and the emptiness. A youth with a large blue visor over his forehead leaned on the counter near the popcorn machine. It felt wrong to be inside, however, and I rushed back out into the street to look for Jennifer. It was improbable that she had lingered. Soon I was running toward the subway stop. She was wearing a thin brown coat and I wanted to catch sight of her shoulders. The sidewalk wasn't very crowded. A smattering of people and small dogs. A hand holding a briefcase raised high in the air to hail a taxi. A woman was walking toward me, pushing a stroller with twin girls. Then I saw Jennifer. She was waiting for the light to change, or maybe the light had changed once already and she hadn't moved.

When I was close, I called her name, and she turned around, her face crumpling. Without warning, she sat down on the ground. This was so uncharacteristic that I first thought she was sick. My appearance had released something in her, or weakened her, it was impossible to tell. She was crying helplessly and people turned to stare. An old woman stopped near us; she was thin, gaunt even, wearing glasses, and she looked at me sternly. She bent down and asked Jennifer if she was okay. Jennifer said loudly, still wailing, *I'm not okay, I'm not okay*. At the same time, however, she reached out and took my hand. I pulled her up gently. The feeling in my heart was one of relief, sure, but also a lot of love. As we quickly walked the two blocks to the subway, I put my arm around Jennifer's shoulders and kissed her hair.

When we woke up the next morning, Jennifer was her composed self again.

—Oh man, she said, her voice strained with cheer. There's something definitely happening with my hormones. I want this to end.

The next time we went to the clinic it was a Friday. I left during Ehsaan's lecture on *Heart of Darkness* to meet Jennifer at the bookstore at two in the afternoon. This time she had brought her car. She broke the silence to say that her friend Jill, who worked at the campus ID office, had said that she ought to have made the appointment for the morning. I didn't ask her why. We were late by about five minutes. A man had been standing outside, his head bowed, and it was only because Jennifer stepped away from him that I even looked at him a second time. The man was praying. Inside, the same guard we had seen the other day, a middle-aged, gray-uniformed black man, fat, with gold-rimmed glasses, checked a register in front of him and said that he didn't have Jennifer's name on it. He spoke in sonorous tones and acted officious, as if he were calling Congress into session.

—I've been talking to someone named Colleen, Jennifer said to the man.

He picked up the phone and dialed three digits.

—Yes, I have an individual named Jennifer here for a two-thirty, but I don't see her name on the list here . . . No, you see, I cannot properly do my work if you don't do yours . . .

He looked up.

—You go ahead, ma'am. You have to understand we keep this list here for your safety. It has to match what is inside. We have security—

But Jennifer wasn't going to wait for him to finish.

Once again, I stayed in the waiting area. Although I had expected to see other men there, the only others in the room were two matronly women, maybe in their forties, sitting together with their bags in their laps. One of them wore a bright red sweater and the other a dazzling white one. I was reading a book by Rachel Carson but now and then my eye wandered outside. The man who had been praying near the door hadn't moved at all. What would happen if he said anything to Jennifer? She was a quiet person but religion brought out her rage.

A young woman came in alone, wearing dark glasses, teetering on high heels, giving to the room a sudden slightly illicit air. After a while, I stopped looking at her and went back to my reading. More than two hours passed. I began to worry why Jennifer wasn't coming out. The woman called Colleen had told Jennifer on the phone that the operation wouldn't take long. They were going to run a couple of tests—"merely procedural"—and that part lasted only a few minutes. Colleen had said the whole affair would take an hour.

The door to the inside opened and a young woman and a man in a camouflage T-shirt came out. They headed for the two women seated together. The women got up and hugged the couple. It was unclear whether the woman had been operated upon, or whether she had only gone in for a consultation. I thought she looked fine. I began to pretend I was reading, aware that my stomach was churning. At least another hour passed. Then the door opened again but it was only the nurse.

I went back to my reading and the nurse came closer and spoke to me.

—Are you with Jennifer?

What had happened to her? Who was to be called in case of an emergency? People died during childbirth in India, I had heard this all the time when I was a boy. Just a few years ago, Smita Patil had died soon after giving birth. But this was an abortion, what could possibly have gone wrong?

The nurse's tag said PAULA. She was in her forties.

—Jennifer would like you to come inside.

A door opened into a narrow hallway and Paula allowed me to walk into the room alone. Jennifer was lying on a bed, a sheet covering her up to her waist. She had been crying, her eyes were red. An untouched cookie and a cup of water waited on the side table. When I asked if she was in a lot of pain, she shook her head and, as if she was cold, pulled the sheet up to her neck.

—I don't want the car to get towed. Can you put more quarters in the meter?

Why hadn't I thought of this myself?

—Yes, yes. Do you want anything else? Would you like me to get you some tea or juice? Why did it take so long?

Jennifer wasn't really saying anything and that is why my questions were so rushed and confused. I went out in a hurry, not waiting at the door for the Middle Eastern woman who was coming into the clinic. She wore the hijab and holding the door for her was a thin man with a toddler in his arms. I shouted back an apology. There was a ticket under the wiper. Twenty-five dollars. I put it in my pocket, telling myself that I would pay it immediately but wouldn't tell Jennifer about it. And, with my hand still inside the pocket of my jacket, I thought I'd cook basmati rice and chicken in coriander for Jennifer. She liked that. And I'd make some dal. Keep some red wine handy, if she wanted it. I must bring her flowers. And wash her sheets if they were bloody. Would the sheets at her home get blood on them? I didn't know the answer to the question but I was certainly going to be generous and attentive.

I didn't recognize at that moment what I already knew, that

nothing I could do would ever be adequate. It seemed that Jennifer had made a discovery about me, a discovery that I wasn't privy to. It was as if a policeman had stopped by one evening when I wasn't there and asked a few disturbing questions about me. And at the end of the conversation, Jennifer had risen and gone to a drawer in my room and found the evidence. All that was required now was for an accusation to be aired in the open.

Late evening. I had placed a bouquet of fresh flowers near her bedroom window, white and red carnations, a couple of asters and yellow daisies, a stem of tiny white spray roses. Now I brought her dinner with a small glass of red wine on the tray. Jennifer sat up on the bed and looked at me.

—I appreciate what you're doing but really I'd just like to be alone. Will you please take that bottle of wine and leave?

—I'll go in a bit. Why don't you first eat? I want to make sure you eat something.

—No, I'm sorry . . . *Why am I even saying sorry?* I'd like to be alone. Go. Please go.

My first thought, Thank god I'm wearing these sandals. I had brought them from India. They were inappropriate for the season. But they were proving useful now, I didn't at least have to upset her by taking time to put on my shoes.

Stepping out of her door, I wondered why she had insisted that I take the wine. Then I realized it was unimportant. I had failed. I knew I had failed in the way one knows one has failed in a dream: you might not know the cause, but the proof is available to you, the train is coming closer, you hear a clanging, there is only the feeling of vast regret that you have no legs and you can't possibly snatch away to safety the small bundle lying on the tracks.

A man was sitting at the bottom of the steps that led up to Jennifer's apartment. He didn't move when I came out. His right hand, with a large sore on one of the fingers, was resting on a shopping cart filled with black garbage bags spilling with rags. I pulled the door shut a bit too forcefully and stepped onto the street telling myself that I needed to eat some rice and curry chicken. The bottle of wine was in my hand. I would eat a bit and drink, and yet, as I said this to myself, I also experienced a clutching sadness.

The world had darkened. A giant hand in the sky had painted the city around me with a black, smudgy substance. Two blocks down, I saw that a basement door opened to a tiny Lebanese restaurant. There were no other customers. I took a seat in the corner and asked for lentil soup and bread. Whenever the waiter was out of sight, I took swigs from my bottle in a manner that wasn't very pleasing. The food and the wine disappeared in some empty place inside me. I called Jennifer's number the next day and for several days that followed but the phone just rang in her apartment. Once I called the bookstore, and God said Jennifer was sick, and that she wouldn't be back until after Christmas. Did he know what was wrong with her? He had heard it was pneumonia. But that couldn't have been correct.

A week passed and I got a card from Jennifer. The first line said that she was sorry but she couldn't talk to me anymore. I didn't read any further than the next line, which said, *All possibilities are stillborn*. The language appeared heavy-handed to me, the too-deliberate, and somewhat inaccurate, metaphor dragging me into waters muddy with misery. I understood that Jennifer was upset and disappointed. I also knew that it wasn't anything I had said, but instead everything that I had left unsaid. She knew that I didn't love her in a deep or lasting way. I felt guilty at first but then another thought took its place. Over the coming weeks, I would start telling myself that it had been a good thing we had done by getting together. We had seized an opportunity for happiness. A part of me would always feel that I had been shallow and opportunistic. But we had also been happy. She had changed me, and I had changed her. This part of what had happened had been a gift.

I was not to see Jennifer till a year had passed and it was winter again. I was with a young woman I liked. We had gone in for a hurried lunch at Ollie's, the Chinese restaurant near the university gates. We had eaten spicy mock duck with steaming bowls of rice. When we stepped out in the cold, I touched my friend's elbow. I was about to tell her that I wished I had drunk a Tsingtao. I stayed silent because I was looking at Jennifer. I knew the coat she was wearing and also the gloves. Our eyes met. She didn't acknowledge me but her upper lip curled up over her teeth in such distress that I was transported to the room in the clinic where I had seen her lying on the bed with the sheet drawn up to her neck. I looked away and walked briskly ahead of my new friend, who, after she became my lover, never asked me anything about Jennifer and so we never discussed what had happened between us.

Part II

Nina

Another clipping in the notebook for this novel. This one from a magazine essay by Abraham Verghese.

His voice took on a conspiratorial tone: "I heard that one of our buggers, when he landed at Kennedy, he met a beautiful woman—a deadly blonde—and her brother outside baggage claim. She was *very, very* friendly. They offered him a lift in a white convertible. They took him to their apartment, and then you know what the brother did? Pulled a bloody gun out and said, 'Screw my sister or I'll kill you.' Can you imagine? What a country!"

(In the Verghese quote, I had identified with the fantasy, but reading it now what catches my eye is the music of that insistent—because it springs from what is dubious—detail: *very, very*.)

We sat with wine in plastic cups.

Coming down the steps outside his apartment building, Ehsaan had stumbled and twisted his ankle. Walking turned out to be difficult for him and our seminar temporarily shifted to his home. The subjects of discussion that day were issues of displacement and exile, focused on the writings of Edward Said ("Reflections on Exile"), Assia Djebar ("There Is No Exile"), and Anton Shammas ("Amérka, Amérka"). One of the students in the seminar, Negin, who was Iranian and had grown up in Los Angeles, said she had really liked Djebar. There is no exile for women. When women lose their country and live somewhere else, the customs of the old country follow them there. They are never able to escape it. Negin's mother had said to Negin's elder sister, who was studying law, Don't be a whore. The mother wanted a marriage in which the family would play a part. But the sister was fighting back. Like one of Djebar's characters, Negin's sister told her parents, I won't marry.

Ehsaan was sitting in a chair with his leg raised and resting on a stool. He tilted his head toward Negin as she told her story and then, when she stopped, he told us about his mother. When Ehsaan left his village, Irki, in 1947, to accompany refugees escaping to Pakistan, his mother remained in India. Her exile was different from Djebar's. Ehsaan said his mother saw the people who were fighting for Pakistan as reactionary and insufficiently anticolonial. That was one side of the picture. On the other side, unlike Ehsaan's older brothers, who had eager plans about what they wanted to do in the new country, their mother was faced with a simpler task. Ehsaan's sister Aba had fallen sick. She had typhoid.

—My mother decided to take care of my sister, who would not have been able to make that arduous journey.

—When did you see them again? Negin asked.

—I didn't, not my sister at least. She died. This was about ten, eleven years later. I saw my mother then. She came to Pakistan for a while before returning again to the village in India. She had liked the life there. We brought her back when she fell ill. She died in Pakistan.

He fell silent. I thought of my mother in Patna. She was waiting for me to come back after I had received my degree. Soon she would be old too. And my grandmother in the village, whom I could see in my mind's eye placing two or three red hibiscus flowers on the shrine in her courtyard. The shrine was a dark stone, no bigger than a fist, on a brick and cement pedestal about four feet high that had projecting from it a tall bamboo with a red jhandi on the top. The brief morning prayer was my grandmother's first act of the day after her bath, her hair still wet, a fresh cotton sari wrapped around her. As it happened, I was never to see her again. On my second Diwali in America, I called my neighbors' phone in Patna so that I could speak to my parents. My sister came to the phone and said that our parents had gone to the village to take care of my grandmother, who was very sick.

—She was asking about you—that's what Ma said.

—Why didn't you go?

—I just got back today. I have my exams in three days.

—Are you celebrating Diwali?

—No fireworks in the house this year, she said.

My sister, older than me, was telling me that our grandmother had died. This clear thought came to me only after I had hung up the phone. My next thought was that my sister must have rushed home from our neighbors' crying. When I imagined this, my own tears came. Before I left India, my grandmother had joked that I would marry a white woman and become a sahib. I would never return home. But I'm going to bring my white bride to the village, I said to her. And she said, No, no, don't do that. She will ask you why your grandmother has got such a flat nose. It is flat like a bedbug's back.

A letter from my mother arrived two weeks later. It wasn't an aerogram letter. Instead, it was an envelope with a photograph inside of my dead grandmother's face with a white garland around her head. My mother had written that I shouldn't feel bad, that my grandmother had passed away peacefully. I was asked to pray for her peace. Light an agarbatti and put it near the photograph. *Think good thoughts,* my mother wrote.

The discussion at Ehsaan's house that day began with Said's line that *exile is strangely compelling to think about but terrible to experience.* Said was Ehsaan's friend; we all knew that both had worked together for the rights of dispossessed Palestinians. But the story that Ehsaan was telling us about his mother and his sister made me think of him as an exile too, suffering what Said had described as *crippling sorrow of estrangement. Your Honor, I've been asked when did it all start? When did I start becoming the person I am today? I don't know whether there is a simple answer to that question. But it was perhaps during that seminar session in Ehsaan's house that, under the influence of Said's words, I started to think of everything heroic or glorious in Ehsaan's life as nothing more than attempts to overcome that great sorrow.*

For this class, we had also read a recent magazine piece by Anton Shammas, a Palestinian writer who grew up in Israel. Ehsaan wanted us to tell him whether the idea of a "portable homeland," the things that migrants carry with them, appealed to us. I spoke up. I said that I had found very moving the story that Shammas had told of a Palestinian man bringing to San Francisco the small plants and seeds that were native to the West Bank. And, hidden in his heavy black coat, the seven representative birds of his homeland: *the duri, the hassoun, the sununu, the shahrur, the bulbul, the summan, and the hudhud, small-talk companion to King Solomon himself.*

Even the names of the different kind of birds were charming. When I read that list, I thought of the birds of my own past, and of the koel's song in the summer.

Ehsaan was smiling. He raised the glass of wine in his hand.

—Kailash, please tell us, when you left home recently and traveled to America, what did you bring with you?

—I was thinking of that question when reading Shammas.

I carried in my suitcase a copy of *The Illustrated Weekly of India* with a photo essay on Bihar. The photos are in black and white. I recognize them as images from the place where I have my roots.

—The magazine with the pictures, Ehsaan said, instead of what someone in an earlier time might have done—the earth from his native place in a jar, perhaps.

He looked at the others.

—I brought pictures of my parents and my dog, Peter said.

Others had probably done the same because they were nodding.

When no one else offered a response, Ehsaan said that Palestinians who left their homeland and were never able to return still keep the keys to the houses they had been forced to abandon. The keys are useless now because the locks are gone. But those keys are the portals to homeland.

I had left home willingly but was still struck by how little I had brought with me. It was as if I imagined I was going to discover a new self. I thought of my own room in the university apartment. The walls were bare—there was a window but no pictures—and the room smelled of the cheap synthetic sheets I used. There was a lemon-yellow electric blanket on the bed. Instead of my parents' photographs, I had carried in my suitcase a magazine, my certificates, my degrees, a fading diploma or two. I had brought with me a few music cassettes in their brittle plastic cases. Geeta Dutt, C. H. Atma, Mohammed Rafi, Hemant Kumar. In my apartment, I read for class while lying in bed, music playing on my radio–cassette player. For many years, often full of self-pity, I would think that Lata Mangeshkar was singing the anthem for people like me: *Tum na jaane kis jahan mein kho gaye . . .* [*]

========

One day in class, my classmate Siobhan, who seemed to be a current or past officeholder in all the progressive student organizations on campus, said that there was going to be a teach-in. War was imminent in the Persian Gulf. President Bush had sent the troops to Saudi Arabia and they were going to proceed to Kuwait to force Saddam to withdraw. There was a goateed speaker from Political Science who spoke for a long time on the role of the oil economy in the war. The Iraqi invasion in Kuwait had actually benefited the oil companies in the West. The rise in oil prices had earned them huge profits. This was true not only of those in the United States but also of companies based in other countries, all the way from Saudi Arabia to Venezuela. It was just that Bush couldn't allow Iraq to dictate terms or control worldwide oil prices. In just the past few years, U.S. reliance on Gulf oil had gone up fourfold, and if we understood this we would know why the U.S. troops had been sent to the Middle East.

When the speaker finished, a group of students began to chant "No Blood for Oil! No Blood for Oil!" Others were hold-

---

[*] A woman's voice coming to you in the night's silence: *You are lost in another world unknown / I am left in this crowded one alone.*

ing up signs. One said, A KINDER GENTLER BLOODBATH. Two young women were holding the ends of a bedsheet on which they had spray-painted the words GEORGE BUSH IS HAVING A WARGASM.

The writer Grace Paley, a tiny woman with a halo of silver hair, was asked to address the crowd. She spoke about a marine named Jeff Patterson, who, back in August, refused to join his unit. He sat down on the airstrip in Hawaii, unwilling to fight in a war he didn't believe in. He had joined the Marine Corps to receive an education, but the time he spent at bases in Okinawa, South Korea, and the Philippines changed his outlook. He was the first protester from among American ranks; others were to join him later. Paley read out a statement from Patterson: "I have, as an artillery controller, directed cannons on Oahu, rained burning white phosphorus and tons of high explosives on the big island, and blasted away at the island of Kahoolawe . . . I can bend no further." Before she ended, Paley said she agreed with what had been said about oil and war. The reality was even worse, she said. There was alternative energy for everything in normal, comfortable American life — television, air conditioners, light, heat, cars. There was only one enterprise that needed such a colossal infusion of energy that no alternative to oil would work — and that was war. A tank could move only seventeen feet on a gallon of gasoline. This war was a war to ensure that America could continue to make war.

Next it was Ehsaan's turn. Siobhan introduced him as her favorite professor. She said he had only recently spent a year teaching in Beirut. Ehsaan was wearing a tan sweater over a black turtleneck. His gray hair was cut short. He looked handsome. He smiled and said that as it was a teach-in he wouldn't waste time making jokes about Vice President Dan Quayle. Except we needed to be clear that in imperialist adventures the children of the rich didn't bear most of the ordeal. In other words, we should note that Quayle didn't enlist to fight in Vietnam, and instead, he joined the National Guard. Nearly sixty thousand Americans were killed in the Vietnam War, but of that number, fewer than a hundred were members of the National Guard.

Despite his cowardly record, Quayle had only the previous day spoken in New York, not two miles away from where we were meeting, in favor of an assault by the United States. Ehsaan had questions for Quayle: Who will fight in our army? Who will be fighting in the Iraqi army? Who will get killed? He followed these questions by saying that, like Grace Paley, he was going to read a letter written by a soldier. The letter had been written by an Indian sepoy during the First World War in what is present-day Iraq. The soldier was fighting in Mesopotamia in the British Army. He had written home in 1916 that a part of the 7th Brigade, in which he was fighting, was besieged and surrounded on all sides by the enemy. *Attempts have been made to rescue them, but without success. There was a fight on 6th March and heavy losses to us in the attempt to relieve them. Some of our men are in the besieged force, twenty in number. They have eaten their horses and mules. They have a quarter of a pound of flour each per diem. We are hopeful of being sent to join the relieving force.* Such precision about the pain and the suffering of comrades fighting in a war. A war, mind you, that has nothing to do with the private destinies and choices of these Indian soldiers themselves. The whole truth is even more unbearable.

Ehsaan's voice rose higher. From records kept during the siege we learn that British officers amused themselves by designing menus featuring horseflesh. We also learn that Major Stewart's *devoted batman was killed while bringing his mule-steak lunch to his dugout*. No need to guess the race of the batman. He was killed because Churchill had acquired for the British government 90 percent of the shares in a corporation called the Anglo-Persian Oil Company. It was necessary to control Basra; the lives of thousands of Indian soldiers be damned. If we are really interested in supporting our troops, which not incidentally are made up of a huge number of disadvantaged youth from minority communities, if we are interested in supporting these young men and women of color, then let's not put them in harm's way to benefit a group of oil companies and the government that promotes their interests everywhere.

Loud applause at the end. I looked around for Nina but she wasn't there. My hands were cold and I liked the idea of sharing one of her Dunhill cigarettes. But I had an ethnography class in Schermerhorn in ten minutes and so I rushed away without even shaking Ehsaan's hand.*

---

* A distinguished Dutch professor whose own research was conducted in Indonesia taught the ethnography course. He also had an interest in South Asia and the previous week he had screened a short documentary about a servant boy in a small town in India. I had found the documentary moving. Growing up, I had witnessed the abuse of children employed as servants in homes all around

=====

Nina and I met in a film seminar that first semester.* She had short-cropped hair, large brown eyes, and impetuous lips. Her movements were full of allure; she was small-built and athletic: a dancer till her late teens. Even when she was not moving, just sitting in the dark watching the films that were screened for us in the small classroom, I was always aware of the outline of her features. Sometimes, instead of watching the film, I'd study the light on her face. We had spoken a few times in class and once

---

me. But my own experience with servants was a bit different. Jeevan, a young, low-caste man from our village, was the domestic help in the house when I was a boy. I must have been around four when Jeevan brought me to the bathroom door and asked me to peer inside. I hadn't noticed the crack in the wood before. And now I saw, as if in a film, my unmarried aunt, my father's younger sister, standing under the shower. I distinctly remember being puzzled, and perhaps embarrassed, by the patch of hair below her stomach. How had Jeevan known that I wouldn't tell my parents about this? This question didn't occur to me till I was in my late teens. I had forgotten the scene for years and cannot now recall what forced its return. I saw Jeevan in the village before I left for the United States. He was a farmer now, prematurely aged, every part of his body shrunken except for the toenails on his cracked, bare feet. The soles of his feet had holes in them, as if a tiny screw had been put in and then taken out before repeating the process elsewhere, holes that Jeevan attributed to his standing for hours in the water in his paddy field. I photographed his feet and used the image in my first book, *Passport Photos* (Berkeley: University of California Press, 2000).

* If the reader in indiscriminate haste has rushed past the epigraph from Abraham Verghese on page 54, this would be a fine occasion to return to it. Even strong and genuine emotions can have their start in pure fantasy. Nina was a site of fantasy, yes, but she was also her own person, passionate and daring.

after a party at Peter's, I trying too hard to be witty, and she managing to be so quite effortlessly.

One day, after the screening of Sidney Lumet's *Dog Day Afternoon,* I saw Nina bent over the water fountain. She raised her face, her mouth still wet.

—I wanted to ask you something, I said to her.

Nina laughed. You want to know whether I'm fertile?

Although she was laughing when she said this, her look was calm and assessing. I too laughed. There was a great deal of nervousness in my laughter because I didn't know what to say.

—No, I told her, I only wanted to know whether you are going to register for Comp Lit 300 next semester.

—As a matter of fact, I am. How can I not enroll in a course that appears on the transcript as CLIT 300?

More laughter.

The following week in the film class we were discussing Nagisa Oshima's *In the Realm of the Senses.* The professor was a small Frenchwoman whose face and neck would get covered in hives if you asked uncomfortable questions.* An Italian girl was

---

* I'm grateful to that professor for the useful advice she gave me later. I was ignorant of all conventions of academic paper writing. At the end of the semester, after giving me a C, she pointed out very gently that I should buy an instruction manual. Many years later, when I was older and wiser, or at least more experienced, I came across a parody of the original writing guide by Strunk and White, written by a duo called Baker and Hansen. I thought their examples would have stuck with me if I had read them in college. Here were their own examples for what Strunk and White had provided under the rule "Omit needless words":

Used for the purpose of sexual pleasure. (wrong)
Used for sexual pleasure. (right)

making a convoluted argument about Japanese cinema; she had recently watched a film about a nuclear explosion on Mount Fuji. Nina was sitting in a chair next to me. I remembered the haiku about the cuckoo that Jennifer had given me. I wanted to write a quick haiku. But not about the cuckoo's lonely call. My fascination with Nina demanded a riskier expression of love. I passed a scrap of paper to her. On it I had written:

> *Wet moss between your thighs*
> *Semen*
> *Rains on Mount Fuji*

She surprised me by putting a small tongue out as if she was licking ice cream.

Suddenly, I was buying magazines like *Cosmopolitan* at the supermarket if they had headlines like TEN HOTTEST THINGS YOU CAN SAY IN BED or SEVENTY-SEVEN SEX POSITIONS. What did I learn from them? That I was supposed to say, *Is it okay with you if I take this slow?*

During a long-ago winter afternoon, in Delhi, in my early teens, I had watched *Tootsie* at the Chanakya cinema hall. Dustin Hoffman, disguised as a woman, listens to the beautiful Jessica Lange complaining.

His penis is a misshapen and uncircumcised one. (wrong)
His penis is misshapen and uncircumcised. (right)

She removed her clothes in a hasty manner. (wrong)
She removed her clothes hastily. (right)

—You know what I wish? That a guy could be honest enough to walk up to me and say, "I could lay a big line on you, but the simple truth is that I find you very interesting, and I'd like to make love to you." Wouldn't that be a relief?

That had given me insight, except that it was short-lived. For, later in the movie, Hoffman, now without his disguise, sees Lange at a cocktail party. He tries out that speech on her and before he has even finished she has thrown a glass of wine in his face.

A better person would have learned to walk a fine line between the two conversations. Not me. I swung from one extreme to the other. Hence my hunger for instruction. When I met Nina I also bought *Romance for Dummies* by Dr. Ruth. Dr. Ruth encouraged you to make noise while having sex: *While you retain the right to remain silent, perhaps you could speak up a little before your final act.* She said you never know how you'll react unless you give it a try at least one time. I enacted a silly pantomime when I came inside Nina that first time, not a war whoop exactly, more of a raised fist celebrating the revolutionary storming of the barricades. She, on the other hand, was silent, even pensive, though later that night she was affectionate, smiling, and this took away some of my foreboding. But here I'm getting ahead of myself.

===

There had been that one time even before Jennifer and I had broken up.

In my department mailbox, just before Thanksgiving, there had appeared a red flyer for a party at Peter's. I showed Jennifer the flyer but she wasn't interested.

> Calling all foreign TAs. Come and learn to speak English by watching *Down by Law* (dir. Jim Jarmusch).
>
> We will begin at 8 PM. 514 W 121st Street, Apt 3B. Door on the Left. Bell doesn't work. Don't let the cat out!
>
> B.Y.O.B. 242-7311.
> Host: Peter Koerner.

I took a bottle of wine for Peter. There was a naked woman on the label with the name Cycles Gladiator printed above her. The woman had a fleshy rump and long, fiery orange-red hair flying behind her. She was floating in the air, her hands on the handlebar of a bicycle outfitted with tiny, colorful wings. This would be to Peter's liking.

Maya from International Relations was already there, looking like the rani of Awadh, a cat in her lap. Flowing silks and a sleepy animal with jeweled eyes. I recognized some of the others. There was Jean, the French graduate student and a black belt, who, I had heard, counted loudly (three hundred forty-three . . . three hundred forty-four . . . three hundred forty-five) when he was fucking. This information had come from Jean's housemate, an Irishman who had described himself, by way of comparison, as a "semisilent fucker." Paulo, one of the Chilean anthropologists, was also someone I knew. He was there in the company of a woman with the semblance of a mustache.

I uncorked the bottle of wine I had brought. Then I saw Nina stepping out of the bathroom, an air of privacy still attached to her. An invisible current, like a rush of air lifting a kite, entered my body. Nina wasn't even a foreign TA—what a lovely surprise! I went up to her hurriedly but she thought I only wanted to go to the bathroom and stood sideways, her back pressed against the wall to let me pass. We smiled at each other and I kept walking. Inside, I studied my face in the mirror. A wild thatch of black curly hair. Round-rimmed glasses that failed to hide thick eyebrows. The face looking back at me wasn't ugly, but it was definitely ordinary. It didn't inspire confidence that a woman in the room outside would look at it and think she wanted to kiss it. I had been with Jennifer earlier in the evening, we had eaten cheap Tibetan food together. But the women in Peter's house, with whom I had sat in classes, were still strangers to me.

When I came back I saw that Nina was sitting on a small sofa with Paulo. I positioned myself on the armrest next to Paulo and stayed silent because Nina and he were discussing the music of Ornette Coleman. Others in the room were also talking among themselves and drinking. Siobhan quoted a line from a short story she had read in an American lit class: *To see her in sunlight was to see Marxism die*. I hadn't heard the writer's name before—and what was he really saying? Siobhan was mocking the politics embedded in such desire. The people around her agreed with the analysis. One of them, Marc, a poet who always carried a tiny tin of Altoids in his hand, touched his hair and said, You can absolutely date this brand of sexuality. It's an artifact of the Cold War! But I liked that line from the story even though I didn't understand what it meant. I wish I had said it myself. Through the glass door on the left I could see the small group standing on the patio outside—another feature of life in America, where you went out into the fresh air to smoke. Inside, just before he put the film on, Peter went up to Maya and kissed her on the cheek. Maya touched Peter's face, and then made space for him on the sofa. The cat jumped off her lap. For a moment, or a little longer, I thought about what I had just seen. Maya's undisguised affection for Peter and her plain, loving gesture in front of everyone else. When had they fallen in love? It gave me a little bit of a shock but it also made me feel guilty: I thought of Jennifer and what she had said once about my not wanting to touch her in public. Even if we had made our love public I wouldn't have acted like Maya. I would not have rubbed our noses together and smiled at one another while our friends pretended not to notice.

The film was in black and white. An Italian man named Roberto was wandering in the night in New Orleans. Roberto carried a notebook with him and he diligently recorded all the American idioms he heard. He ended up in the Orleans Parish Prison, every surface in the film lit up with the dramatic lighting familiar to me from the Hindi films of the fifties or the sixties. Roberto attempted to speak like an American, except that he kept mangling his sentences.

—Jack, do you have some fire? This was Roberto asking his cellmate for a match because he wanted to light his cigarette.

Whenever I laughed, I looked at Nina. She was watching the screen with an amused expression. Roberto was charming; he had killed a man after an altercation at a game of cards, but he insisted that he was "a good egg." And he was! He had found a way to escape from prison. On the run, he lost his "book of English," but he continued to entertain. He had memorized the American poets in translation, Whitman and others. I heard Frost's "The Road Not Taken" in Italian.

On the lam, Roberto found love. During these scenes I would sometimes think of Jennifer and at other times think of Nina. The film made me sentimental, lovesick, and Roberto's good luck gave me courage.

—Are you walking home? I asked Nina when she was leaving.

The sidewalks were darkened by the fallen autumn leaves. A shiny car passed slowly, music coming out of its open windows, and Nina said something about loving Prince. In a high falsetto, she sang, Cause nothing compares . . . and then skipped ahead of me. I ran behind her.

—Do you have some fire?

Nina was game. She pretended to give me a light, and I made as if to shake out a cigarette. When I cupped my hands around the pretend flame, her hands were nesting in mine. I found her touch thrilling. Even before I had reached her building, about five or six blocks from mine, I began to ask myself if I would ever kiss those hands. Her hands, her smooth arms. Her lips.

Despite it not being very cold on the street my teeth began to chatter with excitement.

When we got to her street, Nina stood at the door and said, Do you want to come in?

—No, I said, a bit too quickly, and the hand I half-raised to say goodbye was almost reaching toward her. I turned away into the dark. Jennifer might call soon at home, I thought. That was part of the reason I hesitated. The bigger reason was that I was a coward. I was disappointed that I hadn't had the courage to say yes but I was also secretly exulting. Nina's invitation was an augury for the future.

A week before the Christmas break, papers were to be submitted for all the classes. I could type them in my room or go to the library and use the word processors. I was only just learning to write academic papers, and I feared that I was going to do badly. And what was I going to write about for Ehsaan?* I asked him about the letter he had read at the teach-in. He gave me

---

* We had read E. M. Forster, Joseph Conrad, Frantz Fanon, Patricia Limerick, Assia Djebar, C. L. R. James, and others. Ehsaan's one-paragraph description on the course syllabus read: *This course views Western expansion into the Americas, Asia, and Africa as a development which shaped world history and civilization more decisively than any phenomenon other than capitalism. Beyond broadly surveying the course of Western expansion, our purpose is to explore its legacies to our time and modern civilization. Our focus is primarily on the outlook, cultures and mores, the ways of being and doing that, despite their enormous variety, colonial encounters spawned. Given this concern, the course shall rely primarily on historical narrative, literature, criticism, and cinema. Independently interested students are urged to inquire into art, an area we have not formally included.*

the title of a book by a British historian named David Omissi; in that book, I found other letters by Indian soldiers serving in the First World War, most of them in France. It would be best, I decided, if I could stitch together my commentary by taking excerpts from the letters I liked.

Fateh Mohamed had written in his letter sent to Punjab: *The cold for the last five or six days has been more intense than we have experienced during the two former winters. If one puts water into a vessel it is frozen in ten minutes. At the same time, there is a strong wind. If France had not been such a sympathetic country, existence under such conditions would be impossible. Through the kindness of these people [the French] we pay no regard to the cold. They themselves refrain from sitting near the fire-place and insist on our sitting there. Moreover, instead of water they give us* petit cidre, *which is the juice of apples to drink. Personally, except in the trenches, I have never drunk water.*

Too readily, I identified with what was in the letters: the desire to report on what was new but also to exaggerate, to make things extraordinary, to say that I eat meat every day or that I'm served juice and wine.* In most letters, however, the pathos was the plot. Consider the cry in another letter (less a

---

* There was such emphatic poetry present in the account of everyday reality. Let's read this letter that Kala Khan wrote to Iltaf Hussain in Patiala—*You enquire about the cold? At present I can only say that the earth is white, the sky is white, the trees are white, the stones are white, the mud is white, the water is white, one's spittle freezes into a solid white lump, the water is as hard as stones or bricks, the water in the rivers and canals is like thick plate glass. We are each provided with two pairs of strong, expensive boots. We have whale oil to rub in our feet, and for food we are provided with live Spanish sheep.*

letter than a single keening note) from Muhammad Akbar Khan to his home—*Is my parrot still alive or dead?*

A letter sent to Peshawar—*I have been in Hodson's Horse for the whole thirty-three years. During a railway journey when two people sit side by side for a couple of hours, one of them feels the absence of the other when he alights: how great then must be the anguish which I feel at the thought of having to sever myself from the regiment!* Such fine feeling! When I read the old soldier's letter I found myself thinking that this intense vibration of sentiment, the sense that the sender had about the sorrow of attachment, could only have been the result of a long experience with separation and loneliness.

At times, the soldiers seemed aware that the censor authorities would be reading their letters. They offered praise for the British king. They tried hard to reassure their loved ones. The soldiers were often careful in their phrasing of demands for goods that they could use to make themselves appear sick. Or high. But they also made mistakes. One soldier wrote to say that the next time his relatives sent opium to France they should only say that it was cream to be rubbed into his beard. The letter was withheld by the censors.

Letters like the one by Tura Baz Khan appeared unusual or transgressive to me, full of sexual boasting, and I was left unsure about what to make of them. But other letters, also touched with personal and sexual feeling, drew my attention for other reasons. A letter that I commented on at length in my paper had

A letter from Tura Baz Khan of the 40th Pathans from the Boulogne Depot in France: *[He had enclosed a cigarette card of* The Duchess of Gordon after Sir Joshua Reynolds.*] This is the woman we get. We have recourse to her. I have sent you this [her picture] and if you like it, let me know, and I will send her. We get everything we want. [Letter withheld.]*

been sent by a soldier from the 20th Deccan Horse regiment, stationed in France; I didn't entirely understand the letter or its circumstances, but I was drawn by its quiet undercurrent of sadness and resignation. It was addressed to the headmaster of the soldier's village in Punjab, and though it concerned a matter that was intimate, the language of the letter was formal, even abstract. For me, it was an example of a writer standing on the edge of grief.

My idea is that, since it is now four years since I went to my home, my wife should, if she wishes it, be allowed to have connection according to Vedic rites with some other man, in order that children may be born to my house. If this is not done, then the family dignity will suffer. Indeed, this practice should now be followed in the case of all wives whose husbands have been absent for four years or more. It is permitted by Vedic rites, if the wives are willing. Everyone knows that that article, the consumption of which is increased while the production is stopped, will in time cease to exist.

Other letters were easier to understand but difficult to accept. A brief unambiguous missive from Kabul Singh of the 31st Lancers: *Asil Singh Jat and Harbans have done a vile thing. They forcibly violated a French girl, nineteen years of age. It is a matter of great humiliation and regret that the good name of the 31st Lancers should have been sullied in this way.*

I got the paper back by mail instead of finding it in my department mailbox. In two places on the paper, Ehsaan had written *Good* in the margin. There was a paragraph of typed remarks on notepad paper stapled to the last page. Ehsaan had found my commentary on the letters *a little thin*. There were various questions that I could have considered: What were the rules regarding desertion? How much did the soldiers earn? What was the imperial expenditure during the war? What were the customs as well as the laws regarding marriage? What was the punishment for rape? My eyes went down to the last line of the paragraph. I had escaped grievous bodily harm: he had given me a B.

Your Honor, once again the desire to explain who I am. The stories of the soldiers bring to mind the tale of an ancestor on my mother's side, Veer Kunwar Singh. He had fought not for the British but against them. Kunwar Singh was already eighty years old when he joined the revolt against the East India Company in 1857. He began his campaign by ambushing the British forces near the Sone River. Two days earlier, rebellious sepoys had sacked the treasury in Ara, a stone's throw away from the house where, a little over a century later, Lotan Mamaji was born. The sepoys had also broken open the jail and released the prisoners. The local Europeans, numbering only ten, took refuge in the house of the railway engineer, a man named Boyle; they fortified the door with a billiard table and sandbags. From the nearby garrison town of Buxar, one Major Eyre led loyal troops who helped liberate those hiding in Boyle's home. Eyre's artillery power prevailed against Kunwar Singh's ragtag army, but the old warrior escaped on his horse. His wounded sepoys were executed in the town square. Eyre went to Kunwar Singh's estate and ordered the burning of the fields and huts in the surrounding villages. Singh's estate home was also destroyed and the temple he had built vandalized. In September of that year, two months

after Kunwar Singh began his campaign, the British took into custody in Delhi the aged emperor Bahadur Shah Zafar and sent him into exile to Burma. But Kunwar Singh soldiered on. During the course of an entire year that followed, even during the monsoon months, he participated in battles and led guerrilla attacks up to three hundred miles west of Ara. In April 1858 he defeated the British forces in Azamgarh.

When the enemy returned on the offensive again, Kunwar Singh conducted a brilliant withdrawal of his forces for over 150 miles. Despite their superior firepower and their leadership, which had been tested in the Crimean War, the English soldiers were unable to ever capture Kunwar Singh. He was to die later in his home, his own golden banner flying from his rooftop. But the reason he is remembered today is the story told of his crossing on the Ganges at Shivpur Ghat. The incident took place on April 21, 1858. Kunwar Singh was on a boat, guiding the withdrawal of his troops being pursued by the British infantry.

His boat was receiving fire from the gunboat Meghna, *one of three gunboats deployed on the river. One of the rebel boats capsized and then the boat on which Kunwar Singh stood also took a hit. His left arm was shattered by a cannonball. An amputation was the only cure in those days, and according to the story that is repeated today Kunwar Singh drew his sword with his right hand and, chopping off his left arm, let it fall as an offering to the holy river.*

=====

CLIT 300 was titled Brecht and His Friends. During that second semester, I saw Nina in classes twice a week. I flirted with her more confidently because I saw that she didn't take me seriously—although now that Jennifer and I had parted ways, I prayed constantly that Nina *would* take me seriously. Once, I stepped into the classroom and saw her seated in a circle of four or five others. I noticed right away that her outfit, a pale raw silk vest over a sleeveless cotton shirt, had been made in India. She probably bought it from a place like Bloomingdale's but as far as I was concerned it might well have been a gift from me. Stepping close behind her, I felt the fabric of her vest with my fingertips.

—Nice. I see that my cousin did a good job on his wooden weaving machine.

I didn't check to see if the others were amused or full of contempt. Probably both. All that mattered was that Nina was smiling.

—Your cousin? The one who lost his arm in the war?

—The very same. As a matter of fact, just last month he was brought to London—to present a bolt of the finest silk to the queen at the Festival of India. A thank-you for having ruled over us.

—Well, I thank your cousin for his nimble fingers. I prefer his wooden machine to all the mills of northern England.

Your Honor, by the standards of a court of law, we were full of lies. But how liberating were those lies! They gave me so much pleasure!

I laughed at her remark. I didn't want the banter to end.

—The mills are now closed, I said, and I hear they are all full of regret.

—Yes, serves the English fuckers right. May they suffer from gout and be forced to take the air in Brighton.

Nina was sitting down and, laughing, I put my palm on the back of her neck. She lowered her head as if I had just announced that I was going to give her a massage. And that is what I proceeded to do, making slow circles at the base of her skull with my thumbs, eyes fixed on the point where her hair was the shortest. I was conscious that the talk in the room had grown quiet but I wasn't going to stop. When Nina murmured her thanks I brushed the small bones on the back of her neck with my fingers bunched together. Her skin felt cool. I was flooded with a sense of peace.

This was the first time I had touched Nina. By pressing against the back of her chair, I could hide my erection. I was trying to breathe normally and stay quiet, but silence seemed to weigh the moment with a significance and I didn't dare contribute further to it. I began to blabber.

—Madam, I say this not to brag, but to make myself account-able: I come from a long line of mystic masseurs.

—Your immense promise is evident to me, Mr. Biswas.

The professor, David Lamb, walked in. Quiet, precise, wear-ing glasses that a decade later would be called Franzenesque. Lamb noticed what I was doing. I bet he would have liked to get into bed with Nina. It would no doubt happen very natu-rally with him. The two shared so much, conversation between them would flow without the need to pretend or exaggerate. They would sit at one of the restaurants uptown, drinking wine with cheese and olives, exchanging jokes about a performance they had both seen separately at the Public Theater. One of them would mention dinner, and the other would readily agree. When night came, it would only simplify rather than compli-cate things. And, in the morning, Lamb would pick up his stylish glasses from the side table and look at her smiling at him. When she sat up, he'd say something funny and she would bend down and kiss him on that impressive nose. He saw us, my hands upon her neck, and said nothing.

I removed myself to the remaining seat that was across from Nina. If she was at all conscious that we had engaged in an intimate act she didn't reveal it. Our eyes didn't meet during the rest of the class. I would think of Nina's lowered head and exposed neck when, weeks later, I found a book called *The Art of Sensual Massage* among the seven or eight books stacked in her bathroom. A blue circle on the cover said OVER ONE MILLION COPIES SOLD. Even today I can step into a health food store and the sight of candles or bottles of almond oil will bring back the dreamy, low-lit aura of limbs tensing and then easing under the pressure of my fingers. There is a particular smell I can catch in my nostrils, faintly floral mixed with something more warm and earthy, which is for me the smell of anticipation or, more accurately, the scent of the soon-to-be-fulfilled promise of sex.*

====

One evening students rushed into the university library, screaming, and threw fake blood over each other. The red liquid spilled on the library floor and on some books open on the desks. The students were enacting a scene from the war in the Gulf. General Schwarzkopf's controlled press conferences were clearly

---

* The book that Nina and I were to have the most fun with was one that claimed to help women achieve orgasm. The book wasn't Nina's. We found it in a café in Gardiner, Montana. Hippies, white people with their hair in dreadlocks, ran the café. The book sat on a shelf next to *Catch-22*, a guide to Antarctica, and if I remember right, a new-looking copy of *Blood Meridian*, and several other novels whose spines are now blurred in my memory. The books were there for customers to peruse while they waited for their avocado sandwiches with homemade goat cheese and alfalfa sprouts. In the book on orgasms, Nina found a passage to her liking and showed it to me. I whipped out my notebook, as sensitive and artistic men are supposed to do on such occasions, but then decided to steal the book instead. Tempo is important during sexual activity, the author had noted, before citing the kind of anthropological knowledge that fascinated Nina: according to Dr. Sofie Lazarsfeld in *Woman's Experience of the Male*, *We are reminded of the popular custom in Thuringia. There a couple will not marry until the boy and girl have sawn through a log together. If the rhythm of their movements agrees, the marriage takes place; otherwise the association is broken off.*

too sanitized. In the students' enactment, a few "medics" carried out the "wounded and dying." The leader of the group, Marc Rosenblum, said that the students at Mosul University, where the United States had bombed the cafeteria, "didn't have the opportunity to get pissed off because their books had been damaged." I was in my room and missed out on the whole thing.

I also missed out on a "kiss-in" that Siobhan and her friends in ACT-UP had organized in lieu of a teach-in. The event was reported in the campus newspaper, *Daily Spectator,* with a somewhat obvious picture of two female students kissing while Senator Jesse Helms scowled at them from a poster held aloft in the background. People gathered on the steps of the library nearly each day with banners to protest the war. I often saw Nina among the protesters. I would arrive there and scan the crowd for a beret and a Palestinian scarf. Also, dark shades and often a cigarette in her hand. That was Nina. I dreamed of walking up to her and kissing her hard. I'd run into her in the TA office but I found the public vibe more inviting. She intimidated me. The war was discussed everywhere. I tried to attend the protests but I also had to deal with my own courses and the class I was teaching. It was too much. I would be eating a quick lunch in the café in Pulitzer Hall and catch on the television screen the press briefings that the military conducted. I had missed the show on PBS where both Ehsaan and Said had appeared. To add to everything, there was always the worry about money. If during a particular month I sent a hundred or two hundred dollars to Lotan Mamaji's family in Ara, it put pressure on me to be frugal. In my sleep I would have dreams that were filled with a vague anxiety: I was leaning over a bridge in my village, trying to spit into the river below, but my mouth was dry and nothing came out. In the blank water beneath me, small fish swam.

Soon it wasn't so cold anymore. The war ended; the protests had made no difference. Secretary of Defense Dick Cheney said on television that the Iraqi Army was conducting "the Mother of all Retreats." The scene outside my window changed. Dirty snow that had stayed seemingly for months under the dumpster and mailboxes melted. A dogwood tree in the park put out tight buds that became beautiful red flowers. I could see turtles in the green pond. And there were daffodils! *Your Honor, is there an immigrant from India or Jamaica or Kenya who isn't thrilled to see the first daffodils of spring? The honest person forced to memorize Wordsworth's poem about daffodils without having a clue about what those flowers looked like can celebrate spring with the kind of joy that the native born can never know. This is how we know we have arrived!*

I had just had lunch and was on my way to the library. I told myself that I could read later, when darkness had fallen, and that right now, given how bright and warm it was outside, I should perhaps find a friend to have a beer with. Larry was probably in the TA room, slaving over a critical work on Bellow. He could easily be persuaded to put on his Ray-Bans and sit outside in the sun at Max Caffé. In the office, I saw that the overhead lights were off but Nina was there, sitting at her desk, her face bathed in white under her table lamp. A green frog jumped out of my chest and plopped down in the little pool of light beneath

Nina's chin. Or, that is how it felt. My heart had turned into a frog and escaped from my body. It now lay pulsing under the eye of a woman I loved from a distance.

—Comrade Nina!

In response, an amused shake of the head. A balanced mix of enthusiasm and indifference.

—Comrade IRS to you, my friend. I'm trying to do my taxes.

Taxes! With a dramatic flourish I extracted from my back-pack a yellow folder I had been carrying for a week: my W-2 statement, a dozen receipts from the university bookstore, the bus and hotel receipts from the graduate student conference on Rushdie in Buffalo. My fear of Nina made me bold.

—Nina, I beg you. Please stop. Let's do our taxes together.

—Why would I want to do anything so painful with you?

—Comrade IRS, let's have a beer, then. But let's also do our taxes together. I cannot make head nor tail of those forms.

She agreed that it was glorious outside, gathered her papers, and switched off her lamp.

In the TA office, the light that filtered through the window was weak, half-nocturnal. For a moment, Nina stood still, think-ing. A fish suspended in water. A thin blue sweater hung loosely from her shoulders. Something clicked in her mind, and she darted toward the door, all brisk efficiency.

—Do you have the forms?

—No!

We stopped at the campus post office to pick up the tax return forms. Every chair and sofa at Max Caffé accommodated an affluent law school student, so Nina decided we could go to the tiny park near her apartment instead. She grabbed a blanket and a cooler from her place. A short trudge up a hill till we came to a small stone tower built to commemorate the death of sailors at sea. Was it on that first visit, or later, that she told me all those vessels that had gone down were slave ships? No mention on the plaque of the hundreds crammed together under the grated hatchways, men and women and small children drowned with the manacles still bound to their ankles and necks.

Nina spread out the blanket on the grass. In the cooler that I had carried I found three bottles of beer and, in a silver-foil bag, spoons and a pint of ice cream. In the distance, maybe three hundred yards away, visible through the black trees that were still bare, was the highway. Nina laid herself down on her stomach, pen in hand, the pages of Form 1040NR spread out in front of her. Name and address, she said, and without waiting for me to reply, began to write. But my mind wandered.

Filing Status

Exemptions

Adjusted Gross Income

Line of Your Spine

Your Legs

Oh, Nina's Legs

I readily responded to her questions, mostly by making up my answers, and like a shrewd lawyer she accepted what I told her.

—Don't fuck with the state, Nina warned. She looked up, her

dark glasses hiding her eyes. I don't want to see you deported, she said.

Did she mean it in the way I hoped? Later, she would say yes, but in this and other instances, I kept an open mind. *The only point worth considering, Your Honor, is that it was the solemn enactment of the fundamental duty of the citizen, paying taxes, which brought the two of us closer together.* While she showed her agility with numbers, I smelled the grass and imagined pulling her skirt down the length of her smooth legs. Her breasts were pressed against the hard ground. I wanted to cup them and hold them gently, patiently, while she quickly multiplied 1094.19 by 6.

She brought her calculations to a close. It turned out that $187 was to be refunded to me. I signed my name at the bottom of the form.

—Thank you, I said, thank you.

She pushed her shades up on her head.

—What are you going to do with your dollars?

—Can I take you out for dinner?

We went to La Cucaracha. With the first sip of my margarita, a fine calmness descended on me. I wasn't acting cocky, and to be honest, my mind wasn't entirely free of doubt. Still, I wasn't worried about Nina and me anymore. There was little anxiety. In fact, there were moments when I felt certain that this woman who was laughing and mocking me as she ate tortilla chips was waiting for me to kiss her.

—You are in some terrible situation on a ship, let's say. A field trip gone horribly wrong. And the only way you can escape is if you slept with one of your professors. The question is: who would you *not* sleep with, like never, never, not in a million years to save your fucking life?

—Bonnie Clark, I said after a pause.

—That was too easy. Let me change the question: who would you absolutely want to sleep with, even if you were doing this only because the pirates who had captured you were going to kill you otherwise?

I would sleep with you. Only you. But more important, can't time just stop? I want this minute to last forever.

—I'm not afraid of death, I said instead.

—Why can't a dog tell a lie? Is it because he is too honest, or is it because he is too sly? Poor Wittgenstein!

I had not read Wittgenstein. But David Lamb, our professor from CLIT 300, had read Wittgenstein, and Hegel, and Kant, and Stanley Cavell. Lamb had once said at a party that whenever he suffered from insomnia he read Derrida: Not because he makes me go to sleep but because he makes staying up a pleasure. As I thought of Lamb, a sliver of ice lodged itself in my heart. My earlier assurance ebbed, and I felt stranded on the shore, watching the boat slowly receding. My father had grown up in a hut. I knew in my heart that I was closer to a family of peasants than I was to a couple of intellectuals sitting in a restaurant in New York. Our dinner of skirt steak and jumbo shrimp was nearly over, and now because I was uncertain why we had been laughing only a minute ago, a sense of fatalism began to overtake me. The fickle human heart, prone to despair. How quickly the boredom sets in.

Perhaps Nina noticed a change.

—Okay, truth teller, she said, it is time to get you off this ship and into your bed.

We got into Nina's hatchback and she said she shouldn't have drunk so much. I was relieved when I saw that Nina didn't turn onto her street, that she was going to drive me back to my place first. The tension eased. Now that I didn't have to contemplate whether or not I was going to be asked to come up to her apartment, I could relax again. But to deal with this disappointment, I wanted a cigarette.

—You know what I'd like right now? I said cheerfully.

—A blow job?

I laughed too loudly, and she laughed too.

When she dropped me off, Nina said she needed to use the bathroom. I heard the noise of the flush in the toilet. And I moved away down the corridor, to open the front door for her. Instead, as soon as she came near me, I said, Don't leave.

My hand went up to her cheek.

—*Finally*.

She made those quotation marks in the air with two fingers of both hands when she said that word. She wasn't done.

She said, Jesus, is the paint dry yet?

A person who is laughing is difficult to kiss, so I hesitated a moment. She put a finger on my mouth and leaned in closer, a serious expression on her face. The soft crush of her lips on mine released a fury of desire in me. We kissed for a long time, standing in that hallway, Nina's back pressed against the wall.

I am from a land of famines, Your Honor, and I displayed such hunger, such astonishing greed. Eager to touch every part of her, I turned Nina around so that her back was to me. She raised her arms, her palms flat against the wall. I was the blind man. Her breasts were in my hands. *One afternoon in Delhi, Noni had gone with Deepali from Sociology to Surajkund. They came back late. What did he most like about her? Noni said that Deepali's breasts were like kabootars in his hands, two soft, startled pigeons fluttering under his fingers. Your Honor, this is the truth of my American Dream: to possess the life of a Sikh from Patiala.* At least, that is what the dream was till I met Nina and she took me, almost daily, to other neighborhoods. During my adolescence, I used to make guilty entries in my journal. I never once wrote down the word *masturbation;* I only recorded that I was "distracted."* *In my teens, I had been innocent of even something like a Victoria's Secret catalog. Your Honor, Nina made such self-consciousness a thing of the past. Nina, once we became lovers, rid me of my guilt.* She'd examine the pictures in the catalog and ask me which model I wanted to fuck. Where do you want to do it, the wooden deck visible toward the top of the

---

* Not very sophisticated as a system of notation, I know. Unlike Victor Hugo, who concealed his many sexual activities from his longtime mistress, Juliette Drouet, by adopting a varied system in his notebook. Here is James Salter on Hugo: *Along with a woman's name or initials, he might mark an* N *that stood for naked; something else for caresses;* Suisses, *for breasts; and so forth, a kind of ascending order. For everything, the full act, he wrote* toda, *all. There was something noted for almost every day.* James Salter, *The Art of Fiction* (Charlottesville: University of Virginia Press, 2016).

picture, or right here on the sandy beach where she has planted her red toenails?

All through that afternoon, while she had helped me with my taxes, I had gazed at Nina's legs crisscrossed on the woolen blanket. Now, crouching down in the hallway, beside my bike that I had bought from a Chinese electrical engineering student for twenty bucks, I was kissing the backs of Nina's knees. I kissed her and licked her, pushing my tongue everywhere I could. In touching her, I was touching the sea, I was walking on soft sand, I was tasting the salt of my infinite longing. I heard her sigh when I moved my hands up to her crotch. Then she said, Let's go to your bed.

I apologize, Your Honor. Even at that moment, I could almost hear my mind repeating clichés, Such a long journey. *I was thinking of the long wait for carnal contact with Nina but that phrase—it was the title of a new novel by a writer from Mumbai living in Toronto.* Such a long journey. *I had heard Maya use it after a hunt through different stores for a samosa but it was supposed to encapsulate the immigrant condition. I dreamed of being a writer, and even while fumbling with the clasp on Nina's bra, I sought language for my experience. This search was part of the pleasure of the moment.* It had been a journey not from hallway to bed but from the long wanting to the moment of fulfillment. This is what sex with Nina had meant to me: keen desire and struggle and, just when it seemed that the goal was still so far, success. This ache that I had nursed so long, as if for a lifetime, ended with Nina naked under me. A pair of white thighs opening, legs wrapped around my torso and then spread wide. Her head was inching closer to the wall behind her, and putting my hand protectively on her hair, I moved deeper into her. Her moans soon turned, with a half gasp, into the sentence that the article in *Cosmopolitan* had said every man wants to hear, *I'm going to come.*

Part III

Laura and Francis

umbrella made sense. I could really see him doing something like that." Walker is passionate about Hollinger's sculpture. "The first time I saw Steve's art work was the week I was getting married," she said. "I thought it was so amazing—so complex and sensitive and deep that I said to myself, If I meet this guy, I'm not going to get married!"

This was not the first time a Hollinger

The above clipping in my notebook is, I believe, from 2008. I don't know, or no longer remember, the individuals involved. I must've read it, and liked it, as a startling statement about the meeting of art and desire.

Also, in a child's hand, on a piece of paper torn from a sheet: *Happy Fact: Otters hold hands when they sleep, so they don't float away from each other.*

Mr. Kissinger, you're under arrest.

This was to be said after dessert. Everything would be calm. Nothing out of the ordinary. Ehsaan believed that because they were academics, and had friends in common, they could get invited to a dinner where Kissinger was also a guest. People sipped cognac in such circles. Ehsaan would choose the moment to speak. He was articulate: his words commanded attention. He would get up and make the announcement about the arrest, addressing Kissinger directly.

Then Kissinger was to be taken to a meeting of antiwar activists. He would be questioned about war policies. The police by then would have started a massive manhunt, of course.

The accused was to be moved from one hiding place to another, and within a day or two, a statement would be issued that he had been arrested for the crimes of war. The point was to educate the public. Put the war back on the front pages instead of endless stories about the breakup of the Beatles or Jim Morrison's allegedly lewd and lascivious behavior. They would be clear about their aims. Kissinger was to be released if the government stopped B-52 raids in North Vietnam.

They had been sitting around in a borrowed house in Weston, Connecticut. A white single-story house with a large screened porch in the front. It belonged to Ehsaan's in-laws, who were away in Europe at that time. He had cooked rice pulao and chicken curry. Everyone was drinking chilled vin rosé and, when that was gone, gin and tonic. Out of the ease of the evening, the lingering light of the summer, and the flow of the conversation among friends had come the talk about making a citizen's arrest.

Mr. Kissinger, you're under arrest. This statement was noted more than once in the indictment.

Ehsaan just laughed when I asked him about the Kissinger trial. So many years had passed. But he had a purple mimeographed article, pale with age, from the *Bulletin of the Atomic Scientists*. Noam Chomsky had given it to him, or maybe Howard Zinn, he couldn't remember. At some point during the public trial of Kissinger a member of their group would inform the American public that the B-52 bombings had turned the rice fields of Vietnam into a lunar landscape. The countryside was now useless for crops, gouged by craters, some as large as forty-five feet across and thirty feet deep. Placed end to end, these craters would form a ditch thirty thousand miles long, a distance greater than the circumference of the earth. Unforeseen medical problems now ravaged the population there. That people were living underground day and night, and children were suffering from many disorders, including rickets from living without sunlight.

Ehsaan said that the idea first emerged at an antiwar rally at St. Gregory's Church in New York City. *Yes, Your Honor, ordinary Americans had committed themselves to a plan of administering justice because they felt that their government was acting in a lawless manner.* At any large gathering a person would simply get up and say: We hereby take into custody, in a citizen's arrest, such-and-such people who are government leaders. Then "subpoenas" would be "issued." It was all symbolic, and involved no concrete action. The goal was education.

The idea of arresting Kissinger was an escalation in the war on war, a step-up from earlier actions, like the burning of draft records or the dumping of two buckets of human waste into the Selective Service filing cabinet. But the idea didn't go any further because how would you get to detain somebody like Henry Kissinger without using some form of coercion? It seemed implausible. Ehsaan and his guests spent twenty minutes discussing this plan that evening but abandoned it even before the ice had melted in the glasses from which they were drinking.

Except that a few months later, in November 1970, when

J. Edgar Hoover spoke in a Senate Appropriations Committee hearing, he mentioned this conspiracy and, for good measure, a plan to blow up underground electrical conduits and steam pipes serving the Washington, D.C., area. It was pure fabrication, Ehsaan would say later. Along with Ehsaan, the others named by Hoover were two Catholic priests and two nuns who had been active in the peace movement. After having made the public accusation, Hoover threw hundreds of his agents into the investigation of antiwar activities. A little over a month later, FBI agents knocked on doors to serve federal grand jury subpoenas to scores of people. There was going to be a trial.

For his part, after Hoover's announcement, Kissinger speculated that "sex starved nuns" were behind the plot to kidnap him. President Nixon gave the go-ahead by saying that he would let the Justice Department carry out its prosecution unimpeded. Ehsaan said that they phoned William Kunstler, and after a hurried meeting, the famed counselor released a statement on their behalf: *Mr. Hoover is overgenerous. We have neither the facilities nor personnel to conduct such an enterprise. Nor do we have access to unallocated funds like the government does . . .* Their struggle was to impart a sense of reality into a scenario made feverish by Hoover's paranoid imagination. That is why the lead defense counsel, Ramsey Clark, in his opening statement on the first day of the trial, reminded the jury, Of course we know that Henry Kissinger wasn't kidnapped. He is alive and well in Peking today.

The trial was held in Harrisburg, during the first three months of 1972. *Your Honor, there would have been no indictment,*

and no trial, had it not been for a letter that was written after that
summer meeting in Weston, Connecticut. A love letter, no less. This is
the juncture where I wish to note, once and for all, that the plot of his-
tory advances through the acts of lovers. Oh, the wisdom of love. The
superiority of love and its many follies. I also wish to add that these
details were later to be faithfully communicated to Nina when she and
I fell in love. The discovery of these details I think was a part of the
excitement of being in love with her. Do you understand what I am
getting at here, Your Honor? I beg for the Court's forbearance.

Present at that planning dinner in Weston, Connecticut, on
the night of August 17, 1970, had been a young woman named
Laura Campbell. Laura had just started teaching art history at a
Catholic college in New York. She was also a nun. And she was
falling in love with a man to whom she wrote letters each week
in prison. He was a priest who had waited for the police to come
and arrest him after he had poured blood on draft records to
protest the war.

The priest's name was Francis Hull. He was serving a six-year
sentence in Lewisburg, Pennsylvania, for his antiwar activities;
he was also a participant in the civil rights movement and a
critic of the isolated stance of the church in black communities.
I looked at the black-and-white photographs of him. Hull had
been a baseball player in his youth, and even in his fifties, he
seemed to radiate a youthful energy. Strong face, open smile. In
one of the newspaper reports, his photograph was accompanied
by a quote: *I have faith in the Almighty who will save our souls. I am*
just trying to save the lives of the young blacks being sent to Vietnam.

Father Hull also had faith in a fellow convict, Douglas

Adams. Adams was on a student release program and would go each day to Bucknell University to take classes. While on campus, he would hand over to a librarian named Mary any letters from Hull that he had smuggled out in his notebooks. The letters were for Campbell mostly but also, on occasion, for other activists. Mary, in turn, gave Adams the letters she had received in the mail from Laura. Neither Francis Hull nor Laura Campbell knew that Adams would carefully open each letter and make a photocopy that he would take back with him to prison in a manila envelope. This was because after he had read the first letter from Laura to Francis, and dutifully made a copy, he had approached the FBI and become an informant.

Ehsaan hadn't even laid eyes on Adams till the trial began and Adams, flanked by U.S. marshals, stepped into the courtroom. He was a thickset man in a lavender shirt standing stiffly on the sea of green slime that was the court carpet. He was the main witness for the government. Adams would not look at any of the defendants. In his deposition, he made the claim that Ehsaan had called him twice, at a Laundromat, to discuss plans to kidnap Kissinger. Ehsaan told the press that this was "a complete falsehood." Admittedly, Adams didn't have any qualities that would have incited Ehsaan's interest or trust. Adams had served for a short time in the U.S. military in Korea, and then passed bad checks and stolen a car. Back in America, after escaping from a military stockade, he had once again used forged checks in Las Vegas and then Atlantic City. His father, in conversation with a journalist, said that his son had not spoken the truth even once in his life.

Yet, Adams was kind of a charmer. At Bucknell, he told the young women he befriended that he was very active in the antiwar movement and was probably under surveillance by the authorities. He claimed close friendship with Francis Hull, the mention of whose name stirred people's curiosity and admiration. Adams started dating two female students. He proposed to one of them, a blonde named Jane, but she had doubts about marrying him. To put her in a better frame of mind, Adams went ahead and bought her a bus ticket so that she could travel to New York City for the first time in her life, where she was to meet Sister Laura and open her heart to her. En route, Jane read a letter from Adams that he had said she should wait to take out of the envelope till she was on the bus. The greeting he had used as well as the words he had employed to sign off had been borrowed from what he had seen in Laura's letters to Francis. He had also written that if he sometimes appeared distant in his manner it was because someone close to him had once ratted him out to the FBI. Adams told Jane in the letter that he had proposed to her because he had cancer and he wanted her to give him six months of happiness.

Let us pause here for a moment. The contempt that Ehsaan and others felt toward Adams, that feeling, slightly exaggerated, is in my heart too: in a memory that is not mine, I see Adams stepping into the courtroom flanked by armed marshals, who tower protectively above him, and I hiss in anger. Adams looks nervous because in all the stories we have read liars look around apprehensively while still managing to avoid meeting anyone's eyes. Ehsaan will not even look at him, but I do. My interest in Adams borders on sympathy. He claimed that he was close to Hull, he thought the women he wanted to date would be impressed; I was to do the same with Nina, bringing back to her stories of my encounters with Ehsaan. Adams stole words from Hull and Laura, and used them in the letters he wrote to Jane. I don't want to be Adams in his plaid shirt and oversize glasses, and I don't want to sweat like him, but I am him. *Let me explain with an example, Your Honor.* In Ehsaan's class the previous semester I had read Stuart Hall, who had been born in Jamaica and spent most of his life in England, where he gained a following as an enormously influential cultural theorist. In his essay, Hall said that people like him who came to England in the fifties had actually been there for centuries. He was talking about slavery and sugar plantations. *I am the sugar at the bottom of the English cup of tea.*[*] Symbolically, Hall was saying, the people from the darker nations had a long history in the West. The symbol of English identity was the cup of tea, but where did the tea come from? There were no tea plantations in England. And there was no English history without that other history. Powerful stuff and delivered in Hall's inimitable way. In a poem I was to write for Nina a few months later, I shamelessly put as my closing line: *I'm the sugar at the bottom of your coffee, I'm the color in your cup of tea.* End of pause.

---

[*] Stuart Hall, "Old and New Identities, Old and New Ethnicities." Xeroxed copy of an article in typescript sent to Ehsaan by his old friend Hall. The piece was published a few months later in Anthony D. King, ed., *Culture, Globalization and the World-System* (New York: Palgrave Macmillan, 1991). See pp. 48–49.

Francis Hull and Laura Campbell had hit upon a strategy in their letters. They were afraid that a guard could discover their letters if he checked the pages of the notebooks where Adams used to hide them. So, they would always begin as if they were putting together a college essay. Laura Campbell titled the letter that formed the basis for the indictment "Reflections on Technological Advancement—On the Anniversary of Man's First Landing on the Moon." The first paragraph read:

> Is it possible to reverse the trend of technological advancement—of any advancement? Seems we all have the tendency (& in difficult circumstances almost the need) to look back to days when life was better, air was cleaner, and, with their difficulties, human relationships were easier & more "beautiful." Confession—I do that a lot. But it seems clear that it's not possible to reverse it, to go back. Despite the dangers & difficulties, one must apply a moral consciousness to here & now & all that means & commit one's life to shaping out a future of hope & life. Without knowing what that may mean in terms of proximity to loved ones one still tries to say "yes" at times more weakly than others.

The second paragraph began with the words *What were our thoughts last year as man first walked the moon?* but was quickly followed by a line that dipped into the personal, recording Campbell's pleasure at their last meeting. *The best part was seeing you in the old fighting spirit and to know first hand that beyond physical confinement, they had no control over you.* And then came the part that had given J. Edgar Hoover cause to launch an investigation:

This is in utter confidence & should not be committed to paper & I would want you not even to say a word of it to anyone until we have a fuller grasp of it. I say it to you for two reasons. The first obviously is to get your thinking on it, the second to give you some confidence that people are thinking seriously of escalating resistance. Ehsaan called us up to Connecticut last night. He outlined a plan for an action which would say—escalate seriousness—& we discussed pros and cons for several hours. It needs much more thought & careful selection of personnel. To kidnap—in our terminology make a citizen's arrest of—someone like Henry Kissinger. To issue a set of demands, e.g., cessation of use of B-52s over N. Vietnam, Laos, Cambodia, & release of political prisoners. Hold him for about a week during which time bigwigs of the liberal ilk would be brought to him—also kidnapped if necessary (which, for the most part it would be)—& hold a trial or grand jury affair out of which an indictment would be brought. There is no pretense of these demands being met & he would be released after this with a word that we're nonviolent as opposed to them, who would let a man be killed—one of their own—so that they could go on

killing. The liberals would also be released as would a
film of the whole proceedings in which, hopefully, Kissinger would be far more honest than he is on his own
turf. The impact of such a thing would be phenomenal.

Ehsaan would come and stand behind me, reading the files over
my shoulder. I was his teaching assistant that semester, this
would have been the year 1991, and I was assigned to organize
the papers in his study at home. He saw me reading Sister Laura
Campbell's letter. He was silent for a while and then, leaning
over me, underlined with the nail of his right thumb the words
should not be committed to paper. He laughed a shrill laugh and
turned away to answer a phone call. His voice came from the
next room.

—Edward, how are you? We will discuss that but first I must
tell you: I have found a cheese that will appeal to you . . .

I returned to the papers spread out before me.

We are back during the days of the late summer of 1970.
Adams brought Francis Hull's letter to the librarian. It bore the
title "The Use and Effectiveness of Group Therapy in the Federal Penal System." The opening line: *An emphasis on relationship
seems to have sponsored a growing tendency on the part of the penal
administrators to have inmates in more personal contact with one
another and with staff members.* Immediately followed by a few
lines about how keenly Hull had savored Sister Laura's visit: *the
best part of the afternoon was your glowing person.* Then, as if a dis-

cussion was being conducted in a public meeting, he dived into a critical assessment of kidnapping Kissinger. His main query: *Why not coordinate it with the one against capitol utilities?* Hull expanded on the notion of *effective propaganda and the movement* for the length of two paragraphs. At the end, he added, *Will you permit me a little compliment, Sister? The big difference rests largely with your coming in. And when this odyssey is over, I will learn from you, receiving the education that results from a marriage of minds and souls.*

Among the nine folders related to the trial in the study was a clipping that described Ehsaan as *a slim, debonair 40-year-old with excellent manners and a dazzling smile.* The main story was about Ehsaan raising funds for the defense. Ehsaan had received two thousand letters of support and two that were unfavorable. The most touching letter, the report said, was from a black Vietnam veteran, a former student of Ehsaan's, who thanked him for *being nice to me and treating me like a human being.* This vet had enclosed a three-thousand-dollar check, his entire discharge pay—*because now that my government has done this to you, you need all the help you can get.* The vet had originally intended to use the money as a down payment on a house. Ehsaan returned the check, the report said, suggesting that a hundred dollars would be *a fairer contribution.*

In another clipping it was noted that a marshal inside the courtroom referred to Ehsaan as *that camel driver.* One of the Harrisburg citizens in the court's elevator told the reporter: *that Pakistani should be shishkabobed for bringing the country more trouble than it already has.* This could have prompted outrage or indignation in my postcolonial heart but what interested me more was the following description in another report, this time by a male reporter, in what gets called *a newspaper of public record: Sister Laura frequently wore mini skirts and with her long shapely legs, her smooth complexion, oval face and almond-shaped blue eyes, she looked younger than her thirty-two years.* When I read that, I thought of Hull writing to Campbell, *Will you permit me a little compliment, Sister?* And I saw Ehsaan, near a giant sunlit window in the courtroom, I saw him with his dark, handsome face and his aforementioned dazzling smile, lavishing attention and words on the miniskirt-wearing nun.

=====

Ehsaan came back from talking on the phone and I turned to the page where he had put his finger on the phrase. His leg was hurting again; I saw him grimace when he sat down. I had a question for him.

—Why did she put all that in the letter?

—The first thing you are taught as a guerrilla in Algeria is the following motto: *Quand tu es en prison, tu ne demandes que des oranges.* When you are in prison, you ask only for oranges . . . It takes a lot of revolutionary discipline to resist the temptation to ask for more.

When Ehsaan had been young, that is to say the age I myself was when I first met him, he had gone to Tunisia as a graduate student at Princeton to do research for his doctorate. In nearby Algeria, revolution had caught fire. It was said that Ehsaan had traveled to Algeria and fought in the war against the French. Had he? No one knew for certain. A couple of people remarked to me later that Ehsaan wasn't averse to mythmaking. I myself never got the chance to ask him, and years later, sitting in a restaurant one rainy evening on Broadway, when I asked his widow that question, she quietly said that she didn't know. I had liked her honesty, especially when I pressed her to explain why Ehsaan had chosen to stay in the United States and not return to Pakistan when his studies were over. She laughed and said, "In Pakistan the women wore the hijab. Here they showed their legs." But back in Ehsaan's office that day, I had looked up from the photocopied letter written in the neat, right-sloping hand-writing of Laura Campbell.

— It must have been terrible for them . . . for these letters to be read out in court.

— Oh, it was appalling, Ehsaan said. They were lovely people, with great dignity. It went on for hours. They just stared at the floor.

The defense lawyer had cross-examined the government witnesses. He didn't believe Adams had been left with even a shred of credibility. They didn't need to carry out the charade any longer. The charges were preposterous. He simply got up and said, These defendants will always seek peace. Your Honor, the defense rests. The jury voted ten to two on acquittal for all charges. In the months that followed, both Hull and Campbell quit their religious orders. They got married and opened a community house in a black neighborhood in Baltimore.

—I went to their wedding, Ehsaan said. They now have two children. You should visit them. They will welcome you.

—During the trial, they must have had a chance to see each other in court every day? That must have been a relief.

—They never hid their affection for each other in court. They always embraced when they came together. It shocked some people. I admired them for that . . . And that is how one must understand what Laura did in her letter. She was sharing a secret with her lover—that is all. They had kept him in solitary confinement because of his hunger strike in Danbury prison. She was giving him hope. I have to tell you, they often struck me as naïve, but they were also the most honest people I had met.

=====

Years have passed. It is a hot August day in 2009 and I am at a Starbucks at a rest stop on the New Jersey Turnpike. People come here with their bladders full and their gas tanks empty. In the newspaper someone has left on the table there is mention of a priest who had used bolt cutters to cut a hole in a chain-link fence and then stepped atop the silo of a Minuteman III nuclear missile with an antinuke banner wrapped around his body. It is not Francis Hull. But lower in the report, there is mention of Laura Campbell, and then the phrase *the widow of Francis Hull.* So, like Ehsaan, Hull is gone. Campbell must be in her early seventies now. I call directory information, and a few minutes later, I am asking Laura Campbell for permission to visit.

—Would you like lunch? This is the simple, straightforward question she asks me on the phone.

She is tall, gray-haired. Wearing a T-shirt that says ROTC OFF ALL CAMPUSES. Her denim trousers are splattered with paint. Situated beside a cemetery, the small house behind her serves as a meeting place for activists: on Fridays, which it is today, they distribute food and clothes in the morning. But it is past noon now and on the table set outside the house are scattered the leftovers: an out-of-season woolen jacket, a mustard-colored sweater, old socks, neatly paired. At the far end, I can see a nearly empty container of soup and alongside it an aluminum tray with dry bread crumbs. All around us are tombstones. I ask Laura if it would be possible for her to show me Hull's grave before we have lunch. She introduces me first to a donkey they have in their stable. She pats the donkey, whose name is Vinnie, and rubs her mane. Then we go among the sassafras trees to look for her three pet goats. Planted amidst the thousand dead, Irish working-class folk from early in the nineteenth century, many of them new immigrants, are walnut and maple trees. Also elm and oak. The goats have as their companion and guard a tall llama named Paz. I pet the goats and try to do the same with the llama but Sister Laura stops me.

—They're not used to touch. Their tongues don't distend, so they have never been licked by their mother. But they are very sensitive, very intelligent, oh yes.

A large black marble gravestone with a Celtic cross on it

marks Francis Hull's resting place and Laura slowly runs her hand across the top of the stone. It is a tender gesture. She points out the plum and fig trees close by, and the lettuce bushes and the lines of carrot. When we go inside and sit down for lunch, she holds my hand as she closes her eyes and prays. The meal is simple, pasta, cold cuts, fresh salad. In the car, I had thought I'd ask her questions about Ehsaan and Francis Hull, but I realize that I'm just happy to be in her company. Then I do, anyway.

—All the news reports I had read about the trial mentioned your prettiness and your love for Father Hull. Was that love a part of what you thought of as the revolution?

I feel a bit prurient asking her this, but she doesn't hesitate.

—You want what is good in your life also to be enjoyed by others.

These defendants will always seek love, Your Honor.

=====

Life comes at you in images. Every day this summer the photographs in the news show refugees who in a bid to escape their bombed-out cities risk death on the high seas. Fathers with life jackets clutching their children, women with babies clasped to their breasts. It is not clear what President Obama's response will be to this crisis, but Germany has opened its doors to the new arrivals. On Twitter, the refugees fleeing war compete for my attention with other images of meals people have eaten in restaurants, their pets, or the stunning sunsets seen during beach vacations. I pay attention to what comes my way from

India. Just the other day someone sent me a photograph of a CNG yellow-and-green auto-rickshaw in Delhi. At the back, on its yellow canopy, were the words ASLI JAT in Hindi. That was understandable. But below the words in Hindi, were the words in English:

NOBODY REMAINS VIRGIN

LIFE FUCKS EVERYONE

When I was growing up in India, the common signs in English on public transport were variations of O.K. TATA, HORN PLEASE, USE DIPPER AT NIGHT. When did Delhi's auto-rickshaw drivers become a part of Lord Macaulay's English-speaking army dispensing metaphorical wisdom about getting fucked? This particular four-letter word—short and dominated by consonants, yet malleable and open to a range of inflections. I'll tell you a little later the story of a discovery I made, that there was a whole sermon on it by an Indian guru.

EVENINGS AT 7.

MON	ALCOHOLICS ANONYMOUS
TUES	ABUSED SPOUSES
WED	EATING DISORDERS
THU	SAY NO TO DRUGS
FRI	TEEN SUICIDE WATCH
SAT	SOUP KITCHEN

SUNDAY SERMON 9 A.M. "AMERICA'S JOYOUS FUTURE"

That was the postcard I pinned to the door of the office for the English Department's teaching assistants.* The card showed a notice board of the sort you see at schools and churches, with white plastic alphabets inserted into holes in the black board. (The keen pleasure of embracing shallow stereotypes! I was a foreigner. Still am, after more than twenty years.) An arrow drawn on the postcard with a felt pen pointed to *THU. Office Hrs, 4–6 PM* and my name next to it.

Six of us used the office. Nina's desk was in the same room. And also those of the other teaching assistants: Pushkin Krishnagrahi, Ricardo Morales, and Larry Blofeld. Closest to my desk was my friend Peter's. Near my postcard on the door were his office hours *(Koerner: T–Thu 1–2 PM and by appt)*. Partly out of solidarity and partly to taunt me, he had tacked a print of a five-by-seven photo also showing a sign outside a church.

STAYING IN BED

SHOUTING, OH GOD!

DOES NOT CONSTITUTE

GOING TO CHURCH

I could have pasted above my own desk a picture of the Taj Mahal. This was certainly true during the early days, when I

---

* Nearly all the graduate students in the department were teaching assistants: our tuition fees waived because we were more than willing to serve as anxious, often unconventional, perhaps overqualified, certainly underpaid, but also otherwise unemployable, conscripts in the army maintained by academia. Like many others before me for the past 150 years, I couldn't have made it out of India without this readiness on my part to be an indentured laborer.

wouldn't have thought twice about stealthily tearing out an Air India ad from a magazine in the university library. The record should state clearly, however, that the first thing I tore out was a reproduction in *The Atlantic* of an early painting by Picasso. *Your Honor, Picasso had painted it after first making love. The brown back of a thin male sunk into the flesh of a shapely woman with commodious thighs. What caught my eye was the woman's slim and languid arm, with its high elbow, holding Picasso in place.* Then, when I began reading writers I hadn't read in India I tacked their pictures in place of the notice from the church. Brecht, Baldwin. This was still during my first year in America. One day I found a postcard in Greenwich Village that showed a piece of graffiti on a wall. Where had the photograph been taken? There was no indication. It quoted an exchange between a reporter and Mahatma Gandhi:

— Mr. Gandhi, what do you think of Western
   civilization?
— I think it would be a good idea.

This new postcard had pride of place on the wall: when a visiting student spoke to me, he or she could look past my head and read the postcard. It was like an imagined thought bubble, a witty statement that I wanted to adopt as my line onstage. This was my private version of *To be or not to be* or *Friends, Romans, Countrymen.* But then one day, a flyer appeared in my mailbox. The opening words were *If God is dead, then you lose the most*

important word in your language. And you need a substitute. Instead
of God, Fuck has become the most important word in our language.
The words were from a speech by Osho, who was also known
as Bhagwan Rajneesh. All kinds of flyers, pamphlets, announcements were put in our mailboxes every day. The difference was
that an Indian had written these words. Therefore, I treated
them as my own. I made copies for all my friends and officemates. The following day, or the day after that, there was a tape
in my mailbox. Both the flyer and the tape had come from a
Bengali grad student, Biman, who otherwise kept himself busy
with work on his thesis on Naguib Mahfouz. I listened to the
tape with great interest. Osho spoke with what in this country
was called a pronounced accent. For me, his voice was like the
voices of my relatives and friends, even the word *English* uttered
with a sibilant hiss. Osho's whole lecture was a disquisition on
the word *fuck*. The guru's talk was repeatedly interrupted by
laughter from his American audience. This filled me with ela-
tion. I ignored the awful shallowness. An Indian was holding
forth on the English language, offering a sermon from below,
an unholy discourse on how sex was the new divine, and all the
white people couldn't have enough of it!

Fuck, we belonged!

—First thing, when you wake up, if you repeat the mantra
Fuck you five times it clears your throat too.

That was Osho speaking. I played the tape on the boom box
in the office.

Osho started as a teacher in a small town in Madhya Pradesh

but later became an international guru. People gave up their lives, and their property, to flock to his ashram in Pune. I had heard that Osho told people to free their minds and that, inevitably, there were orgies at his ashram. Sometime in the eighties he moved his ashram to Oregon. My father had a friend from college who was a psychologist from Chapra; he read Osho's books and wanted to follow him to America. One evening, when I was a teenager, this man arrived at our house in Patna wearing a saffron kurta. He asked my mother for some sindoor so that he could put a red mark on his forehead. Did my mother have a necklace of rudraksha beads? She did! He wet the tips of his fingers at the sink and touched his curls. He was going to a spiritual meeting, he had hopes of impressing a linguist who had come from America. I had always thought my father's friend was good-looking, he had a lazy charisma, and now, as I listened to Osho's tape, the memory of my father's friend came back to me. Some months later he died in a car accident; he never got a chance to travel to America. But Osho, from a similar place, from a similar caste, had made it. He was a role model.

—One of the most interesting words in the English language today is *fuck*. It is a magical word.

This was Osho again, speaking out from the tape.

And then there was a weird, quite exact, and also quite inaccurate, in fact plain wrong, listing of the usages of that word. Osho, in the manner of a schoolteacher, named the grammatical category and then provided an example. And each item was followed by uncontrollable laughter from his devotees. I heard the laughter and imagined half-naked hippies, who had flocked to the huge ranch in Oregon, laughing with tears running down their cheeks.

> Transitive verb: John fucked Mary.
>
> Intransitive verb: Mary was fucked by John.
>
> Noun: Mary is a fine fuck.
>
> Adjective: Mary is fucking beautiful.
>
> Ignorance: Fucked if I know.
>
> Trouble: I guess I'm fucked now.
>
> Fraud: I got fucked at the used-car lot.
>
> Aggression: Fuck you.
>
> Displeasure: What the fuck is going on here?
>
> Difficulty: I can't understand this fucking job.

It was weird and incoherent, but my friends were laughing. Here was an example of what Americans meant when they said: *It is so bad that it is good.* Every now and then, we would press the play button and listen. For weeks, my officemates tried to speak like Osho.

It was funny because it was Osho, the small-town Indian accent mixed with the ready report on American idioms. That was part of the humor. As was the fact that here was a spiritual leader holding forth on the word *fuck.* And then there was that part too, which was surely present in the reaction of my friends, about how banal it was in the end. They were laughing at the fact that something quite stupid was actually succeeding. It was fun. (E.g., *Surprise: Fuck, you scared the shit* — pronounced by Osho as *sit — out of me.*)

Rajneesh, for that was Osho's original name, gave up teaching after he became the "Sex Guru" and began to gather followers from all over the world. Before Manmohan Singh and other political leaders engineered a liberal reform of the Indian economy, at least twenty years earlier than them, Rajneesh was preaching that socialism would only socialize poverty. What India needed was not more Gandhis but more capitalists.

—But your Osho is a Jain. He comes from a family of merchants. He might speak of God, but he is a man after money.

This was my father, in his own small-town way, talking about Osho with his psychologist friend one day.

Osho had no use for scholars. He had no use for religion either. But although he read little, he had made it a point to read the Bible. He read it, he said, like a detective story. It had everything, the Bible—love, life, murder, suspense. It was sensational. He said that his thinking about scholars was the same as that of Mullah Nasruddin. This was the story he narrated: A man came to Mullah Nasruddin and said, Nasruddin, have you heard? The great scholar of the town has died and twenty rupees are needed to bury him. Mullah Nasruddin gave the man a hundred-rupee note and said, Take it, and while you're doing it, why not bury five scholars?

The orgies at Osho's ashram had been reported even in *U.S. News & World Report*. Peter claimed he had read about them as a teenager in Germany; he had an aunt in Cologne who abandoned her studies, got Chinese tattoos on her stomach, and dreamed of joining an ashram. At Osho's ashram in Oregon, there were reports of bioterrorism and his followers were accused of plotting the assassination of a U.S. attorney. After Osho was deported from the United States, twenty-one countries denied him entry. He had gone back to India and died recently. That, as they say in America, was a downer. In Oregon, there had been arrests and all kinds of charges by the police. His longtime secretary, Ma Anand Sheela, a woman born in India but married to an American, was arrested on charges of attempted murder. Asked by journalists in Australia about the fears people had concerning the Osho cult taking over that country, Ma Anand Sheela said, Tough titties.

Tough titties!

I asked Larry Blofeld, my officemate who was writing a novel, what that phrase meant.* He smiled and flexed his pectorals.

Larry openly accepted my failings and took a consistent tack in his responses. I once discussed Faulkner with him, but even if

---

* Larry's novel was titled *Pop.* Not about a father, as I had first assumed, but about popular culture. Young people dropping out of college to become singers. It began with a young man driving down from Chicago to the university in St. Louis with his girlfriend. I knew this because I once asked Larry to read me the opening page. It was a magical thing for me, the fact that someone I knew had written a novel. Larry took out his manuscript from a folder with an elastic band around it. His protagonist, Blake, was at the wheel. This was the line I asked Larry to repeat so that I could write it down: *Illinois is a large state and during the four hours or so they were on I-55, across the distance that stretched roughly between the block from where Al Capone directed his operations and the small house in which President Ronald Reagan was born, Jessica twice removed her seat belt to blow him.*

I were asking a question about a character in *Absalom, Absalom!*, for example, Larry would answer my query only by making some connection to India. Even if the sole connection he could make was to Indian food served in a restaurant he regularly visited. If he couldn't make such a connection, he would slip into barely disguised mockery.

Now, in response to my question, he leaned back and said, *Tough titty, said the kitty, when the milk went dry.* Ever heard that? It's not such a hot phrase in New Delhi?

I didn't say anything and just smiled politely.

—Tell me how far is India? Larry asked.

I shrugged.

—Okay, answer this question for me, please. What's closer to New York? India or the moon? I'll give you a hint. You can see the moon.

Bile rose in my throat. I was aware of the effort I was making to keep smiling.

Larry raised his eyebrows. He was asking if I had anything to say.

No, Larry. As Osho would say, Fuck you.

Part IV

Wolf Number Three

They know I'm a foreigner. It makes me a little uneasy.

—JAMES SALTER, *A Sport and a Pastime*

"There are only three things to be done with a woman," said Clea once. "You can love her, suffer for her, or turn her into literature." I was experiencing a failure in all these domains of feeling.

—LAWRENCE DURRELL, *Justine*

There had been a complaint. So even before the new academic year began, my second year in America, all foreign teaching assistants were required to attend a workshop where there would be free doughnuts and coffee. The predictable demographic—Chinese and Indians—filled the room. Pushkin was there because attendance was mandatory. Otherwise, he wouldn't deign to come to such things. He had a volume of Nirala's poetry with him; he said he was translating it for a London publisher. Pushkin was from Gwalior, from a Brahmin family close to Nehru. He was the son of a politician who had written a book of poems in Hindi. I didn't know this then but in a few years Pushkin would surprise Ehsaan by being invited to have dinner with Kissinger after he had published an article on Afghanistan in *The New York Review of Books*.

His full name was Pushkin Krishnagrahi. He didn't offer an easy entry into his world but he gave thrilling glimpses of it through some of the things he said. For instance, he once explained he was unimpressed by a particular author because "literary reputations in the United States are merely a function of real estate." He was rangy and wore his hair long. He had a beard. His seriousness was a part of his getup. He presented his seriousness first at conferences and academic festivals. Yet, even Pushkin was there in the room. Nina, however, was not. Nina, who was American. A native speaker. But she and I had by now become a new tribe of two, speaking with each other in a private tongue, a language of love and lust. I could be reading a book about a peasant rebellion in Portugal but it was easy to look out the window and slip into a reverie. We were sitting on a bench overlooking the Hudson, my hand on Nina's thigh, sharing a memory. As an American, she considered it her duty to inform me about facts native to the land. For instance, the precise size in miles, length and breadth, of the locust swarm that arrived in Texas in 1875. Eighteen hundred miles long and 110 miles wide. The locusts ate everything in their path, not just vegetation but also harnesses off horses or the clothing hanging from laundry lines. In her presence, I embraced the apocalypse. Nina said that farmers would attempt to scare away the locusts by running into the swarm but they had their clothes eaten right off their bodies. I would lean over to eat away her clothes and she would laugh and push me away. We would kiss, my hand joyfully cupping her breast. But I was not with Nina now. *Your Honor, in that room that day they were talking about translation and I suddenly wanted to tell Nina a story. The flight that brought me to America traveled first from Delhi to Frankfurt and then from Frankfurt to New York. On the second leg of the journey, the flight attendant was handing out dinner. The flight attendant was asking, as she came down the aisle, "Veal or chicken?" An old Punjabi woman was sitting next to me. I hadn't spoken to her. Earlier, I had watched her struggle with the bathroom door and thought to myself that this might be the first time she was traveling in a plane. Was she visiting a son or a daughter who now worked abroad? I hadn't asked. When at last the trolley reached us, the attendant repeated her question and the old woman said, "No chicken. No chicken." She didn't speak English and I understood that she was saying she was a vegetarian. But the flight attendant said, "Okay, veal for you. And you, sir?" I had to stop. I said to the Punjabi lady in Hindi, "Mataji, you probably don't want it. This is meat. Do you eat meat?" She lifted her hand from the tray as if her fingers had been singed. The attendant said that they probably had pasta left at the back. She gave me pasta too, even though I would have preferred the veal, but I wasn't in a mood to protest. I was also angry with myself. Your Honor, I've never held myself above blame. After all, why hadn't I left my seat and helped the old woman when she was standing outside the bathroom? I had noticed that she hadn't even known how to lock the door.*

Right then, at that orientation for the foreign TAs, a woman named Donna was handing out photocopies of an article from *The Spectator*. A girl was sitting on the grass in front of Farrow Hall. Under the picture it said, *Melanie Olson, Astronomy major, dropped a Math course because she had trouble understanding her foreign TA.* The girl was wearing a denim skirt and the photographer had taken the shot with the camera tilted up from the ground. Blades of grass shot up in the foreground.

Peter was seated next to me. He put his finger on the photograph and spoke in a half whisper.

—Actually, she said she likes taking it in the ass but her foreign TA couldn't seem to understand her.

Peter wore thick glasses and smelled of cigarettes and sweat. On the other side of him sat Maya. She was trading barbs with Donna.

Maya was looking especially beautiful and full of mystery. She had lined her dark smoky eyes with kohl, and her neck and arms sported delicate silver jewelry. She was from Delhi and spoke in a fake British accent. I could see her spending afternoons in air-conditioned rooms in South Extension or Golf Links: lush green potted plants, and cushions on low wooden diwans arranged creatively in patterns of gold, magenta, and red. When I had first arrived in Delhi from Patna for college, people like Maya attracted me. I envied them. And this feeling of envy produced in turn a sense of revulsion. I still hadn't escaped that confusion of feeling.

—I'm not here to rid American undergraduates of their provincialism, Maya said to Donna. That is emphatically not a part of my job description.

Her Chilean friend from Anthropology, Paulo, enthusiastically bobbed his head and beat his hand on the table. Donna pulled her jacket over her stomach and said that there would be time for discussion at the end of the workshop. Maya said that Bush was bombing Iraq. Perhaps this could be the subject of their later discussion.

Peter raised his rounded chin toward Maya, and said quietly, Do you know this annoying woman sitting next to me?

His faint show of sarcasm hid a fascination with Maya. Within three weeks of their first meeting, they had become lovers. It was one of the things that I would always think about when I thought about love: acerbic and fragrant Maya in love with the acerbic and slovenly Peter. Did they fall in love because, in a sense, they spoke the same language, their poisonous tongues entwined in a beautiful private dance? Except that when they were together, they seemed quiet and subdued, not at all given to angry pronouncements about the world. Instead, they were attentive to each other, solicitous, generous with their gestures of affection. It seemed they were very happy just to sit in each other's company. I'd see them with mugs of coffee beside them, reading under the red-and-white awning of the Hungarian Pastry Shop, or standing outside West End Bar smoking endless cigarettes.

Putting all the participants in pairs, Donna said we were now to engage in role play.

—You are a teacher who is talking to a student who has missed class because he or she has had to deal with an emergency.

There were titters. Donna held up three ringed fingers. She read from a chart that said:

> *Please pay attention to*
>> *A. making eye contact,*
>> *B. clarity of expression,*
>> *C. showing a friendly attitude.*

Before taking turns playing teacher and student we were to talk to our partners for five minutes. My partner was one of the Chinese students, and the sticker on her chest said CAI YAN. I had seen her before talking to Maya, and guessed she was in International Relations. I felt an inward dread that I wouldn't understand what she said, but she was calm and spoke clearly. Her manner made me self-conscious and I tried to speak less hurriedly.

Cai Yan's parents lived in Quanzhou. Her mother was a schoolteacher. Her older brother was a well-known pianist in Shanghai. Her father had been a bureaucrat but had resigned some years ago and owned a factory in nearby Guangdong. I asked her what the factory manufactured. She had so far maintained a slightly imperturbable smile but now she gave a short laugh.

—Black Dragon Brand Rollerblades.

—Indian names always mean something. Is that true of Chinese names too? What does Cai Yan mean?

—My name . . . I think it means a bird in spring, or a spring swallow.

Cai Yan was slim and elegant. The jacket she wore had small buttons shaped like horseshoes. Her hair was black and covered her head like a fine helmet.

—How are things? I asked.

—There was a fire in the Laundromat on Saturday.

—Oh.

—On One Hundred and Twenty-second Street.

—I know the place.

—I was able to save my clothes. But I couldn't go back in. I tried but was aware of the utility . . .

Had she meant to say *futility*? A little later, when I heard *breeze,* it is likely she had said *breathe*. "I found it difficult to breathe." Did my speech also confound her in the same way? I felt that both of us were playing a guessing game. But there was no mistaking the word *fire*.

—Why did you want to go back inside?

—My bag with my library books was inside. And my journal.

—You lost them, I asked.

—A fireman brought them out for me. The library books had charred pages. The journal had turned to wet black ash.

—I'm so sorry, I said.

I felt this was the first time Cai Yan was sharing this news with anyone.

—I wanted to tell you, she said. The fire was the reason I couldn't complete my homework. I also missed class.

She saw my expression and raised an eyebrow. Then she gave a slight smile.

—You see, she said, it was an emergency.

I laughed when I understood that this was a story, but she didn't alter her Mona Lisa smile. Apparently she was unwilling to be amused by the stupidity of others.

Donna had wanted us to play the part of the affable teacher, listening patiently to a student's brittle fabrications. I had made an error and assumed at first that Cai Yan was describing what had actually happened to her. When it was my turn, I started with the truth. I told Cai Yan that when I was in my teens in India, the walls of the huts close to my village had graffiti on them with slogans like *Chairman Mao is our Chairman*. We could be on a bus on the highway and it would be held up in traffic for half an hour because of a march denouncing the massacre of protesting peasants. Thin, kurta-clad young men and women singing on the highway: The East is Red! The sun rises! China produces Mao Tse-tung!

—*"Dong Fang Hong,"* Cai Yan said, with a trace of excitement. That is the name of that song.

She said she had sung it in school.

As Donna had instructed, I maintained eye contact with my partner and exhibited a pleasant and friendly manner. I began to show off.

I asked, Do you know Lin Biao?

Even in the eighties, with Mao and Zhou Enlai already long dead, and the reformist Deng in power, China meant something different in India. There were still communist groups in the villages around my hometown that were fighting for a peasant revolution. Mao was their god. Often in the trains going past Ara, there would be motley crowds of young men and older folk who would sing songs about the social change about to come with the blessings of Mao. Everyone in those groups had the same look of zealous certainty on his bearded face, and their singing needed no further accompaniment than the sound of the train and a tambourine.

The name that I had thrown at Cai Yan, Lin Biao, belonged to a legendary associate of Mao's. Lin Biao was later accused of political treason and died while attempting to flee in an airplane. I knew his name because I would read in the papers that the Maoists in the Bihar countryside were following the "Lin Biao line." This meant the belief that one day the villages would rebel and overwhelm the passive, decadent cities. For Cai Yan's benefit, I invoked danger. In my late teens, I would be sitting at breakfast with toast and scrambled eggs, a novel by Somerset Maugham beside my plate, and a crowd would surge at the mouth of the street. I added color. I said that the radicals, waving red flags, would sometimes allow me to leave for my classes. When I came back, there would be three cows standing in the garden outside. In the bedroom in which my parents slept, a new family would be sleeping after having chopped up the bed for use as firewood.

She listened seriously but without any curiosity.

—I was exaggerating, I said.

—I know, she said. She spoke softly, even serenely. There was no smugness in her.

But I was wrong to think that she hadn't been curious. As I realized much later, the mention of Lin Biao's name was a mistake. I had invoked it on a whim, but to Cai Yan it meant nostalgia. Nostalgia not for the China of her childhood but for the poor villages of my past. In such fleeting connections are destinies shaped. Before two years of our graduate study were over, Cai Yan would talk to Ehsaan and decide she would write about Maoist struggles in various parts of India.* By the time that happened my romance with Nina would have gone the way of operator-assisted trunk calls and mimeograph machines.

═══

Hanif Kureishi's book *The Buddha of Suburbia* was published the same year that I came to the United States, and I discovered it a year later when I read the novel for one of my courses, the one called Black Britain. The book presented an England strung out on what one character in *Buddha* called *race, class, fucking, and farce.* I embraced this eclectic attention. (*Race & Class* incidentally was the name of a serious journal—Ehsaan was on their editorial board—but Kureishi wanted to mix it up with *Fucking & Farce.* Mind and body, together!) Then I watched a video of *Sammy and Rosie Get Laid* in the library. Kureishi had written the screenplay. Shashi Kapoor played Rafi Rahman. A handsome

---

* I have in my notebook this advice on writing about place, advice presented in the black-and-white shades of noir lighting, apparently for men only—although Cai, as a woman, called into question the fungibility of all these categories:

> Chandler always prided himself on being, as he said, the "first to write about Southern California in a realistic way," going on to note that "to write about a place you have to love it or hate it or do both by turns, which is usually the way you love a woman."

Pakistani politician who is charged with having introduced martial law in his country and other attendant abuses like torture and maiming. One episode in the film affected me the most. Rahman goes to meet Alice, the woman he had loved when he was a student in London. In Alice, Rafi had found his white woman. She had loved him. He had made promises to return, but never did. Alice, played with a kind of luminous fragility by Claire Bloom, takes Rafi to her cellar and shows him the clothes she had packed, the books, the shoes, the bottles of perfume. She shows him the diaries from 1954, 1955, 1956, inscribed with letters to "My Darling Rafi." But Rafi has no response for Alice when she says to him bitterly: *I waited for you, for years! Every day I thought of you! Until I began to heal up. What I wanted was a true marriage. But you wanted power. Now you must be content with having introduced flogging for minor offenses, nuclear capability, and partridge shooting into your country.* I thought of Jennifer as I sat alone in the library carrel watching this scene. Would she ever say that she had waited for me?*

---

* Alice reminded me of Jennifer and no one else. That memory, and the accompanying feeling, was special to her. I read somewhere that Bobby Fischer could run into someone and say, about a game they had played fifteen years earlier, You should have moved your bishop to e7. I'm very bad at chess but the remark spoke to me because I'm aware I sit outside a cave with a hoard of precise memories. Each half-eaten meal, filet mignon abandoned on the table in a Spanish restaurant, each darkened window and accompanying hangover, each sunrise, each sunset, Patsy Cline on a jukebox in a grimy rural bar in Montana, each touch, its temperature, each empty bottle of wine thrown in the trash but now locked in that cave behind me, belongs to a particular moment and a particular woman I'm in love with at that moment in the past.

While writing a paper on Kureishi I came across a remark he had made to an interviewer: "I like to write about sex as a focus of social, psychological, emotional, political energy—it's so central to people's lives, who you fuck, how much you love them, the dance that goes around it, all the seduction, betrayal, loyalty, failure, loneliness." This appeared like a credo I wanted to adopt. Not so much about writing but about sex being central to our lives. Still, I wasn't very confident and took the quote, which I had copied down on an index card, to my friend Peter. He sucked on his cigarette and nodded his head when I read out Kureishi's words to him. Right on, he said, and then asked if I wanted a beer.

We sipped our beers. The light of the setting sun flooded the room. Peter got up and put on a music tape, one that he used to play in our shared office, Keith Jarrett's *The Köln Concert*. When he sat down with a fresh beer bottle, I thought Peter looked thoughtful, maybe even sad.

—Sex is a difficult thing, he said.

I stayed silent.

—It's important, of course, as Kureishi says. I guess I'm saying it's a huge and complicated thing and it's not always possible to get to everything underneath.

Peter had so much heart, and such honesty always. He had spoken to me in the past about his struggle with depression, an illness that ran on his father's side of the family. I think Peter was open with private matters because there wasn't a trace of malice in his heart. Still, he surprised me by telling me about

Maya. He said he stayed up late one night at Maya's place. It might have been TA work. Then, in the dark, he felt his way to the bed where Maya was already asleep, and accidentally bumped into a package left on the floor. At the sound, Maya screamed and getting up from the bed rushed into her closet. Peter couldn't understand what was going on. In fact, he said to me, he was perhaps screaming too. He was scared of what had happened, and quickly put on the light.

—It's only me, it's only me.

Maya said nothing in response. Peter said that Maya always slept naked in bed and she looked especially vulnerable coming out of the closet. He got into bed next to her. He had been scared, Peter thought now, because he was seeing Maya suddenly as someone alien. She went back to sleep or that is what he thought but then Maya sighed and adjusted her head on his shoulder.

—Sorry, she said quietly to him. It has to do with something that happened in my childhood.

Peter waited in the dark. She didn't say another word. The next morning he mentioned what had happened but Maya wouldn't say anything more. He took the hint and never brought it up again, but just the previous week, after Maya was angry with Peter about his staying quiet for hours not speaking to anyone, Maya told him about her past. She said that when she was in high school in Delhi, her parents were in Moscow for two years. Her dad had a position in the Indian embassy. Maya was left behind to complete her school year in Delhi. She stayed with her uncle in Jor Bagh. This man wasn't really her uncle, he was her father's closest friend from college, a successful lawyer and on the governing board of the Delhi cricket association. He came home from the club late and raped her every night except when she had her period.

—Every night. Forget rape. Just think, every night. How do you wrap your head around such a thing? She was sixteen. I didn't even ask her how long she stayed in that house.*

═══

I didn't mention any of this to Nina perhaps because I almost instinctively felt that she would think it was wrong of Peter to tell me about Maya. After all, Maya wasn't my friend. I was tempted to tell her about my conversation with Peter when we came back from watching *Thelma & Louise,* but in the end I said nothing.

---

* Where could Maya have found help or taken her complaint? Here is another newspaper clipping pasted in my notebook:

covering up for him.
    "When I treat rape victims, I tell the girls not to go to the police," Dr. Shershah Syed, a prominent gynecologist in Karachi, told me. "Because if she goes to the police, the police will rape her."
    That's the way the world

The film had been playing for several weeks at the movie theater near Eighty-fourth Street on Broadway. A light drizzle was falling. In the early afternoon Nina and I walked over to the theater and settled down with popcorn and giant sodas. Thelma's ridiculous husband reminded me of a cousin of mine in Dhanbad. I had seen him hold his hands out and wait for his wife to button his sleeves and strap his watch on his wrist.

When the two women stopped at the roadhouse, I felt the tension growing within me. Thelma was drinking and dancing with a man named Harlan. Later, just as Harlan was about to rape Thelma in the parking lot, Louise stepped into the frame with a gun. A minute later, when Louise shot him, Nina let go of my hand and surprised me by clapping. I clapped too, and then a few others in the theater joined in, although at least one person, a man from a row behind us, asked us to quiet down.

There were funny moments in the film but it wrung the sadness out of us. Thelma, played by Geena Davis, undergoes a huge change (she gets radicalized, as Ehsaan would say), and Louise, the Susan Sarandon character, is strong and clearheaded and entirely without illusions. While watching the movie I knew that Nina would later ask me which scene was my favorite. I had very much liked Thelma's resolve at the end when she says, I can't go back . . . I mean, I just couldn't live. Or earlier, her saying to the cop before locking him in the trunk of his squad car that he should be nice to his wife: My husband wasn't sweet to me. See how I turned out. In another scene, Louise is a bit dismissive of her boyfriend Jimmy's affection. She tells Thelma, He just loves the chase, that's all. It made me think of something Jennifer had once said about me, but I wasn't going to say this to Nina.

The popcorn and the soda robbed us of our appetite. We sat on the steps outside Nina's building with a couple of Coronas.

—Did you immediately know why Louise didn't want to drive through Texas?

—I didn't, I said.

An old woman walked past us on the sidewalk with her tiny dog on a leash.

—Did you? I asked.

—It was the most powerful thing about the movie. The past that lies there under the surface.

When I heard Nina say this, I thought of Peter and what he had told me about Maya. I didn't have the courage to say anything about Maya. Instead I said, I liked that song about the woman who realizes that she's never going to ride through Paris in a sports car . . .

—Marianne Faithfull, Nina said. The song is about a suicide. You should listen to another song of hers called "Broken English." I should have it upstairs.

This was the moment during the evening, with the street darkening as we sat on the steps, when I began telling Nina about the teenage daughter of my father's first cousin. Suneeta lived in the village where my father had grown up. Her father was a farmer like everyone else in the family, but he was also a drunk. He got into scraps and often beat his wife, a tall woman who people said was very strong herself. Their house was separated from my grandmother's by a narrow dirt lane. Deepak, Suneeta's elder brother, had taken after his father. When he was a boy, he would follow me all day when I visited the village, eager to bring me fruit or jump into the village pond if I asked him to. But he was now grown up. My grandmother complained that Deepak stole her grain. Like his father, he would climb the khajur tree and drink the toddy straight from the pots that the tappers had hung there.

Suneeta was tall like her mother. Her skin was fair and she had light brown eyes. When Suneeta entered her teens, she was shy with me. I had barely exchanged a few words with Suneeta, but there were many complaints about her. Suneeta sneaked into my grandmother's small kitchen garden and stole the spinach. I remember her in a cheap, orange cotton sari, her hair slightly unkempt, looking attractive and just a little bit dissolute. The news of her death came as a shock. At first, the story in the family was that the girl had been trapped in love by an older, wily man, a distant relative of ours. I was told that Suneeta would go into the mango grove behind my grandmother's house to meet her lover. He lived in the village too, and was married, and this man had killed her. This story, like all stories in my family, hid something even darker. Later, I learned that one night Suneeta had gone into the house of a distant relative of ours to steal and was caught. The man kept her imprisoned in a room for a couple of days and raped her. Another friend of his also joined in. When word got out, Deepak and his father walked into that house and slit Suneeta's throat. When the police arrived from a nearby town, things were so handled that it was the rapists who were charged with the murder. They were now in prison and would die there. I was told that Deepak didn't even return home; he disappeared from the village and was working as a day laborer on a railway line in Assam. A few people believed that he had come back and was a rickshaw puller in Patna. When I next went to the village, Suneeta's mother held my hand and cried for the children she had lost.

Night had fallen now. After a while, Nina had a question.

—Did she approve of what Deepak had done?

—I didn't pry for details.

—I don't mean, Did you ask her if he was able to behead her in a single motion?

—I know what you mean.

—I guess I'm saying—

—Well, I was finding it difficult to talk to her. She was holding my hand and crying. I was also distressed because, every few seconds, she kept lifting my hand to her eyes, using it to wipe her tears.

=====

Nina enrolled in a course taught by Ehsaan called Flags and Rags. She hadn't been in Ehsaan's class during the first semester I studied with him. That fall, Nina was taking a course in Marxism and deconstruction with an Indian professor and another course in Victorian literature. The class on Victorian novelists was taught by a star in her field whom I had once met at a party—the Victorianist sat on the floor in the kitchen, drunk, snot running down her nose, while her husband entertained the nervous students in the living room with his stories about teaching in Africa. Flags and Rags was structured as a critique of nationalism. I was in that class with Nina and Cai Yan and several others. We read Gramsci and Tagore because Ehsaan's heroes were failed revolutionaries and poets. Nina liked the syllabus, she liked Ehsaan too, but she often joked that she had signed up because of a mistake. She had at first thought the course was about fashion and it was called Fags and Rags.

We began going to a bar on Thursday nights. Starting at nine, anyone could take the microphone and recite poetry. Five people in the audience chosen at random used scorecards to mark poems on a scale of one to ten. One night a slim man, clean-shaven and bald, reading a poem about queer love and clear rage. Then someone with Bobby Kennedy's face printed on her trousers reading a poem about her lover, and an Indian woman in the audience shouting that she wanted a ten for that one: I love poems which have nipples in them. The emcee tilting his bearded face and saying, Let's have a tête-à-tête about that, ha-ha. A young black woman in a baseball shirt with JUN-GLE FEVER written on the back softly reciting a lament about the many moons of unwanted pregnancies and deaths in poor homes. That first time, on the late-night subway bringing us back uptown to our apartments, I put my mouth close to Nina's ear. As if I were standing in the bar speaking into the microphone, I improvised words that were delivered to the backbeat of the train's moving wheels:

> I read in a book, baby, that this is the hour of the immigrant worker—after the milkman and just before the dustman.
> With his immigrant love, his love poem is a stammer at your doorstep at dawn,
> a terrible, trapped-up hope in this hour of becoming.
> It has nothing of the certainties of those who give names to bottles of wine in the languages of Europe.
> A woman just into her twenties, from Shanghai, alone at an underground train station
> in the middle of New York at night
> after working overtime in a garment factory,
> looks at her hands for a long moment
> in the bluish light of the station.

Such were the discoveries during that semester. Nina gave me a book of poems by radical Latin American poets. Pablo Neruda had written odes to ordinary things like the tomato and the onion; I composed rapturous lines about Nina's mirror, her favorite scarf, and a pair of spoons in her kitchen drawer. I was also reading modernist poets who wrote in Hindi. My poetic interest widened and I had soon compiled a set of political poems that began with a rousing line I had stolen from Joseph Heller: Even that fat little fuck Henry Kissinger was writing a book!*

Tongues untied, Your Honor. The language of liberation that came through language itself. And then the liberation of the body. In the cabinet where I store my passport there is a yellow ticket from Billy Bragg's Rumours of War concert. The ticket was stapled by Nina to a card on which she had copied down a line that Antonio Gramsci had written in a letter to his future wife: *How many times have I wondered if it is really possible to forge links with a mass of people when one has never had strong feelings for anyone: if it is possible to have a collectivity when one has not been deeply loved oneself by individual human creatures?*[†]

The Billy Bragg concert was at the nearby Beacon. Nina and I walked there together, holding hands. It was a small theater and it was packed. Bragg wore a black T-shirt and black jeans, the guitar hanging from his shoulder. His songs were against war and against greed. It seemed to me that if he kept singing any longer, all the punks in the front row who were dancing by simply bouncing up and down would start tonguing each other. Nina and I went drinking afterward, and when we were walking back to her apartment, she sang Bragg's line over and over

* Joseph Heller, *Good as Gold* (New York: Simon & Schuster, 1979), p. 328.

† Antonio Gramsci, *Selections from Cultural Writings,* eds. David Forgacs and Geoffrey Nowell-Smith; trans. William Boelhower (Cambridge, MA: Harvard University Press, 1991), see p. 147.

again: I dreamed I saw Phil Ochs last night. When we got back, she didn't lead me to her bed, where we often made love and slept with our legs entangled three or four times a week; instead, carrying a blanket in one hand and a small flashlight in another, she led me to the roof. We were in the dark on the top but all around us were the lights of the city.* On our right, spanning the darkness, the towers of the George Washington Bridge. The illuminated bits of Cliffside Park in distant Jersey afloat in the waters of the Hudson. Nearby the red glow of a sign for a parking garage.

The narrow beam of the light that had climbed up the stairs, three or four steps at a time, has now jumped across twenty-odd years. It comes to rest beside Nina and switches off. She is lying on the blanket on her stomach. She has spread some clear gel in her hand and put it on my cock.

—Higher, she says.

I haven't done it this way. It excites me but I'm also, quite honestly, afraid that it might hurt her. I feel the tightness of her muscle and its release, and she is soon pushing against me, making a sound that makes me want to thrust back.

---

* This immense solitude in the middle of the city. I'm reminded now of another clipping in my notebook. *A flourishing slum* is written on the top and the following section pasted below: *Parapa then fixed a man-sized plank to the hutment wall, so that while his father and brother made love to their wives below, he could stay chastely on the shelf. Still, he sometimes sleeps outside, beside an open sewer, in the blissful quietude of the street.* (A Google search reveals that this clipping is from *The Economist,* December 19, 2007. I conducted this search because I wanted to find out why I had written *A flourishing slum* on the top of the page. It is the title that was used in the magazine.)

—Do you want me to come harder?

Somewhere among her moans a murmured yes, and the fingers of her right hand touching the back of her own neck. By then was I standing or kneeling? I came in a rush and her back arched, and she bucked again and again.

—I love you, I love you, Nina said. And then, Let's go down and catch the end of *Saturday Night Live*.

That semester in CLIT 300, David Lamb used a book whose title, *The Tremulous Private Body,* would come back to me after Nina and I had finished making love. She would be holding me and I'd feel her body rocked by a passing shudder. During that moment, she'd clutch me tighter and when the moment had passed, she would turn away and promptly go to sleep. I once mentioned *The Tremulous Private Body* to her and she immediately began to mock Lamb. I liked this. It took away my feelings of fascination and jealousy. A week or two earlier Lamb had wanted a book report from us on another book he was teaching, *Roland Barthes by Roland Barthes*. Barthes had quoted a letter from a man in Morocco identified only as Jilali. Jilali's letter was about what he himself called *a disturbing subject: I have a younger brother, a student in the third-form AS, a very musical boy (the guitar) and a very loving one; but poverty conceals and hides him in his terrible world (he suffers in the present, "as your poet says") and I am asking you, dear Roland, to find him a job in your kind country as soon as you can, since he leads a life filled with anxiety and concern; now you know the situation of young Moroccans, and this indeed astounds me and denies me all radiant smiles . . .* Barthes described the language of the letter as *"sumptuous," "brilliant,"* and *"literal and none-*

theless immediately literary." Everyone in Lamb's seminar focused on what Barthes had called *"the pleasures of language"* that spoke "at the same time *truth and desire: all of Jilali's desire (the guitar, love), all of the political truth of Morocco."* I penned a mini-essay on utopian discourse. But Nina's book report was considerably shorter. She Xeroxed a section of the letter quoted in *Roland Barthes by Roland Barthes* and then distributed copies to everyone in the class. Nina had used a felt pen to write across the page the following question for us: *Did that bastard Barthes give Jilali's brother a job?*[*]

Only a few months had passed since Jennifer, but I was deeply in love with Nina. It is possible that an objective viewer would have thought that I was obsessed with her; maybe Nina thought this too, although she never said it. For several weeks during that first summer, she was gone. She was staying at her parents' summer home. Her parents lived in Pittsburgh but they spent the summers in Cape Elizabeth, Maine, where they had a cabin. During her childhood, Nina had spent summers in Rome, which is where her father was from—Nina's parents met in Rome when her mother had traveled there as a junior from Dartmouth on her study abroad program. But for many

---

[*] The affectations of graduate student life: love expressed in the idiom of required reading in the doctoral seminars. A reader of *The Village Voice* on Valentine's Day that year (1991) would have encountered in the personals, in the section captioned "Public Display of Affection," the following message for Nina, which had cost me thirty dollars: *Hey babe: Let's snuggle in bed and read the poetry of the future or even the missionary-position Marxist writing you so greatly admire. XOXO.*

years now the family had summered in Maine. Nina told me that they didn't have a phone in the cottage; so I waited for her letters. The letters arrived every few days, though not as often as I wanted, in envelopes that had pictures stuck on them and, once, a section of a map showing the beach and the ocean. Inside were messages that were invariably brief. They were crumbs that stoked a hunger and only left me famished. *I'm aware, Your Honor, of the language I'm using but may I proceed to the bench to present evidence? This is Nina in a letter stamped June 29, 1991: What I have to say about what you have called your situation is this. I want your constant hand on my back, your unwaged agricultural labor in the fields of my nightly dreams, I want your back pressed into my front, your warm Brazil and shy Tierra del Fuegos. I want your cumspattered shirts and your baby, baby.*

Another time she wrote: *Today I've got something which I've never had before, which is laryngitis. I can scarcely make a sound. Today I could whisper sweet filth in your ear. Have you ever wanted to fuck a half mute, honey?*

Filth!

Your Honor, I have entered the body of America. I have spoken filth in the ear of one of your fair citizens when I was inside her.

Your Honor, this was something new for me.

She was hospitable in the extreme, meeting me with laughter. Her laughter alone saved me from my self-ridicule. Or what I imagined as the world's ridicule. *Your Honor, when I was on the phone with her I spoke in a high British accent, having stooped to using words used by Prince Charles in his conversation with Camilla Parker Bowles.* (I was a boy in school when Charles kissed Diana on the balcony of Buckingham Palace. A decade was to pass before I read of his long, continuing affair with the aforementioned Parker Bowles, who had approached him at a polo match with an unforgettable proposition: "My great-grandmother was the mistress of your great-great-grandfather—so how about it?") Such has been my pathetic, unsentimental education! I have relied in my games of seduction on words plucked from the airwaves by a scanner and published by British tabloids for laughs:

> CHARLES: The trouble is I need you several times a week. Oh, God. I'll just live inside your trousers or something. It would be much easier . . .

> CAMILLA: (in a falsetto) What are you going to turn into, a pair of knickers?

> CHARLES: Or, God forbid, a Tampax.

> CAMILLA: (shrieking) Oh, darling!

No one had ever talked to me like Nina did. Before she left for Maine, she gave me a leather bracelet with a silver clasp in the middle. I thanked her with a kiss.

—Try not to let any woman touch it while you're having sex, she said.

I had often thought of other women. Did she know this? I might have laughed nervously.

She said, Do I have dibs on your sperm?

—Yes, I said. I was unsure what *dibs* meant but I didn't care. My sperm, I said, and the scented mangoes from my mango orchards, all the fruits of my toil too, the tree of my childhood, the furnished apartment of my soul.

These florid speeches. Was she mocking my feverish syntax when she sent me her occasional letters written with great rhetorical flourish? More than once I thought we were like two porn artists hamming it up for the camera. This was not the greatest danger. The biggest challenge to love is not when you pretend you are in a porn film: no, no, it's when you believe that you are in a bad Hindi film, delivering reassuring saccharine platitudes to each other. Nina lived her life in a B. R. Chopra movie for a while and then made her escape.

What was Nina's natural mode of talking? When you phoned her, the answering machine picked up the call. She never answered. Instead, you got Laurie Anderson's voice saying, Hi, I'm not home right now . . . A series of electronic beeps, punctuated by a detached repetition of clichés, a language removed from sentimentalism. It was intelligent and all incredibly hip even if a little remote and maybe chilly.

But this is wrong, of course. Back in April, on my birthday, we had been drinking beer and I said I wanted to see a fish tattooed on her arm. Some weeks later, on her own birthday, she had acquired a tattoo. The new oil on her arm formed a pool in which hung a single fish. Nina owned two eight-pound dumbbells that she used to strengthen her muscles. She watched the fish as, weight in hand, she flexed her arm.

—Will you marry me?

I asked her this impulsively, as I watched her exercising. I laughed when I said that, but the words still hurt in my throat.

—You want to do it for the green card?

She was smiling. The dumbbell rose and fell in a precise arc.

—Yes, when they ask me over at Immigration, Did you marry her for love? I'll say, Yeah, I love the way she climbs on top and fucks me. Nina, I'll say, lick my mouth and show them how wet it is when you are done with me.

I might have babbled on. There was always just that hint of seriousness between us that made me nervous and talkative. I recognized, not for the first time in my life, that as far as women were concerned I preferred taking the low road of indelicate candor. *But I was also, Your Honor, exploring language. I was the poet of my own sexual liberation.*

After the dumbbells and a run, Nina and I ate a simple dinner of rice and beans in her kitchen. The television was on in the next room. Maybe it was something said on the news, Nina turned to me and asked whether the Immigration and Naturalization Service had a uniform.

—Yes, I said.

—Do you ever imagine having sex with the Border Patrol? You know, the way porn in Israel has sometimes much to do with the Nazis.

I was aware that Nina had been in long relationships with others before me, one with a man who was much older than her, a designer of yachts. Then she had dated, for two years, a man named Jonathan who was a labor organizer. Compared to her, I was inexperienced. When Nina put to me this fairly innocent question about the Border Patrol, I asked myself anxiously if she liked to imagine having sex with someone else. The thought of loving Nina forever, and only her, passed through my mind, as it often did, in some kind of quick, sad, dulling way. And, characteristically, what emerged from my mouth was more insincere banter propped up with academic jargon.

—You're asking me do I want to be fucked by the state?

—Well, have you watched *The Night Porter*?

I hadn't. Nina said it was a story about a former SS officer, now a night porter in a hotel in Vienna, and a woman who was a survivor from the same camp. The officer and the prisoner had been lovers in the camp. I interrupted Nina.

—No, I would like to fuck Susan Sontag. Or maybe Susan Sarandon.

Nina considered the point. I wanted very badly to be in love with intelligent, well-read women. And Nina was exactly that. I had fallen in love with her, and with her prose. Her perfume and her lips too. No, with her prose and her lipstick. Even plain words seemed so potent. Once, I came out of the shower and she was lying naked in bed, a lovely creature stretched on the dark sheet: on the inside of her thigh, in dark red lipstick, she had written *Here*.*

---

* After Katherine Mansfield's death from tuberculosis, Virginia Woolf noted in her diary on January 28, 1923: *Our friendship had so much that was writing in it.*

I came home from the library and checked the tiny tin mailbox before entering the apartment. There was a postcard from Maine with a picture of a cowboy stuck on it. The photo had probably been cut from a trashy magazine. On the other side, Nina had written: *Just saw a program on TV about American cowboys. There was one small bit that was interesting. These rodeo wrestlers hold a steer by the horns and bite its (very) sensitive lower lip to bring the animal down to the ground.*

I felt an onrush of blood, a sudden heat and an upheaval. This is the effect that many of Nina's letters had on me. At other times, I was left uncertain. Mystery surrounded her words. One day she wrote that she had fallen asleep in the dentist's chair and she had a dream about us. We were seated in front of a hypnotist who was putting her to sleep. The two of us were holding hands. Even as she was drifting off to sleep, she was telegraphing a message with her fingers. She was saying that she loved me, she was asking for my help. *Help me!* I found this appeal indecipherable. And then Nina had added: *I'm not at my parents' place right now but I'm going to drive down there tomorrow. If you are a good one you'll soon mail me a letter tasting of pears and licorice and your own sweet self.*

Not at her parents' place? Where was she, and why hadn't she called? I sent her a card. I was like a man waiting for the bus on a long strip of empty road, uncertain whether the bus ever came on that route. In the food co-op that evening, while purchasing my groceries, I also picked up pear and licorice.

But there was no call from Nina. Finally, four days later, a post-card arrived. I couldn't tell where it had been posted. In Nina's neat, angular hand, the following message: *I heard on the radio today that Columbus's men, unfamiliar with the migration patterns of American birds, regularly mistook the mid-Atlantic presence of feath-ered companions (en route to Africa) for signs of landfall. Continually disappointed. Where are you? I tried your office and your house. White featherless biped (f) seeks warm-blooded tropical creature (m) for new world adventures and more.*

It helped that she had mentioned the radio; her story appeared anchored in some sort of reality. But how could she have missed me? If I wasn't at the office, I was to be found in my apartment, reading all the books that Ehsaan wanted me to read. The truth was that I had grown suspicious of Nina and there were often occasions when I didn't even know whether what she had written was true. Then I'd feel guilty and simply wonder whether I had misjudged her.* At other times, I questioned her judgment. After I was rejected for a journalism internship, she wrote: *I'm sorry that you didn't get the job. Is it at all liberating, I wonder. It's come to be that I can't imagine anyone really likes to go to work. The Great Depression was such a fertile period, you know. The things that were invented in that decade include the TV, the helicopter,*

---

* I told Nina that last Christmas, I was thinking of her while sitting alone in the dark at a movie theater watching *Pretty Woman*. I was weighed down by self-pity. But Nina wasn't much concerned. She said, Ugh . . . Couldn't you have found another movie? That film represented the dream of Reaganomics: that the recession could be brought to an end by giving a blow job.

How could I not love her! She gave me a map of the world in which we lived!

nylon stockings, the jet plane, and that thing that is a jet plane in nylon tights, Superman. Think of the many classics of literature that were written during that time!

Was she right? I was so taken by the drama surrounding the messages that I don't think I got the chance to really understand what she was actually saying in any letter of hers. *Such drama!* On some days, two or even three letters. She would write, *I'm so happy to be tearing the letter I had begun.* And I'd spend the day wondering what it was that she had written or not written. And then I would find another one, *It's your world, I'm just livin' in it.* (I checked Nina's horoscope in *Mirabella* when I was at a hair salon. This is what I read and, naturally, I tore the page out to take home with me and stick in my journal: *If you thought you had your fill of personal and professional dramas, forget it. The fireworks are far from over. You, and sexy Virgo Richard Gere, have spent a considerable amount of emotional energy this year trying to figure out the state of your love life. Now it's time to move on. The lunar eclipse on June 8 will make you even more intense and sensitive to others' whims. Surprising events around the solar eclipse on June 23 will clear the air, and you will be ready, willing, and able to do battle for the best reason of all: true happiness.*) Clear the air! Clear the air!

It doesn't matter if I can't remember what the fight was about: it was always in a way about the same thing. She was often in another city, she would say she would call, and didn't; her small lies, which she said were the results of her nervousness from my continually testing her, drove me to the brink of madness.* She sent me letters. All her letters were so beautifully crafted—which only added to my suspicion. The mention of any other name in a letter she had sent me would take away all the pleasure of receiving any words of affection from her. I discovered jealousy was a disease whose first symptoms were a sudden darkening of the universe followed by a faint prickling on the surface of the skin, especially the face, before a hammering commenced in the heart.

I always complained to Nina that she didn't love me enough, and I didn't realize for a long time that in doing this I had already lost the game. It was all futile really. There could never be a cure. I had become attached to a story that started one night: I got up in the middle of the night and the thought came to me out of nowhere that Nina wasn't in Maine. She was in Pittsburgh with her ex Jonathan. As soon as the thought came to me, I knew with deep certainty that it was true. I said this to her when we next spoke on the phone, and she surprised me by accepting my charge, only adding that while the details were correct I had drawn the wrong conclusion. Jonathan's mother was dying, first

---

* I have now looked in all the four notebooks I have from that period but I can't find a sheet I had torn from a magazine: it was a "found text" that a man had left behind in his airplane seat, with the names of two women on top of the page and the attributes, both positive and negative, listed under each name. "Great cook," "honest," "good in bed," "bad breath," "kind to my parents," and the like. How many times I had drawn lists about Nina! And sometimes matched them with another name next to hers! "Gracious," "sexy," "smells nice," "little lies," "careless," "forgets to mail letters," "good scotch," "doesn't cook," "smokes too much," "distant," "beautiful laugh," et cetera. No mention of "love."

her kidneys had failed and then her other organs went kaput. Nina spoke about her for a long time.

—This is a woman who has been very kind to me, particularly during one long sickness. I wanted to do the right thing by her, but wasn't at all sure that you would understand. I'm sorry. In retrospect, I should have been honest with you.

I accepted this explanation but my doubts lay in repose only for a short while. I had been naïve. I had been blind to the fact that Nina was still in a relationship with Jonathan when I stepped into the picture, and then I treated the discovery of this fact as a revolutionary breakthrough in the way in which knowledge was to be forever organized. I'm certain I was tedious. More than once, Nina protested against my absurd complaints.

—I'm boxed into a historical corner. One that I cannot seem to get out of, even when I'd give anything to be able to do that.

—I love you and am not always sure you love me.

—I sometimes think that if you really loved me you'd let me out of this mess.

—Are you saying you want to end this?

—No, I'm just saying that if you could ever let the test be over, I could stop failing.

Whenever we had a conversation like this, I felt immediately chastened. There was another thing. I fumed, I accused, but Nina never. She didn't raise her voice. In fact, I don't think she regarded blunt statements at all as truths. If you weren't being decent, were you being truthful? When I was bitter, I would think it was a class thing, this obligation to be polite. At other times, I felt like a real heel.

Sometimes after we fought, I would come back into the apartment and hear her voice on my answering machine. When this happened, I relented quickly and called her back. But there were times when I didn't care. The stab of guilt I had experienced earlier was no longer there; its place had been taken by rage. I was too angry that she hadn't written, or hadn't called, or had been out late with friends.

Nina and I didn't only fight. Back in February, maybe only ten days after I had placed the Valentine's Day ad in the *Voice*, we went through a breakup. It didn't last long but a change had come: nothing was to be taken for granted anymore. Why do couples fight, or where do such fights have their origin? A minor irritation or a misheard remark is linked to a barely articulated but long-established hurt or resentment. It is as if a closet with a secret trapdoor opened into a dark tunnel that allowed you to crawl to a distant hiding place.

The occasion was a Friday night dinner. Maya and Peter were our guests. We were at Nina's but I was doing the cooking. Nina was the teaching assistant that semester in a nineteenth-century American lit class and there had been a big guest lecture earlier that evening. She came back with the report that a distinguished professor emeritus had gone to sleep in the chair next to her soon after the lecture started. The visitor adjusted the rhythm of her delivery to minimize the sound of the gentle exhalations coming from the first row. Nina liked giving titles to events, and here was another one: "The Speaker and the Sleeper." For Maya, I had brought my tape of Hemant Kumar songs. She sat close to Peter, and she looked happy. We drank wine and then it was time for dinner.

I had made a special effort and prepared rogan josh even though the smell of the lamb cooking in the spices made Nina throw open the kitchen window as soon as she entered the apartment. Also, chana masala, raita, grilled cauliflower. For dessert, I had bought kulfi from Maharaja Palace on Frederick Douglass Boulevard. Peter had been quiet but he liked the food. When he was eating his pistachio and cardamom kulfi, Maya looked at Peter and started on a story.

—I was outside the Pastry Shop yesterday. A woman was kneeling on the sidewalk, feeding her terrier small treats. "You like it?" she would ask, and then as if the dog had said something in response, she would stroke its face and say, "I love you too!" This went on for a long time. The terrier never tired of her question, which she must have asked a dozen times, or her declarations of love.

Maya touched Peter's nose instead of asking him whether he liked his food. I saw Nina looking at me.

—Thank you for dinner, honey.

—But did you like it?

There was an edge in my voice because I didn't really think Nina enjoyed eating Indian food. She was always gracious, of course, but whenever she praised me I felt she was lying. I couldn't keep a feeling of humiliation out of my heart. Now, at the dinner, I made the mistake of pointing out the truth.

—You ate a spoon of rice, a few forkfuls of cauliflower. Anything else?

Nina laughed. She said she had been so hungry she ate cheese and crackers at the reception after the lecture.

—Why are you complaining? Maya asked me. Look at Peter! He's eating enough for all of us.

Peter pretended to stop eating, returning his fork to his plate. The conversation shifted, and after the wine was gone, we said our goodbyes. I'd have spent the night in Nina's apartment but when Maya and Peter had left I said I'd go back to my place. Nothing would shake Nina's calm.

—Are you sure? Please stay.

—No, I think I should go. I'd like to read a book that's in my room right now.

—It's Saturday tomorrow. We'll wake up late and then eat the leftovers.

—Why do you work so hard at pretending? You don't need to like what you don't like.

In asking that question, was I trying to get rid of my shame? But shame at what exactly? Or did I only want to find a tear in the equability in which Nina wrapped herself at moments like this? Nina was standing at the door, smiling her smile of smiles. And then the literal translated into the metaphorical: in the expression in her eyes, I saw a door closing. When I turned to leave, I was certain she wasn't going to tolerate any more of this unpleasantness, and as I went down the stairs of Nina's building, the taste of food turned to ash in my mouth. I was sad, yes, but I also experienced relief. I told myself that there would be no occasion again to wonder whether Nina was being genuine. If this relationship were to be over, and it was acceptable for this frivolous quarrel to be embraced as the cause, I would now forever be free of guilt.

In my bed, I lay with my face buried in my pillow for a long time. Ultimately, I fell asleep and when I woke up I was relieved that there was no message from Nina on the answering machine. She hadn't called. And as the days passed, I discovered that she wasn't going to call. No blinking light near the phone when I returned from my classes. A polite nod in the one weekly seminar, that was all. In my effort to start a new life, I went to the gym. At the university pool, I swam for a while but my thoughts returned to Nina. A young woman in a far lane with a cap on her head and goggles could have been her, I thought crazily. One night, I took out from my wardrobe the black silk dress that Nina had left there after a party. Her perfume lingered in the fabric. There is no love more real than the kind experienced after a breakup. I felt it was important to spread the black dress on my bed and then cover it with my body. When I sank my face in my pillow this time, I must have murmured Nina's name many times.

In the months to come, I often repeated this story to Nina, about my embrace of her dress. She listened without mocking me at first but then this story too was folded into her larger narrative about me. I was continually performing in a play in my head and she was enlisted as a player in a role that wasn't of her own devising.

When she returned from her visit with Jonathan's mother, Nina said we could go on a trip together. She came to my apartment.

We fucked with a mix of efficiency and impatience, we ate Chinese takeout, and then we fucked again as if we were getting rid of the memories of the past weeks. Or, that's what I thought later as I watched Nina lather her hair with shampoo when we stood under the shower together. No one I had seen in my life, except maybe two half-naked men once beside a village road near Hajipur, bathing next to a water pump after a day's labor in the fields, rubbed soap on their limbs more vigorously than Nina. She manufactured a skin of foam and was scarcely recognizable when she transformed herself into an unworldly creature with suds in her hair and froth covering even her face. I heard this creature asking me where I wanted to go.

—Grand Canyon.

In her silence I knew I had said the wrong thing.

—No, but there's Las Vegas close by.

It was now my turn to remain silent.

Florida was too close. Hawaii too far away.

—Can you land somewhere in the middle of the country and then drive through Yellowstone?

If we were going to drive, Nina wanted to go to California instead.

—We will drive down Highway One with the Pacific outside the car window. You'll love it.

Water had washed away all the soap bubbles from her hair and face: she appeared beautiful and gleaming, scrubbed clean, with dark glittering eyes and a peachy mouth.

I liked the idea of the drive with the ocean outside but all I had seen of this country were cities on the East and the West

Coasts. What would I have known of India if I had visited only Bombay and Calcutta? I wanted to drive through parts of the United States, its vast middle, and then roam in the wilderness. I suspected we weren't going to the Grand Canyon because of some past association.

—We'll land somewhere and just drive through Yellowstone, I said.

The tickets we bought were for mid-July. When the date drew close we went to the Countee Cullen Library on 136th Street and checked out a batch of Books on Tape: Norman Mailer's *The Executioner's Song* (because it was the thickest and had the largest number of tapes in it); *The Great Gatsby;* a three-in-one set of Toni Morrison's works, *Sula, Song of Solomon,* and *Beloved;* also Alice Munro (*Selected Stories,* read by, yes, Susan Sarandon); a book by Elmore Leonard; and Nabokov's *Lolita.* Nina didn't think we'd have that much time but she didn't protest. She chose a book called *Middle Passage,* which I'm quite sure we never listened to.

Next step: a trip to AAA to get a TripTik made for the drive. From Cheyenne, Wyoming, to Missoula, Montana.

—Yes, madam, thank you, the route should pass through Yellowstone, yes.

The heavily perfumed woman, of sixty or thereabouts, held three different-colored markers between the fingers of her left hand. She would select one of them and highlight a highway so that the yellow would light up like a runway through the flat green of the paper. Our trip was going to take three or four days.

Nina felt we should give ourselves a week; we were flying into Cheyenne and out of Missoula. These names, till now unfamiliar to me, came to possess a kind of magic.

We were graduate students; we used words like *research*. So, on our second day in Yellowstone, we found ourselves using that word. When we discovered that even though it was still summer, there was snow in some of the park, and that we should have brought jackets and sweaters, we began to tell each other that we hadn't done the right research. Here we were in a forest of fir, the setting sun having slipped behind the horizon of rock, and the cold hung like desolation among the lodgepole pines stripped by summer wildfires. It was evening and nearly dark, but we weren't worried. On the contrary, all the uncertainty and the cold outside added an edge of excitement to our drive. We were going to find a motel among the three places marked as *X*s on our map. It appeared that we still had anywhere between thirty and seventy or eighty miles to go. We should have bought a travel guide. Instead, we had concentrated on finding the right books. Elmore Leonard was in the cassette player just then, as we drove with our dashboard light lit up in green, white, and red as if it were Christmas. A voice said in the dark: *They watched Jackie Burke come off the Bahamas shuttle in her tan Islands Air uniform, then watched her walk through Customs and Immigration without opening her bag, a brown nylon case she pulled along behind her on wheels, the kind flight attendants used.*

I leaned forward in the passenger seat and switched the

voice off. The tension in the story was making me jangly. It affected my nerves and I sought release.

—I read a story once by Milan Kundera. This woman pretends she is a hitchhiker when she gets into her boyfriend's car. It is an erotic story but a very messed-up one . . .

—Did you tell me your name, sir?

Nina was smiling a little bit.

It was not very dark, but there was no one else around. Nina stopped the car on the side of the road. I got out to stretch my legs. When I was back at the door Nina slid into the passenger seat and then turned back, facing the road we had driven on. She said she didn't want her skirt on. I was eager and felt her wetness with one hand—and as I remember this, or think I remember, I cannot help asking if Nina, wherever she may be now, also remembers the same things from our relationship. (I took a picture of her in New York City under the sign of a bar named Chameleon. That's you, I said. Such cruelty. She must remember that.) I want to believe that she remembers how the sound of our breathing filled the car. In the distance, through the rear windshield, I could see a point of light traveling high up on the mountain: the car's light appeared and disappeared as if I were watching the flight of a firefly. When I entered her from behind, even in that cramped space, does she remember thrusting her ass back into me with tiny, ecstatic jolts? In the story that I have formed in my head, though this could be from another time, I remember that when I made a caressing gesture, gently touching Nina's breast, she pushed my hand away and said, *Fuck me.*

≡

An earlier journey, before I had left India. It was summer and I
was taking the train back to Patna from Delhi. The other pas-
sengers in my compartment were sleeping; I was reading a novel
by Lawrence Durrell, a writer who was born in Jamshedpur,
only a few hours away from Patna.* The book had been recom-
mended to me by a woman I'd met at college in Delhi. She was
an undergraduate too, studying literature, and her parents were
professors at a college nearby. I thought of her as modern—
which I was not—because she had acted onstage and traveled
abroad. She had a high forehead and light-colored eyes. We had
drunk tea together and smoked cigarettes outside the college
canteen but we weren't lovers. We were too shy or too young
to have even held hands. I had in my bag the address she had
given me for her aunt's home in Baroda, where she would be visiting that summer; she had asked me to write letters to her and
I was already writing one in my head as I turned to look at the
moon outside the train window. There wasn't then, nor would
there be in the future, any real intimacy between us. What did
we know of love? No one in my family had married outside our
caste. Love was the province ruled by kids with cars and mem-
berships to clubs; the young men I saw around me bathed in

---

* Durrell's novel has an enigmatic epigraph from one of Sigmund Freud's letters: *I am accustoming myself to the idea of regarding every sexual act as a process in
which four persons are involved. We shall have a lot to discuss about that.*

cologne, peeling sticks of Wrigley's chewing gum before going up to say hello to a woman. I had taken the young woman's notes from a lecture to a student in the dorm who claimed to be an expert at handwriting analysis. I realized it was a bit like going to an astrologer. He looked at her closed letters and described her as "emotionally reserved and suspicious of others." Looking at my notebook he traced in the air the long tails beneath my letters and said, with a hint of indecision, that those loops "represented a vivid imagination but might also mean that you are mired in sensuousness." If there had been any romance it had been entirely in my vivid imagination! But I had acted with exorbitant passion in one respect. On the night before our exams, another student brought to me the question papers that were meant to be unsealed the next day. I didn't ask him how he got his hands on the leaked papers; without thinking twice, I got into an auto-rickshaw and went to the woman's house. She was surprised to see me, and to discover that I knew where she lived, and she was more surprised still to find out the reason I was standing at her door. I didn't study that night. I was nervous and eager to know whether I had given the woman I liked so much the correct information. The test papers turned out to be authentic and she laughed when I confessed that I had performed badly. I hadn't done the work. Our friendship didn't grow although we exchanged a few letters in which we enclosed some wan attempts at poetry. A year before I left India, I read in the newspaper that she had been awarded a prestigious fellowship that would allow her to write about Tagore at the University College in London. Then I heard from someone that she had come out as a lesbian, and this news, which I received in New York, pleased me. Both of us had stepped out of the protective armor of our earlier weak transgressions. We had become ourselves.

Gallatin National Forest. Our cabin had a heater but the cold seemed to seep through invisible cracks and pool near our feet. A little before dawn, I felt Nina stirring and then saw that her eyes were open. She complained about the cold and said she wanted pancakes. Pancakes and coffee brewed over a wood fire. I huddled closer to her.

The Gujarati man at reception said we would have to wait an hour to get breakfast, but if we drove north, we could see wolves at this time. Where would we find them? We had discovered the lodge with much difficulty. But the man was assuring.

—Turn left when you come out of the gate. Drive north for half an hour, and you'll see them crossing the road or in the grass leading to the river.

—Okay, so the wolves are out at this time. What about pancakes? Isn't there an International House of Pancakes out there somewhere?

—You'd have to drive to Bozeman for that. They will be open when you reach them because it'll take you two hours to get there.

Of course, we didn't go. We fed each other chocolate and drank bad coffee, lying in bed, listening to the dry, detached voice of Jeremy Irons reading *Lolita* on the tiny cassette player that Nina used to record interviews. *To any other type of tourist accommodation I soon grew to prefer the Functional Motel—clean, neat, safe nooks, ideal places for sleep, argument, reconciliation, insatiable illicit love.* We looked around the cold room, its pink walls and the framed picture of a young grizzly stepping into a frothy stream, and we laughed. As if by agreement, Nina hunched herself under the blanket and crawled up until she was lying on top of me. She sat up and made small, deft adjustments so that we fitted well together. Jeremy Irons was saying, *I have never seen such smooth amiable roads as those that now radiated before us, across the crazy quilt of forty-eight states. Voraciously we consumed those long highways, in rapt silence we glided over their glossy black dance floors.*

═══

Six months later, I thought of Nina's face in the motel room that morning when I heard mention of wolves on the radio. It was my father's birthday and I was going to call him in India. But first I was waiting for Nina to call me from her conference in Boston. I didn't want her to get a busy signal if she called. On important days, I called my parents. Half a world away, the phone rang in Patna. At that time, my parents still didn't have a phone. Nowadays every milkman walking on the road ahead of his cows has a mobile phone in his front shirt pocket. *Your*

Honor, I'm describing another time. Calls used to be expensive, and it could take an hour to get a connection. When I called the neighbor's number, someone would run out to get my father. I usually hung up and then called AT&T to complain that the line had been disconnected. The operator would apologize and then call for me without charge. As far as I was concerned, immigration was the original sin. Someone owed me something. This half-expressed thought had found a home in my heart. It provided me an exaggerated sense of identity, and granted me permission to do anything I wanted. I'm not trying to justify anything; I only intend to explain.[*]

I had never spoken to my family about Nina. My father's questions when I was on a visit to India were like the following: Can you tell me why Americans are more punctual as a people? Or, Is there any way of explaining why Indians spit so much? For her part, Nina had never asked me much about my parents. This surprised me a bit. Not just my parents, I don't think even India interested her. I remember her saying once that if she ever visited India, she would be sure to skip the Taj Mahal. In Grand Central, we had seen an ad for travel to India: in the sky above the marble dome of the Taj, a monument to Shah Jahan's love for Mumtaz Mahal, were the words *And to think these days men get away with flowers and chocolates*. Nina wasn't very impressed.

—Don't you think it's somewhat perverse—beautiful monuments built for women when they are completely dead?

---

[*] I have the following quote in my notebook: *I carry a brick on my shoulder, in order that the world may know what my house was like.* —Bertolt Brecht

She chuckled when she said that. To show that she meant well, she kissed me on the ear.

A few months after we had been together, I decided to introduce India to her by showing her one or two films by Satyajit Ray, starting with *Pather Panchali;* but then I grew nervous, fearing that she would get bored. Another evening we went to Blockbuster to find a video. Nina was standing behind me in the store, her breast pressed against my back. I told her I wanted to watch a movie neither of us had seen before. I picked *The Silence of the Lambs*. She said that she had always wanted to see that movie. I liked it from the very first scene. After a while, I put the new VCR on pause to reach across and kiss Nina because, unlike Jodie Foster, she had a full, insolent mouth. Later, while we were still watching the movie, she made a comment that told me right away that she had seen it before. I didn't ask her about it. I had stopped doing that now, but I kept a private count of the times she lied to me. *Insidious intent on my part, yes, Your Honor. This was a small obsession. The way in which a country will stamp your passport every time you enter and leave. An exercise in record keeping.* I was in love with Nina and afterward, when the film was over, I said to her, in my best Anthony Hopkins impersonation, I'll have you with a little Chianti and some fava beans. Her dark eyes brightened and she made an eager swallowing sound with her tongue.

A week later, I woke up in the middle of the night and grew conscious of a memory that I had forgotten. I recalled Nina telling me once while we were out on a walk that she had a history professor as an undergrad whom she now called Hannibal Lecter. After she had graduated, she had gone to thank the man in his office. And the professor, reserved and more than twenty years her senior, had left his chair and come to her. He had stuck his tongue into her mouth and sucked hard for a moment and then as abruptly withdrawn and sunk back sheepishly into his chair.

I was now sitting waiting for Nina's call from Boston and the story crossed my mind—a thin cloud moving across the face of the sun—about that night we had together watched *The Silence of the Lambs*. In a self-pitying way I told myself that I had come so far from my roots: there was nothing of my day-to-day affairs that I could share with my parents. I wondered what I would say to my father on his birthday when he came to the phone in Patna. I was sitting close to the phone. Nina hadn't called even though she had said she would. The conference in Boston was titled Moving Image. The coffee I was drinking was a Sumatran variety called Mandheling that she liked. We had bought it together, not that it really mattered. I didn't even like drinking coffee, but there I was, with a cup in front of me, waiting, pretending to listen to the radio. That is what mattered, that I drank coffee now. I also let people smoke in my car because then Nina's doing the same wouldn't bother me as much. I switched on National Public Radio most mornings because she liked to wake up to it and I told myself that this way we'd have more things to say to each other.

Immigrant, Montana. Those were the words I suddenly heard

on the radio. The name of a place. NPR's Liane Hansen said that federal officers had killed a wolf at a ranch near Immigrant, Montana. I was instantly back in Yellowstone with Nina, listening to tapes as we drove through the forest. Her mock fear of bears when she took off her clothes. And the wolves. That morning in the motel, they were only half an hour north of us!

—Wolf Number Three, Hansen said with a slight smack of her lips, had developed a taste for sheep.

A man from the National Park Service said that Number Three had killed at least one sheep, maybe three, and then he was moved sixty air miles away, but he came back and another sheep was attacked.

—Three made a mistake, we gave him a second chance, he made a second mistake; we removed him from the population.

I felt like laughing. In the quietness of my apartment, I heard this man trying to sound like Harvey Keitel. I realized I was doing what Nina always did—talking back to the radio.

—This is NPR! When did you hire Quentin Tarantino?

I yearned for Nina. Now I felt I understood why she listened to the radio: it was as if she was walking alone down a crowded street and the world reached her in the form of scraps of overheard conversation and shouts. I wanted my voice in her ear. It was my father's birthday, he was now sixty-five, and his weak heart was killing him. He would not live long. So I told myself that on this special day the least I could do was love my girlfriend. If Nina were around—or even if she would simply call me that day—I'd say to her, I love you. I wanted to see her laughing when she heard me say that I liked Wolf Number Three and his preference for unbrainy sheep over vixen. I had this image of the wolf running through sixty miles of undergrowth, across frozen lakes he had never seen before, never pausing because his eyes were hungry for home, for the sight of the familiar fence and the sheep ranged inside.

—Honey, I hope he got to pull one down by the throat, the sheep's head thrown back and the blood warm near his mouth, before some stupid, solemn jerk with a hard-on nailed him with a three-thousand-dollar rifle.

Part V

Agnes Smedley

In a magazine, the list of 237 reasons people have sex, from a poll conducted by University of Texas psychologists Cindy Meston and David Buss. The list started with "I was bored" and ended with "I wanted to change the topic of conversation." In between were others like "I was feeling lonely" and "I wanted the person to love me." And "I wanted to burn calories."

Nina didn't forget the wolves.

Months after we had broken up I looked inside my mailbox and found a postcard showing Old Faithful with a small news clipping stuck on it. Nina's handwriting was recognizable in the address she had written, but she had written nothing else.

> The reintroduction of wolves to Yellowstone National Park has failed to stop elk from eating quaking aspens, disappointing scientists who had hoped that the wolves would do so by creating a "landscape of fear."

That was the last note I received from Nina after she told me that she no longer had the stomach for any more fights. When she said she was going to just walk away, I began to apologize. We were outside my apartment on Morningside Drive, standing on the broad sidewalk. The day was cool, the locust tree had put out white flowers, and fresh leaves covered its branches. A garbage truck was idling on the corner. The breeze carried a faint stench, I remember this clearly. A graduate student in art history, who had had beers with me, saw our serious faces and kept walking. Nina looked sad but she had made up her mind. She left me admiring the strength of her decision. I had nothing to support my despair. So many times I had complained to Nina about our relationship, and not once had she been the one to say it was over; now it was she who was walking away and it was clear that nothing I said would make a difference.

—I love you. You know I love you.

—Try to find someone who loves you, and love her back.

She was right about that, but she was wrong about the wolves. Just the other day I watched a video called *How Wolves Change Rivers*. The introduction of wolves in Yellowstone changed the ecology in unexpected ways. The wolves didn't just kill the deer. Their presence meant that deer and elk avoided certain areas like valleys and gorges. Vegetation returned to these parts and so too did other forms of life like birds and beavers. Grass grew on the banks. The new grass held the soil together, reducing erosion, and the rivers stopped changing course. On the brief video, the presenter, George Monbiot, spoke about this as a miracle. He spoke in a voice that was gushing, often breathless, wholeheartedly enthusiastic, even optimistic.

I wonder whether Nina has watched the video. Because of the lies. I don't mean Monbiot, with his fast-flowing words. Instead, I'm talking about my lies. Once, after we had been arguing for an hour, Nina had said she had read my journal. My anger vanished, replaced by panic.

—Kailash, she said, I found it depressing to just read those pages. How do you even manage to live the life they describe?

She usually called me AK but used my formal name when she was upset. Which pages had she read? I kept quiet.

—I always knew about the girl from the coffee place.

When we had been fighting, fighting and then making up the same day or three days later, then, in between those days, or maybe after dinner, or in the morning, I would try to wrangle a bit of intimacy with someone else. There was Amy from the organic coffee place down the block from the university; after a fight with Nina, I had gone to watch *Cape Fear* with Amy. For much of the movie, I had my hand between Amy's thighs. I'm sure I put this detail down in my journal. (I had probably also noted what Amy had said to me after we first slept together. She said that a friend of hers had acted in a porn film in which she had given a blow job to a dog. A German shepherd. I put this in a poem. Peter used to go to the café where Amy worked. He heard me read the poem and his only comment was that Amy was describing not her friend's experience but her own.) There was a second Amy too, a photographer at the student newspaper, who was going through a breakup. I had kissed her in the darkroom while working on my own prints. It didn't matter who you fucked in the dark. One face became transposed on another; anyone's body could be Nina's. Had Nina read about her too? I had written about the night I spent with Trish from Comp Lit. She rode a motorcycle; Trish was the only grad student in our cohort who had slept with a professor, a man who taught Lacan. Trish had delivered a conference paper about phone sex. She wore tiny black skirts and I had admired her in the couple of classes we had taken together because she appeared fearless. There was very little emotion in Trish's brief encounter with me, however, and she had barely concealed her boredom, even her contempt, when I started talking about Nina in bed. If she had read my terse but accurate description, Nina didn't say anything. It was clearly too depressing to even talk about it.

When we broke up, I made an entry in the journal about a young visiting assistant professor who had been hired to teach screenwriting for that semester. She was French-Algerian and had a boyfriend back in Lyon who was away teaching in Dubai for a year. My journal records that I told Fadela about Nina, and she was frank about her boyfriend. When we went to Kinko's to make a photocopy of her manuscript we kissed in the store for twenty minutes.

======

More than two decades have passed since that last morning on Morningside Drive. Not even work has brought us together again, although at airports, for some reason, I look around to see if Nina is there. *Airports, Your Honor, are the places where immigrants feel most at home. And also most uneasy.* The closest I came to a sense of her, except for the sudden dreams that appear in my sleep and catch me unawares, her lips on mine, her hot tears on my shoulder, was when I rented a car in Denver and drove through the day to Yellowstone Park. I had gone to Denver on behalf of an Indian newspaper to report on the Democratic National Convention when Barack Obama accepted his party's nomination. Hope was in the air. But even the expression of hope can very quickly appear routine, as in the ritual of the roll call, when the different states offered their electoral votes to each nominee. "Madam Secretary, Maine, the sun comes out in Maine the first in the nation . . ." "Illinois, home of Abraham Lincoln." "Mississippi, home of the blues." "Ladies and gentlemen, fellow Democrats and friends, we bring you greetings from the great state of Georgia, the thirteenth state in our union, birthplace of Dr. Martin Luther King Jr. . . . where we look to the future with an optimistic gaze . . . we, the empire state of the South, the jewel of the South, the great state of Georgia . . ." *No, Your Honor, I mean no disrespect. I only mention this to communicate my interest in the democratic process and in the sweet, folksy music of American speech. And I wouldn't put too fine a point on the manner in which, even in that moment, when the votes were announced, the bland and cheerful tribute to homeliness barely hid the preceding battles over political real estate.* But that was in Denver. After a day and half on the road, in the tiny pale green Mazda, I was at the mouth of Yellowstone National Park.

It was three o'clock in the morning and I drove past the unmanned ticket booth. The car's lights grazed bushes of sedge and boulders beside which grew small yellow flowers. Near a turn, three elk appeared right in front of me, as if they had conjured themselves out of the darkness. Like ladies of the night, stepping on high heels, the animals gingerly crossed the asphalt and disappeared into the pines on the other side. I rolled down the window. The air was cool and I saw above the dark outline of the hill to the right a small moon. Over the sound of the car, I heard the nearby howling of the wolves. In another half an hour, when the first tattered signs of day appeared in the east, I could see that the dark shapes that looked like boulders in the field were bison. And when it became lighter, closer to the river, were visible the gray wolves trotting amidst the solitary pine and the rows of cactus. Number Three, where have you gone!

Immigrant, Montana, was a small town with an old saloon and two stores that rented canoes and fly-fishing equipment. For a souvenir, I bought a fly, an iridescent form speckled with blue and gray; under its belly was a shining hook. Black granite mountains rose high on the other side of the Yellowstone River. The river flowed a short distance away from U.S. Highway 89, which cut through town. When I walked down toward the water, small grasshoppers leapt out of my way. The river water shimmered in the sunlight, and it was difficult to see the trout. The sun and the infinite blue sky, everything was beautiful, and yet this place could well have been a ghost town. It was a name that I had long carried in my imagination; it now belonged to the past. For all these years it was a name that brought together, like the two hands of a clock meeting at the right hour, the two most deeply felt needs of mine, the desire for love and the hankering for home. But there was nothing here for me.

=====

Last summer, I was at a writers' colony in Portland, Maine. The town in which Nina's parents had a cabin was only fifteen minutes away. I looked up their name in the phone book and was surprised not to find anything. But an online search quickly yielded results. There was an obituary in *The Cape Courier,* the local paper. Nina's mother had died due to heart failure. The first paragraph gave the date and cause of death. The short paragraph that followed made me certain Nina had written it. *For Mrs. Robin, the day imposed a simple rigor that had to be met with an aesthetic offering; her instincts were democratic, and she aimed for elegance and economy. She cast an equal, but critical, eye, on the layout of the morning newspaper, the township's budget allocation for the area schools, the arrangement of flowers on the desk in her study. She was an artist and an activist. Over the past year, during her convalescence, she wrote many letters to editors of newspapers on matters of concern like rent control and graduated income tax; when she had energy left from such endeavors, she painted lovely watercolors of the kestrels and bohemian waxwings that sat on the branches of scrub pine and juniper behind her house. She spoke amiably to the ringed plover and red-necked stints she encountered during her strolls on the beach, and came home to play a wicked game of rummy. Mrs. Robin is survived by her husband, Joseph; her daughter, Nina; and her twin grandchildren, Rebecca and Adam.* Suddenly, in that familiar land called language, the painful past was alive again.

While working on this book, I was searching for a particular postcard from Nina. I didn't find it, but look—here's a detail from that reproduction I had torn out of a magazine during my first days in this country. *The Lovers* by Picasso, 1904. *The draw-*

ing was done after Picasso first made love to Fernande. (He would have been twenty-two at that time. Had he really not made love to anyone else before? I think I unconsciously decided this was his first time because I was older than he.)*

A couple of days or maybe a week after our final breakup, I had seen Nina at Riverside Church, where a teach-in was being held to discuss the acquittal of the cops who had beaten Rodney King. I was seated in the last row but had a clear view of Nina as she stood with her back to the wall. She had joined her palms together as if she were praying. How many times had I held

---

* The torn sheet with Picasso's drawing. Proof against any argument that my report on desire is a recent preoccupation. It is true that I have published nothing over the past ten years, but I have notes. E.g., a clipping in my notebook has the following two bits of information: *1. Scientists could not say why some Australian women felt sad after otherwise satisfactory sex. 2. Mares are more likely to intentionally miscarry when they have mated with foreign stallions* ("Findings," *Harper's Magazine,* June 2011, p. 88).

Also, scribbled on an earlier page, the following observation: *Prairie dogs kiss more often if humans are watching* ("Findings," *Harper's Magazine,* April 2011).

Your Honor, was it fair on my part to wonder who was the researcher at Harper's Magazine *during those months in 2011 when I was paying attention to that section? Such an avid interest in the quiddities of sex! Young journalist, where are you now? Did you find in love the satisfaction you wanted? In March 2011, for instance, the "Findings" section reported the following: "The sexual arousal of men is dampened by sniffing the tears of a woman." "Young straight American couples who agree to be monogamous often aren't." "Apologies are disappointing." Such are the gifts of the Internet, Your Honor, a basic Google search revealed that the journalist in question, now an editor at* Harper's, *had been born in Delhi! Onward!*

Dear Editor, may your curiosity and interest in the world be rewarded a thousandfold!

those hands! I could go up to her and kiss her fingers, if she would let me. After ten minutes, I rose from my seat and left the meeting. It was too sad to keep looking at Nina.

In the days that followed I felt that I had failed not only in love but also in life. I fretted and moped because others around me were doing far more interesting things. My friend Peter had gone to Hamburg with Maya; from Germany, they were going to travel to France. Maya's parents were flying from Delhi to Paris, and they would come down to the South of France, to a village near Avignon, where Peter's uncle, a gay man and a successful painter, owned a farmhouse and several acres of land. Peter and Maya were getting married there. Maya was hoping that being married would make Peter happy. She was tremendously excited about having a Hindu wedding in the French countryside. We had all been invited, but no one could afford it. (Except Pushkin, but he had indicated that there was a conflict.) Larry was working as a teacher at a summer camp for teenagers among the California redwoods. His novel was going to be published in a year. Kurt Vonnegut had given him a blurb. Our officemate Ricardo was preparing a paper on cities and slums. Cai Yan was interviewing an Indian sociologist in London who had once been a member of the Naxalite underground in Bihar. Even Nina, despite the distractions of our troubled relationship, was making progress with her project on those she called the daughters of Mother Jones—Grace Lee Boggs, Audre Lorde, and Angela Davis.

Pushkin had received a grant for a translation project that was now nearly complete. He was translating from Hindi into English the story of a fifty-eight-year-old, low-caste man who had spent his life as a manual scavenger on the outskirts of Delhi, carrying shit on his head or on a cart, shit collected from row upon row of old houses. When I read the section that Pushkin showed me, I felt envy. Pushkin was already the writer I wanted to be. And, in translating the testimony of the untouchable man, he had done good work, not just because it was time well spent but because the story, even in translation, carried the hurt of the real. As a young reviewer in Delhi, Pushkin had railed against academics and activists on the left; in a surprise turn, which of course made sense, after coming to New York he had become the voice of the oppressed.

I had once known a man named Prabhunath whose father had been a minister in the Charan Singh cabinet. This fellow Prabhunath was a landlord in Palamu, and he had said to me that the low-caste people would always remain under the upper castes.

—You see, balls. He was pointing at his crotch. Balls will always hang under the cock, he said.

People like Prabhunath belonged to an older India. That particular India was alive in news reports that came to us about young couples lynched for marrying across caste lines or a Dalit beaten to death after drinking water from a well for Brahmins. Unlike Prabhunath, Pushkin was a member of the new India. He was a Brahmin, and his place in the world owed a lot to his past, but he had disavowed his origins and was now at home anywhere in the world. He wouldn't talk of a Hindi writer from Jaipur without also mentioning Jorge Luis Borges and Buenos Aires or Nâzim Hikmet and the Sea of Marmara.* When it came

---

* I liked Pushkin for saying things like You know I can see why Pico Iyer says, "One reason why Melbourne looks ever more like Houston is that both of them are filling up with Vietnamese pho cafés." It gave me a sense of what it meant to possess a global identity. It was something I wanted for myself too. But when I was getting drunk in Delhi with my friend Shankar, a journalist at *The Telegraph*, he had harsh words about Pushkin. Shankar said that Pushkin was only a jet-setter. He quoted from a piece he had just read to underline his point. "He isn't global at all. He's just from another planet. It's called the First World."

to romance, he probably thought it would be provincial to sleep with someone who was taking classes with you. He was more adventurous. I heard he was dating an opera singer in London. She was famous for her radical views. The previous winter she had gone to South Africa to sing for Nelson Mandela. If you caught Pushkin walking across campus on a Thursday night, he would, always very humbly, turn down your invitation for a drink. He was going to wait till he was in the air, he might add a bit later. He was on his way to La Guardia, where he was going to catch the late Virgin Atlantic flight to London.

I must sound bitter. I have good reason. One night during a conversation that went exactly along those lines, I asked Pushkin why he wasn't going to France for the wedding of our friends. Pushkin said he had already said yes to the organizers of a literary festival in London. Usually, he was parsimonious with information, but now and then he threw me a crumb. He was going to moderate a discussion on the representation of violence. Who was going to participate in that discussion? Oh, it was going to be the writer J. M. Coetzee and the philosopher Judith Butler. Pushkin then asked me politely what I was planning to do that night. The desi taxi drivers were going on a strike the next day in New York and I was meeting one of them to perhaps file a little report for a newspaper in Delhi. Pushkin nodded and we soon went our separate ways.

That night, after making me wait half an hour, Imran pulled up in his cab at the corner of Amsterdam and 121st. We sat talking in the car for a bit and then he started driving. He took a fare

down to Wall Street. From there we went to the East Village to
drop off another customer. It would be midnight soon. Imran
asked me if I'd like to watch dancers and I said yes. We drove
uptown for another fifteen minutes. Heavily weighted curtains
inside the front door and then in the darkness, the glow of bodies: young women, completely naked, stood like mannequins in
a row behind glass walls. Imran was my knowledgeable host. He
led me inside toward the music that flowed out into the semi-
dark in an intensely pleasurable stream. Here customers, mostly
men but also women, sat around tables. On both sides were
wooden benches where women were performing lap dances.
Waitresses milled about carrying trays with drinks. At one
table, two Indian men, young and stylish, were smoking cigars.
A beautiful black woman, wearing a golden thong, her breasts
bare, came up to Imran and me. We exchanged hellos. Imran
offered her a drink. She wanted a Cosmo, she said, and I asked
for a gin and tonic. A moment later I thought of Pushkin. It was
his favorite drink. He must be having his drink by now. In a little
while, Imran was going to pay the black girl twenty-five dollars
to do a little lap dance for me. She would put a hand lightly on
the back of my chair and dance, her mouth close to mine, her
breath smelling faintly of a mint-flavored gum, and then she'd
pull herself higher, coming closer, so that she brushed her nipples against my cheeks. All the while, she never stopped making conversation, asking me to name my favorite restaurants, as
she turned one breast and then the other toward me. I said I
couldn't recall the names just then and she laughed and, taking

my hand, pushed it down under her thong, snapping the band on my fingertips. I turned my head and saw just five feet away an old man, maybe seventy years old, staring impassively in front of him as a girl sat on his lap. That night, when Imran brought me back to my apartment, I was aware that I hadn't even asked him enough questions to be able to write a newspaper report about the strike. Instead, I had visited a nightclub. Anyone wanting to become a writer couldn't say no to experience. As I was falling asleep it occurred to me that I, unlike Pushkin, was doing no writing. I didn't dwell on that thought. I was mostly thinking of the thin black girl in the bar with the fragrant breasts who had said her name was Zaire. I was never going to see her again but the scent of her body clung to me. In the dark of my room I shut my eyes and saw the glitter on her skin. I wanted to make love to her. She had said, Remember I'm Zaire, just like the country, come and visit me again real soon.

═══

I needed to write another paper for Ehsaan. On my transcript, I still had an "Incomplete" from my second semester. We had read Fanon in his class. In one of the chapters Fanon had written about love between a black man and a white woman. I asked Ehsaan if I could write about desire. I was thinking of what Nina had once asked me about the movie *The Night Porter*. The messiness of love. The complications of desire, especially forbidden desire. Love *despite,* or *in spite of;* love beyond and across dividing lines. That must have been at the back of my mind when I thought of that movie's presentation of love between the Nazi officer and the woman in the concentration camp.* Was there a film in the postcolonial context that I could focus on? Ehsaan said yes. He mentioned the films made about love during the Partition. Then he stopped.

—Are you familiar with the name Agnes Smedley?

I hadn't heard of Agnes Smedley. She had died in 1950, and although I didn't know this then, she would change the course of my life.

Early in the century, in March 1918, a trial was held in New York City—*United States of America vs. Virendranath Chatto-padhyaya and Agnes Smedley*. Chattopadhyaya, or Chatto as he was called, was a nationalist who had arrived from Calcutta under the pretext of pursuing graduate study in physics. He was from a famous, well-educated Brahmin family; the poet Sarojini Naidu was his sister. Smedley had been born in a poor family in Missouri, and she was trained as a teacher. After hearing a lecture at Columbia University by the great Indian leader Lajpat Rai, she offered help. He asked her to type a manuscript about his experiences in the United States in return for private classes on Indian history. Smedley admired Rai immensely but didn't follow his moderate politics; after his departure, she fell in step

---

* It would be years before I would find out that the words that appeared in the opening paragraph of Roger Ebert's dismissive one-star review of *The Night Porter* included the following: *nasty, lubricious, despicable, obscene,* and *trash.*

with the Bengali revolutionaries who were looking for allies in their battle with the British. Virendranath Chattopadhyaya was one of them. The trial in which Chatto and Smedley were charged with treason was based on the discovery, the previous March, of thousands of dollars in cash as well as machine guns and ammunition in a Houston Street warehouse in Manhattan. The money and the weapons had been supplied by the German military attaché. The defendants were accused of smuggling arms supplied by the Germans to aid radicals fighting for independence in British India.

While in prison, Smedley wrote stories about the prostitutes, alcoholics, lunatics, and thieves who surrounded her. She had been familiar with poverty in her childhood and youth. Perhaps because of her past, and also because of her politics, her portraits of those she met in prison were a not-so-subtle denunciation of the immense class divide in American society. And later, upon her release, after she had witnessed for another decade the struggles of the Indian revolutionaries in exile, she also wrote an autobiographical novel. Ehsaan wanted me to study Agnes Smedley's literary outpourings and conduct research on the trials of the Indian radicals on both coasts. Maybe my thesis, he suggested, could grow out of this project.

The lives I was reading about quickly seized my interest. The accounts of the early Indian revolutionaries in New York and California filled me with energy. And envy. I wanted to inhabit more and more deeply the stories of their precarious but exciting lives and their loves. Slowly at first, and then with a rush, I saw in the strange relationship between Chatto and Smedley an omen.

Chatto was held in prison for eight months and Smedley for seven to eight weeks. When he was released, Chatto was a physical wreck, unable to walk even a few steps without Smedley's help. In January 1919, they traveled together to France to take part in the Paris Peace Conference, and later, in 1921, to Russia to attend the Comintern gathering. They didn't obtain an audience with Lenin and had to leave disappointed. Assured of German support, they traveled to Weimar Berlin to escape British spies. Berlin was staggering under inflation. Smedley found out to her dismay that six weeks' wages could get a working person only a pair of boots. The economic crisis also forced Chatto to give up his plans of founding an organization in Germany that would build support for India. By the fall of 1923, the inflation in Berlin had reached its peak. Smedley wrote in a letter that she had been mutely observing people dying a slow death. There was a small church on her street, and she'd watch funeral processions arrive and leave. Workers used all of their wages for just a couple of loaves of bread, some potatoes, and margarine. Meat and fruit were beyond their reach. She could not find sugar in any of the stores.

When Smedley first met Chatto, she thought he looked fierce but also ugly, with dark, glittering eyes set in a pockmarked face. He was a short and thin man, in his early forties but with already gray hair. In the reminiscences of a well-known Danish

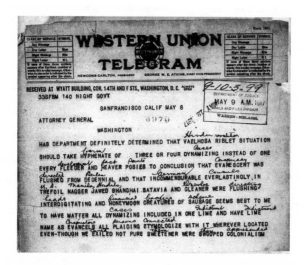

U.S. attorney's encrypted telegram regarding Indian
nationalist activity in California. Dated May 8, 1917.

novelist, Agnes Smedley was described as bright and vivacious,
full of vigor, fond of wearing costumes and dancing. But despite
their physical differences, Smedley and Chatto were attracted
to each other and became lovers. They discussed politics with
great excitement, and she later said that he was the first man to
whom she hadn't lied that her father was a physician.

I was soon immersed in the account of their relationship.
Smedley's education had been haphazard, and her childhood
had been harsh. Chatto, on the other hand, was a polyglot who
had been educated at Oxford, and had lived a luxurious life.
However, neither his education nor his family's wealth saved
him from pettiness. In more than one letter, Smedley discussed
her problems. In one she wrote that Chatto was *suspicious as hell*

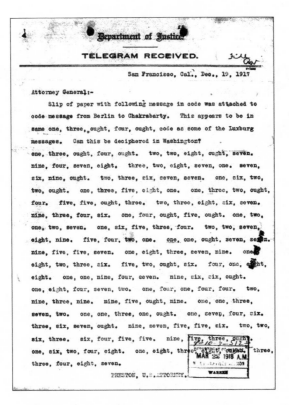

U.S. attorney's query about cracking the code in an intercepted note sent from Germany to Indian nationalists in the United States. Dated December 19, 1917.

of every man near me. There was also some professional jealousy. Smedley published an article about Indian immigrants in *The Nation,* and Chatto commented disapprovingly that she was *showing off.* Smedley had other complaints. All the time she was in Berlin, the small home that she shared with Chatto was overrun by guests. Smedley wrote, *Moslems and Hindus of every caste streamed through as though a railway station or a hotel. Students came directly from their boats, carting all their bedding and cooking utensils.* Smedley didn't really know how to cook, but she was now expected to do just that. In the margins of the same letter, she wrote: *I cook until the very walls of our home seem to be permeated with the odor of curry.*

When she had been only twenty-two and working as a teacher in Missouri, Smedley had married an Irish socialist. (This was some years before she met Chatto.) Her husband was a union organizer and journalist. He lived in St. Louis and traveled a great deal; this suited Smedley because she didn't want to be tied down to a domestic life. She was squeamish about sex. She was opposed to the idea that the mere act of marriage should require that a woman suddenly welcome a physical relationship with a male; she also detested the prospect of becoming a vessel for bearing children on a regular basis, which had been the fate of her own mother, who had succumbed to madness after giving birth to her seventh child.

To make matters worse, only four months into her marriage, Smedley found out that she was pregnant. Abortion was illegal and she had to go to Kansas City for the operation. On the train ride back, Smedley was in pain and she sweated and moaned in distress, and according to her biographer, Smedley's husband asked her to stay quiet and sit up straight in her seat because of the looks she was attracting. Smedley refused to speak to him for several weeks. Six months later, she wrote to her husband, *I take the blame. I do not want to be married; marriage is too terrible and I should never have entered it. I was wrong—for you loved me and I do not know what love means. I want my name back, also.*

A shift came in 1917, when Smedley met the legendary birth control pioneer Margaret Sanger. Sanger had launched a public education campaign. Her attempt to popularize contraception was aimed at liberating women, encouraging them to think about sexual behavior as not only appropriate but also pleasurable. Smedley was twenty-five now. Quite soon after the divorce was finalized she plunged into an affair with a journalist named David Lee Willoughby. The affair left her feeling unsatisfied and lonely, and she tried to quell these feelings by entering into short-lived relationships with other men. One of the biographies I read had this to say: *A pessary might allow Smedley to be as sexually predatory as any man. Her inability to trust anyone sufficiently to permit real intimacy, though, denied her the happiness she sought. If she were to feel, as she wished, that her life had meaning, she needed more meaningful work.* This search for meaningful activity led Smedley to active engagement with the struggle for Indian independence and her meeting the man who would be the center of her life for so many years.

There was one disturbing detour, however. Smedley had an encounter with M. N. Roy, a well-known communist leader, an encounter that hurt Smedley and cast a pall on her relationship with Chatto. In late March 1917, after a meeting of a group of Indian and Irish revolutionaries at the Mayflower Hotel in New York City, Roy asked Smedley to accompany him to Grand Central Terminal, where he was to meet two men who were bringing letters from Moscow. It was cold outside and Roy needed to fetch his coat. Smedley accompanied him to his fifth-floor room. Roy came out of the bathroom, where he had gone to wash his face, and found Smedley near the radiator warming her hands. He turned her around and kissed her. For a moment or a little longer, Smedley told a friend later, she liked the pressure of Roy's lips on hers. But then an older unease suddenly bloomed inside her and she tried to get out of the embrace. Roy was adamant, however, and pinned her down on the bed. Many years later, when Smedley felt that her relationship with Chatto had drawn her into an abyss of self-loathing, and that each day brought with it the threat of a nervous breakdown, a psychiatrist suggested that she write a memoir. She sat down to work on a thinly disguised autobiographical novel, *Daughter of Earth.*[*] For the first time, the episode with Roy found its fullest mention in this book's pages, and Smedley also revealed how what had happened in the hotel room lingered in her life with Chatto. Within the space of three pages in *Daughter of Earth*, Smedley moves from the love that an Indian revolutionary felt for the narrator, to their quick marriage a week after their first meeting, to the husband's inquiry whether Roy was one of the

---

[*] In *Daughter of Earth*, Smedley transcribed from her life. Even the fictional name that she gave to her protagonist, Marie Rogers, had its basis in reality. Marie Rogers was a name that Smedley had invented years earlier: she had used it to sign all her letters during her involvement with the rebellious Indian nationalists in America. Her book is neither a memoir nor simply a novel. And when I read it, I thought Smedley offered us a model for writing.

men that Smedley had been intimate with earlier in her life. On the night of her hurried wedding, Smedley's protagonist wakes up to find her Indian husband staring at her, speechless, with a strange, drawn face. He finally asks her a question— *Tell me what men said to you . . . The men you lived with.*

I began working on my master's thesis for Ehsaan. For a few pages, I would see the world with Smedley's eyes, and then, with a feeling of uneasy identification, with Chatto's. That sexual tension, born out of jealousy, was so vivid. *Your Honor, I saw myself as if in a mirror, my face night-lit with jealous rage, standing beside Nina's bed. I was asking her about Jonathan. So many times I had contemplated her past. I imagined her sitting on the deck of a yacht off the coast of Maine. The yacht was owned by a former lover of hers. The two of them were sipping white wine and eating grilled lobster. I returned to such scenes in my mind as I read more. Here was Jawaharlal Nehru, in* An Autobiography *(1936), remembering Virendranath Chattopadhyaya: "Popularly known as Chatto he was a very able and a very delightful person. He was always hard up, his clothes were very much the worse for wear and often he found it difficult to raise the wherewithal for a meal. But his humor and lightheartedness never left him. He had been some years senior to me during my educational days in England. He was at Oxford when I was at Harrow. Since those days he had not returned to India and sometimes a fit of homesickness came to him when he longed to be back. All his home ties had long been severed and it is quite certain that if he came to India he would feel unhappy and out of joint. But in spite of the passage of time the home pull remains. No exile can escape the malady of his tribe, that consump-*

tion of the soul, as Mazzini called it." Your Honor, I was in pain, I suffered from the consumption of the soul.

There were also other aspects of Smedley's story that affected me deeply. Earlier in her book, her heroine described receiving a letter from jail: *I read and re-read a letter lying before me. It was from my brother George. I could tell no one of its contents, for I feared that none of the people I lived with would understand. They idealized the working class, and I feared they might not understand the things that grew in poverty and ignorance. They would say my brother would have been justified had he stolen bread, when hungry, but he should not have stolen a horse. Even I, who loved him so dearly, felt this.* These words had come from a great distance and found a place close to my heart. What Smedley had written about the unfeeling hypocrisy of those who idealized the working class also applied to the people sitting around me at the seminar table in Ehsaan's classes. But, more than that, her words took me back to my own relatives in Bihar. Their small worlds, their plain poverty, and the ordinary complications of their difficult lives. Ehsaan had once told us that he did not see a lightbulb, hear a radio, or ride in a car till he was eight or nine years old and he did not fly in an airplane till he was twenty-one. I shared a bit of that past with him and wanted to write out of that experience. Was this only nostalgia on my part? I had left home, and the immensity of that departure sought recognition in my new life. I think that was the main thing. What I was learning in America was new and illuminating but it became valuable only when it was linked to my past.

=====

Ehsaan told me to read a short story by Somerset Maugham called "Giulia Lazzari" because it had a connection to Agnes Smedley. The story is narrated by a dapper fellow named Ashenden. He is a British novelist working as a spy in Europe for his country. Now he is on a mission to arrest Chandra Lal, an Indian revolutionary in Berlin. Chandra is a lawyer by training and bitterly opposed to British rule in India. Although he receives funds from German agents, he doesn't use the money on himself. He is hardworking, principled, and abstemious; he keeps his word. In all these respects, Chandra resembled the man who was his model, Agnes Smedley's lover, Virendranath Chattopadhyaya. The title character is Italian, a performer of Spanish dances, and a prostitute.

More than the discussion of politics in the story, the smaller personal details arrested my attention. Here were the two Englishmen in the Maugham story discussing Chandra's looks. Looking at the Indian's photograph, the narrator observed, *It showed a fat-faced, swarthy man, with full lips and a fleshy nose; his hair was black, thick, and straight, and his very large eyes even in the photograph were liquid and cow-like. He looked ill-at-ease in European clothes.* Ashenden's superior expressed surprise that Lazzari could have fallen for Chandra.* He said, *You wouldn't*

---

* *Your Honor, the sting of such judgment but also the comfort! The comfort of knowing that if I too was being judged in this way, then I wasn't alone. Let the record state that*

have thought there was anything very attractive in that greasy little nigger. God, how they run to fat! I went back to the description that Smedley had offered of the Chatto character in her novel, *Daughter of Earth*: *He was thin, with a light brown skin, and his hair was black and very glossy. His eyes, shaded by heavy eyebrows, made me think of a black Indian night when the stars hang from an intensely purple heaven. Over the eyes was an intangible veil of sadness—how could a man with such an intense face have sad eyes! He was perhaps in his early thirties.* I wasn't thinking just of myself, dear reader, and how a white woman might regard me. I was thinking of Ehsaan and his charm. He was my idol. I had not forgotten a news report from the Kissinger trial. A reporter, who was female, had written: *Ehsaan is an exquisitely polite man with dazzling white teeth and large divergent eyes which give him an abstracted look.*

In the paper I submitted to Ehsaan, I adopted a more academic tone. I pointed out that the tale written by Maugham invested the British with control and cunning. The qualities of those who populated the fringes of this colonial narrative, the swarthy-skinned inhabitants of a world that was unstable and filled with need, were questionable. Chandra and his ilk were suspect, and their judgment, if not their moral nature, was defi-

---

Nina and I had made love in a small patch of grass near the university's administration building one afternoon. It was the Fourth of July. The U.S. flag flapped above us. I was aware of all kinds of negative judgment, Your Honor. How could she have fallen for me? I suffered under an invisible indictment. And, in response, it was as if I was saying to Nina, I kiss you with my alien tongue, your body taking me in against Article 274 of the Immigration and Nationality Laws, which presses on bodies penalties for encouraging or inducing an alien to come to, enter, or reside in the United States.

cient. These characters might have some fleeting nobility, or passion, and even pathos, but they didn't have the gift of narrative. Their words didn't have coherence, and their lives didn't have the unity that comes from the power to tell a story. There was also the crucial question of love. Ashenden had asked Lazzari if she really loved Chandra, the man he wanted to catch. Lazzari replied: *He's the only man who's ever been kind to me.* In Smedley's novel, her protagonist said to her Indian lover: *I have loved no one but you.* (Did I think of the women I have loved when I read those words? Yes, I did. Did I find myself judged? I surely did.)

In what I wrote for Ehsaan I do not remember whether I examined the congruences or the differences between Maugham's Chandra and Smedley's Chatto. In Maugham's story, Ashenden uses Lazzari to lure Chandra to a port town. Upon discovering that he has been trapped, Chandra swallows poison and dies. It is more likely that I only pointed out that the real-life Chandra Lal eluded the British rulers in a different way than Maugham had imagined. But his end was tragic too. Chatto had been active during the last years of his life in communist Russia. The British still ruled India and would not permit his return. He was arrested on July 15, 1937, during Stalin's purge. His name appears on a death list signed by Stalin on August 31 that year. He was probably executed on September 2, 1937.

═══

There was a party at Ehsaan's house. I went to pick up Peter as planned, but when I rang his bell Maya came to the door. Her face was puffy. She said that Peter wasn't well. *Was it serious this time? No? But in that case he could have called!* Over subsequent months, this conversation became routine, following a pattern; and for too long, till it was too late, I thought only that Peter was withdrawing from us because he was falling deeper and deeper in love with Maya. This had been Maya's hope when they got married, and we were all susceptible to this hope.

The invitation to the party had come from Prakash Mathan, an older student. He was completing his doctorate in international relations, something about the informal sectors of lending in the Brazilian and Russian economies. Prakash wore beautiful silk shirts. That was something I had noticed about him. He had come as a boy from Kerala with his mother after she found a job as a nurse in Houston. His father worked as a car mechanic in India, and he followed his wife to America. At the party, while Ehsaan cooked, Prakash served drinks. While Prakash was mixing Manhattans for us, Cai Yan wanted him to tell me a story he had told her earlier about Ehsaan. Prakash raised his eyes and asked, Which one?

That was another thing about Ehsaan, there were always stories. The previous week he'd had me over for lunch at his house. The lunch was for a Pakistani friend of his, a doctor at Columbia Medical, whom he had known for many years. He had cooked keema, baingan bharta, and his trademark dal, with a tadka of onion and garlic fried in oil floating on the surface. The doctor was in her late thirties, pretty, and stylishly dressed. Her husband was an American, a well-regarded scientist.

—Did Harvey tell you about his first scientific experiment? Ehsaan asked the doctor about her husband.

The doctor had probably already heard about the experiment, probably from Ehsaan himself, but she smiled and shook her head.

—This was when Harvey was four years old and living in Brooklyn. He was in the backyard and decided that he was going to pee right there. To his surprise, a worm emerged from the little puddle he was making. He promptly concluded that worms came from your urine. He was a scientist. In order to prove his hypothesis, he went back the next day and repeated the experiment. To his satisfaction, another worm appeared from the puddle, just as before. Here was reproducible proof! He told me he held on to this scientific belief till he was nine years old.

Now, at Ehsaan's party, Prakash embarked on the story that Cai Yan wanted him to tell me. We were standing on Ehsaan's balcony with our drinks. Prakash was balancing his drink and a cigarette in the same hand.

When Ehsaan was in his twenties in Pakistan, some years after he had migrated there from Bihar, he received a Rotary Fellowship to study abroad. He knew he wanted to visit four places when he left the subcontinent. Three of those four places he visited en route to the United States. Now Prakash put his free hand to use, holding up one finger after another:

1. He went to the Highgate Cemetery in London to pay homage to Karl Marx.

2. He also visited 221B Baker Street, for its well-known literary landmark.

3. And he made sure he got the opportunity to wander through the British Museum, where his reaction was, Return the loot!

The fourth place he wanted to visit was the site of the Haymarket riot in 1886 Chicago. Ehsaan wanted to go there because, as a boy, he had been taken to May Day celebrations in India. He wanted to lay flowers at the Haymarket monument to honor the striking workers who had marched in the first May Day parade. But several years were to pass before he could visit Chicago. He had, by then, been in and out of the country, doing research and political work for several years in Tunisia. In 1967, ten years after he first arrived in the United States, Ehsaan found himself in Chicago. He left his hotel and bought a bouquet of flowers; however, when he got to Haymarket, he could not find the monument. He asked several people, but none seemed to know about the landmark struggle for an eight-hour working day. Finally, someone pointed the monument out to him. It was the statue of a policeman who had preserved law and order on that day long ago. Ehsaan brought the flowers back and gave them to a young woman he liked at the conference he was attending. She later became his wife.

I clapped my hands.

—Wait, wait, there is more, Cai Yan said.

—Well, here's the thing, Prakash said. All this happens and

just a year later Ehsaan gets a fellowship in Chicago. This is at the Adlai Stevenson Institute. And he is giving a speech at an antiwar meeting. He recounts the story about his search for the Haymarket monument. He tells the audience how shocked he was that the historical memory of workers' resistance, recognized and celebrated around the world, hasn't been honored in its own place of origin. Not long after, two FBI agents show up at his door. They want to know what he had said at the sit-in about Haymarket and who had been among the audience. It turned out that the Weathermen had just blown up the offending statue of the Chicago policeman.

—Let's call him here, Cai Yan said.

All three of us turned to look at Ehsaan, who was chatting with an old man with a Moses-like beard.

—Would you like a real drink? Prakash called out.

Ehsaan heard the question, excused himself, and walked over to where we were standing.

—Prakash told us the story of how you got to see the four great sights. Including Haymarket, Cai said.

—Did he tell you that I got a visit from the FBI after I had spoken about Haymarket?

—What did you say to them? I asked.

Ehsaan was a master of pauses.

—They first asked me if I was a citizen of the United States. I said, No. They said, Don't you feel that as a guest in this country you should not be going about criticizing the host country's government? I said, I hear your point, but I do want you to know that while I am not a citizen, I am a taxpayer. And I thought it was a fundamental principle of American democracy that there is no taxation without representation. I have not been represented in this war in Vietnam. And my people, Asian people, are being bombed right now. Surprisingly, the FBI agents looked deeply moved. They blushed at my throwing this argument at them. They were speechless.

He was smiling. A couple other students had joined us to catch the end of the story. One of them asked Ehsaan how he understood what had happened with the FBI agents that day.

—Well, at that time, I understood something about the importance of having some correspondence between American liberal traditions and our own rhetoric and tactics.

It is a tenet of graduate student life to debate such pronouncements. The more serious-minded among us, Pushkin perhaps, had maybe taken a lesson from this tenet, a lesson about aligning pronouncements with practice. But what was to remain with me after all those years was the example of Ehsaan seeking Marx and Sherlock Holmes together in London. It was as if someone from my town had expressed the ambition to read everything by Mahatma Gandhi and watch every Dilip Kumar film! Or better still, a friend showing devotion to the revolutionary life of Bhagat Singh and also taking joy in reciting the batting and bowling figures of Ranjitsinhji.

From Ehsaan we wanted narrative. We didn't always care how much of it was nonfiction or fiction. Ehsaan lived—and narrated—his life along the blurry Line of Control between the two genres. Others responded in kind.

For instance.

Standing in a kitchen in Amsterdam, where he headed the Transnational Institute, Ehsaan narrated the story of his childhood to the great writer John Berger. Later, Berger gave a fictional name to the Ehsaan character in *Photocopies*. The details belonged to Ehsaan's life but the broader narrative was about the Partition. Ehsaan was only thirteen years old and living near Gaya in Bihar when it became clear that India would be divided and there was going to be a new country for Muslims. Riots broke out in the cities. A man in Ehsaan's village who worked in a printing shop in Calcutta came back with the report that Hindus and Muslims who till yesterday had been neighbors were at each other's throats. But Ehsaan had seen his own relatives murder his father—he didn't believe it was religion that taught people to kill.

Ehsaan's eldest brother held a senior position in the tax ministry; he wanted to claim his place in Pakistan. Ehsaan went with his brother's family on a train to Delhi, where they were put in a camp in an old fort called the Purana Qila. Although there was a separate section for officials and their families, cholera was already spreading among the thousands of refugees waiting there. The new government in Karachi was providing planes for senior officials and their families. Ehsaan's family was to board a plane for the short flight to Lahore, but there had been a mistake. They were a seat short. Ehsaan was asked to stay behind and wait for the next available flight. His brother gave him a rifle and some money. However, no plane came and Ehsaan was forced to join a long column of refugees leaving for the border. The lines of people fleeing in both directions stretched for miles, raising dust that hid the distant horizon. As a boy, Ehsaan had seen the river Ganga in flood, carrying away huts and cattle and branches torn from trees. Now, in a daze, he felt he was being carried away in a flood of strangers.

In their group, there was an opium eater. He had been a beggar in the refugee camp, but in the column, unable to feed his addiction, he began to recover. Even his gait changed. The opium eater, whose name was Abdul Ghafoor, assumed leadership of the group, and he put Ehsaan on sentry duty. Ehsaan carried his rifle with him at all times and he felt protective of the young women among the refugees. He would look at them furtively, admiring the shape of their lips. In the open fields at night, lying under the stars, he imagined their breasts brushing his cheeks.

On occasion, as dusk approached, Abdul Ghafoor would ask the group to take shelter in an abandoned mosque or the courtyard of a village school. This was better than spending the night in the fields, where fires flared around them and human cries mixed with the sounds of animals. Early one night, the column camped close to a rural railway station, drawn by the sight of a police tent pitched at the other end of the single platform.

During dinner, four young Muslim men came to the camp, swords in hand, with a woman walking behind them. They were given food, rotis cooked on a small fire and eaten with onions dug from a field. Abdul Ghafoor instructed Ehsaan to stay alert. The four youth had slit the throats of the two Hindu policemen in the tent at the other end of the platform. The woman with them was the wife of a Muslim carpenter from a nearby village. Ehsaan looked at her. She was sitting by herself, speaking to no one. Her name was Jamila. She must have been in her early twenties; a parrot-green dupatta hid most of her face, but a silver nose stud glinted in the faint firelight. After her husband was found knifed in his shed, the villagers had brought the woman to the police tent. The two guardsmen stationed there promised to arrange for Jamila's transfer to a refugee camp if they weren't immediately able to put her on one of the trains going to the Wagah border. After a week, word leaked out that the woman hadn't been allowed to leave. The guardsmen had kept her to cook for them and give them company at night.

The arrival of the young men and the woman had introduced a disturbance. Ehsaan noticed that people in small groups conversed in quiet, uneasy voices. But after they had eaten, the young men, especially a small-faced man among them, a blue handkerchief tied on his head, had much to say. Ehsaan was on duty and didn't hear the stories himself. The next morning, an old hakeem in the group, a medicine man from Agra who always had a sprig of mint, or fennel, or a basil leaf on his tongue, told him, not without consternation, that the youth had some nights ago attacked the home of a Sikh shopkeeper. One of the four had been close to the family. The Sikh had a grown-up daughter, still unmarried, and his wife was a tall and beautiful woman. She was known in the community because of her embroidery work.

When the young men were about to break down his door, the Sikh rushed out in the dark to fight. In one hand, he carried a flaming torch, rags tied to a piece of wood and probably dipped in kerosene. In the other, a long sword. But the four of them were too much for the shopkeeper; they got away with cuts on their arms and a slashed thigh. Inside they found the rest of the family in the kitchen. After giving them a drink, opium mixed with water, the Sikh shopkeeper had used a small kirpan to kill both his wife and daughter. The youth with the blue handkerchief on his head said that all he got were the thin gold earrings worn by the dead girl.

By midday, the young men and the widow had disappeared down a side road. Ehsaan and his group passed another column going in the opposite direction. The people in the other kafila looked no different: they had tired and drawn faces, they carried meager belongings and food in sacks or in baskets on their heads. Most were on foot. One woman led two goats on a rope. A tall, thin man, wearing only a strip of cotton around his waist, carried on his back a shrunken old woman who looked as small as a child. That night, Abdul Ghafoor sat down with Ehsaan outside the circle of sleeping bodies. Ehsaan asked Ghafoor where the young men and the widow had gone.

—They told me they were taking her to a camp. I didn't want to fight them. It is possible they will have sold her to someone by now.

Ehsaan sat in silence. Perhaps he could have pointed his rifle at the small-faced man and ordered him and his companions to leave the woman with them. He was pondering this when Abdul Ghafoor pointed to the bright moon.

—Look at that, he said. It looks like a freshly made roti. You reach for it and find that it is burned black on the other side. That is the freedom we have been given.

In the Ehsaan Ali archives at Hampshire College in Massachusetts, there is a letter from John Berger asking him if he approved of the brief narrative that he, Berger, had written about Ehsaan's past. I must assume that Ehsaan had liked the form that Berger had given to his story. I can only speculate that the choice of a fictional name for Ehsaan's character was necessary because one or both of these men—Berger and Ehsaan—understood that memory is unreliable.

———

> Tell me with true frankness
> — should these few pages be published?
> The question concerns not only their
> quality but, much more important, the
> circumstances and convenience and integrity
> of your life? You can just as well
> say no as yes. Or; I'm not sure;
> let's forget it, please. Out of friendships,
> be true to me.
> ~ ~ any chance you want to say yes —

You can reach Irki, the village where Ehsaan was born, by road from Patna. I went there last summer. It took me about four hours. It was a hot July day, late monsoon season, and the highway went past paddy fields filled with water. Small towns appeared at regular intervals, and the car I was traveling in would need to slow down to a crawl. At one point we stopped to look at a crumbling mausoleum built beside a vast lake whose waters appeared a dark green, the mausoleum's archways framing the shadows of lovers. We continued on our way, passing tight clusters of crowds on the narrow highway, medicine stores, sheds for grinding wheat, cramped tailor shops, and stalls where chickens were sold from cages in which the birds had plucked each other's feathers out. A thin road branched off from National Highway 83, past huts and houses built close together, and then a sharp turn to the left near a mosque, a sign that we were in a Muslim part of the village. If we had remained on the

highway, in another hour we would have reached Bodh Gaya, where Gautama Buddha had found enlightenment.

The house where Ehsaan was born has now been divided between relatives by brick walls. A small metal gate stood locked near the wall where Ehsaan's father had been sleeping on the night he was murdered. I was invited to come inside through a door on the side. The middle-aged woman who answered the door introduced me to her mother, Sadrunissa, who was eighty-two years old and almost completely deaf. Sadrunissa was Ehsaan's first cousin. Her son-in-law shouted Ehsaan's name into Sadrunissa's ear and then, to make it clear whom he was talking about, he patted in the air as if he were touching a child's head before miming with his fingers the gesture of a throat being slit.

Sadrunissa began to speak in a high-pitched voice. She had very few teeth left. She spoke of her father, who loved Ehsaan, and then of her uncle, Ehsaan's father, who believed in justice and equality for all. He used to say, Do not oppress anyone. They killed him for it. She spoke of Ehsaan as if he was still alive and living in America. I didn't correct her. Her son-in-law told her that I was a journalist. Sadrunissa nodded her head and asked if I was from *The Searchlight* or *The Indian Nation*. These had been the two Patna newspapers from my childhood; they'd ceased publication decades ago.

The *azaan* sounded from the mosque. I had delayed things; it was time for my hosts to break their Ramzan fast. I was left alone while Sadrunissa and her family went inside to pray. While I waited on the veranda, small frogs hopped on the floor and a thin cat crawled down the clay tiles of the roof. After ten minutes, Sadrunissa came out and sat down with me. She took a cracker from the plate on the table and drank water. Her daughter brought out slices of mango and a couple of glasses of Rooh Afza. The son-in-law was a journalist for a small Hindi paper with its headquarters in Punjab. He had stopped asking Sadrunissa the questions I wanted to ask and would try to give replies himself. He said the family that had killed Ehsaan's father had met with ruin. Their two sons had both gone mad. The family had been cursed. Sadrunissa's son-in-law was curious about Ehsaan. He urged me to write about him because, he said, no one knew about him in his own birthplace. While he spoke, geckos darted swiftly on the green walls, trapping in their jaws the insects that were attracted by the naked lights. It was turning dark and I wanted to get to Bodh Gaya so I could find

a hotel to spend the night. Sadrunissa would interrupt our conversation to repeat, very loudly, what she had already told me
earlier. When I got up to leave, she held my sleeve and said that
the family had done well. By the time he retired from service,
her father was a deputy superintendent of police, and her son
had become a doctor.

Part VI

Cai Yan

I want to share these lines from a Xeroxed page left so many years ago in my mailbox, with Ehsaan's scribbled *EA* in the corner, after we had discussed my possible thesis topic. It is a quote from "Speeches on Religion to Its Cultured Despisers" (1799) by Friedrich Schleiermacher:

"What seizes you when you find the holy most intimately mixed with the profane, the sublime with the lowly and transitory? And what do you call the mood that sometimes forces you to presuppose the universality of this mixture and to search for it everywhere?"

And this note I had scribbled along with a quote from Gandhi's autobiography, *The Story of My Experiments with Truth: I was devoted to my parents. But no less was I devoted to the passions that flesh is heir to.**

---

* Morality is of interest to him, but morality always in conflict with itself. This is what makes the Mahatma more interesting than a box of tissue paper or, for that matter, a source of inspirational quotes printed under Gandhi's toothless smile on the covers of children's notebooks all over India.

I remember being awoken once a little before dawn by a sound that I didn't recognize at first. An Indonesian student lived in the unit next to me in that apartment building on Morningside Drive; his girlfriend was visiting from Cleveland or Cincinnati or some such place, where she too was a grad student. Was someone screaming? No, was she laughing? The sound, a moaning punctuated by rhythmic silence in a way that no ordinary screaming or even laughing can accommodate, went on for a while. Such shameless joy. Alone in my bed, wide awake now, I marveled at the matutinal sexual athleticism of the Indonesian fellow, Katon. He was thin, serious-looking, in wire-rimmed glasses. I think he was studying forestry. What had he done to the white girl from Ohio, what forest spirit had he been keeping secretly stored in a bottle, what animal instinct for pleasure had he released in her now? She was shrieking with happiness and all the birds in the forest were surely going to wake up any moment now and release their song.

I waited till nine to call Cai Yan. Nina had been gone several months now. I hadn't slept with Cai Yan yet, although we had spent a lot of time together in classes and even at Ehsaan's home. Of late, I had started humming a snatch of *"Dong Fang*

Hong" (The East is Red! The sun rises! China produces Mao Tse-tung!) whenever we passed each other in Butler Library or the corridors of Schapiro Hall. She would shake her head in amusement. A month ago, Maya had formed a writing group; Cai Yan and I were a part of that; we often sat next to each other on Maya's sofa, and I had noticed that each of us agreed with nearly everything that the other said. *(Your Honor, how fierce is the romance whose fires are fed by throwing on the flames torn pages of Bakhtin and subaltern studies!)* We were ready to spend hours together, I felt. I thought this could be the day. Katon had gifted me an omen. Cai Yan was grading papers for the international relations class where she was a teaching assistant. I asked her to come over to my apartment; she could grade at my place while I cooked an early lunch for her. I told her I would keep up an endless supply of fragrant tea.

In half an hour, the bell rang.

I had an old pot, an antique piece that had been Nina's gift, and I set this on the small desk. While Cai Yan did her work, I prepared lunch. Kadhai chicken, fried gobhi mattar, a tomato and cucumber salad on the side. For a thin girl, she had an enormous appetite. The rice was ready first and Cai Yan didn't want to wait, she scooped spoons of rice into a bowl and ate using a pair of old chopsticks that had come with a meal I had once ordered from Chinee Takee Outee.* Later, I gave her the rice

---

* *Your Honor, that name! You decide. Open and plainly literal pandering to the stereotype of a pidgin-speaking Oriental—or, instead, a playful linguistic mockery practiced by a consciousness primed by Asian-American critiques of representation?*

with the cauliflower and the chicken. She devoured it all. It reminded me of a small animal, and it excited me to watch her eat with such hunger.

Cai Yan laughed easily, but not when I flirted with her. That kind of play didn't appeal to her. She received each statement with some earnestness and then evaluated it seriously.

—Is it true that in China the word for *hello* translates as "have you eaten rice"?

She laughed and said yes. Then she said that actually it was usual for a hello to be accompanied by the second inquiry about food.

—Ehsaan is Chinese in that way, Cai Yan said. He first asks, Are you hungry? Oh, I like him so much.

We were sipping tea after lunch.

—I wonder whether there are other expressions that are also very different in Chinese. How might someone ask another person, So, are we on a date?

Your Honor, believing flirtatiousness to be foreign to Cai Yan, I spoke in an earnest manner. The gates didn't open. No one can keep the foreign away, or not for long, but Cai Yan was untouchable. Although she smiled she didn't seem to admit the thought that I was trying to seduce her. I stood, a stranger, a supplicant, a homeless alien, at the gates of an implacable continent. I saw her as if at a huge distance, standing alone at the end of a long road.

—I don't think anyone says things like that. People just know.

Which, of course, left me not knowing much. Nothing troubled Cai Yan's serenity. She still spoke with a half smile. While I waited, she remarked that she was making such swift progress, she must keep grading papers. I left her at my desk and went away to read in bed.

Cai Yan finished all her grading work in the evening and announced that she was going to step out for an hour. She didn't give any reason why she was going to come back to my apartment. When she returned, she was carrying two heavy grocery bags. She had brought beer and also pork and shrimp for home-made dumplings.* We drank beer and after I had chopped cabbage, chives, and ginger, Cai Yan mixed them with the pork and shrimp that she then put on rows of dumpling wrappers. The smell of sesame oil filled the apartment. Soon it was time to eat. The dumplings were delicious. They were first dipped in ponzu sauce and we sprinkled scallion on them before popping them in our mouths.

I didn't think anyone else in the entire apartment building could be having better food that evening. It was a date, I felt

---

* Cai Yan's report from her shopping expedition was that the cashier was a white girl dressed all in black and with black lipstick. Her black T-shirt said in white letters: JESUS SAVES I SPEND. When she was growing up, Cai Yan said, people in China wore clothes that were nondescript and didn't make any statement. It surprised her but also interested her that in America people wore T-shirts that made all kinds of bold assertions about the wearer. Had she observed this because she was Chinese? I didn't think so. I feel it is a shared immigrant trait. You come to America and just like you try to understand road signs you also take note of T-shirts. The affluent-looking middle-aged white man in Coney Island with the T-shirt shamelessly announcing: MY INDIAN NAME IS RUNS WITH BEER. Or, more recently, the somewhat cheerful and overweight woman, possibly a Latina, who passed me on the street wearing a T-shirt that said: FCK, and below that, ALL THAT'S MISSING IS YOU.

it. To make conversation, I said that I was ashamed that I had done so little work all week. This is the kind of thing all graduate students say. But Cai Yan paused. She wanted to know if I had ever felt shame.

Real shame?

I thought of the time I was caught stealing two books from the book fair in Delhi. I thought about that incident but didn't allude to it. Cai Yan was looking at me without any impatience or, for that matter, heightened expectation.

Then I remembered lying to my parents about my exam results when I was in high school. I wasn't ashamed of what I had done till my mother found out. There was also the shame of not having gone to see my friend when his father died. I was in my first year of college. My friend was someone I hung out with often, but I had never been to his house before, and I used this as an excuse to stay away. But it hurt when I saw him at the tea stall in Patna. He was standing there, his head shaven, and I had said nothing. Yes, it wasn't that I hadn't gone to his house. Instead, it was the fact that I hadn't had the courage or grace to offer condolences to a friend who had lost his father. I was ashamed also when a teacher I liked in school saw that I was cheating and turned his head away to give me a chance to hide my notes. All these incidents came back to me, but again, I didn't offer them to Cai Yan.

My silence didn't appear to disturb her.

—I was ashamed, Cai Yan said, when my cousin's husband called me on my phone and asked me to meet him. He was a doctor in Shanghai. I had just finished high school. He said he didn't love my cousin anymore. When I didn't say anything, he said, I mean it, I don't even like her smell. I would like to take you out for a drive. I have bought a new car and when I bought it I told myself that I want to take my dear cousin-in-law Cai Yan for a drive. I know a place about an hour away where we can have a special lunch and then take a walk in a garden. There are luxury cabins beside a lake if we want to rest. When he was saying these things, I said nothing. At a birthday party some weeks later, he pressed my breast and I felt I was going to vomit over his hand. I told my cousin what had happened. She slapped me on my left cheek but after that her husband never came near me.

I sipped my beer while Cai Yan spoke. She spoke matter-of-factly, with her mysterious half smile, as if she was amused by what she was saying. When she stopped, I began talking, perhaps because I didn't know how best to respond to her.

I recalled a half-forgotten incident from the time when I was a teen and my family had gone on a trip to Gujarat. I have repressed the name of the small town we were visiting. We had arrived at an old stone monument and looked around first for a bathroom. There wasn't one. Then we climbed up the medieval monument, several floors of narrow stairs, and arrived at the top. My mother said she was helpless. She continued to apologize before I understood that she needed to urinate. I told her to use a corner of the room while I stood on the staircase blocking access. Where was my father? I think he had climbed down already. My sisters were with me. Ma chose to relieve herself near a small drain hole in the corner. But this was a mistake.

When we came down, it became clear that the men below, those who sold entry tickets to the monument and also manned the tea shop, knew what had happened. Did I turn back and look up at the large wet patch visible on the wall high above? Perhaps that was the first sign. I remember clearly what the men were saying and without looking at her I tried to imagine the confusion and shame on my mother's face.

We talked like this that night and several other nights. I slept on the couch in Cai Yan's apartment; on one of those nights I said to her that we needn't sleep apart, we could share the bed, but it was as if I hadn't spoken at all. Her expression didn't change. She retained her serene half smile and brought me a pillow and a blanket where I was sitting on the couch. I had begun enjoying these nights, finding comfort in the acceptance of a near intimacy. One night, a cat was in her apartment. The cat was named Frida Kahlo and belonged to Maya, who had gone out of town for the week. Late that night, I lay on Cai Yan's couch watching television. The PBS station was showing a documentary on Christa McAuliffe, the schoolteacher who died in the *Challenger* disaster. Cai Yan had already gone to sleep in the bedroom. The cat was with her. When the shuttle had burst into flames, I was in high school in Patna, but I had watched on television McAuliffe's students counting down five-four-three-two-one. Their teacher lived for seventy-three more seconds.

When the documentary ended, I realized that I had probably never watched the footage of the kids: we didn't have a television in Patna. It is possible I had read about it in the newspaper. McAuliffe had taken with her on the flight an apple that her students had given her. That is how I learned about this custom in America. The scene stayed with me. As well as what Ronald Reagan had said to the schoolchildren, using words that I later found out were borrowed from a World War II poet: *We will never forget them, nor the last time we saw them, this morning, as they prepared for their journey and waved goodbye, and slipped the surly bonds of earth to touch the face of God.* I went to sleep thinking that when I had read about the disaster I hadn't foreseen the trip to America and my life as a student in New York City. There was no way I could have imagined or expected the experiences I was going to have. This moment in Cai Yan's apartment, and all the moments that had preceded it during the past three years, was alien to me. There was nothing that connected them to what I had known in Patna or the years I'd spent in college in Delhi. On those days when I sat in the university library, reading *The Times of India* or *The Statesman,* which arrived from India a week or sometimes a fortnight later, I allowed self-pity to take root in me like an affliction. Sachin Tendulkar had scored a big century against England in Chennai, but by the time I read about it the next Test match in Mumbai was already over and India had won the series 3–0. Weddings and deaths happened at a distance, and the distance was also inscribed in time. Which is to say, if you'll indulge me for a drowsy minute, I had often felt as if I had been sent into space.

Sometime during the night, Cai Yan touched my shoulder and woke me up.

—Frida is impossible, she said. She is keeping me up. I'm going to put her here and close the door. You come and sleep in the bedroom.

Who was Frida? As I stumbled into the bed I remembered the cat that Cai Yan was looking after and then I promptly fell asleep. When I woke up again, it was still dark and I became conscious that I had my arm around Cai. This thrilled me. I brought my face closer to her hair. The familiar smell of ginger was mixed with something else. I moved closer to her and felt her push her ass against me in her sleep. My heart was beating wildly, and I was certain that this hammering would wake her up. I put my hand on her breast. Was Cai awake? She was. She turned toward me in the dark and allowed me to press my lips on hers.

The next morning she acted as if nothing had happened. She didn't talk about it and I didn't either, but it was impossible to go back. In September, I returned from a three-day visit to the National Archives in Washington, D.C. Cai was very interested in my photocopied letters of Indian radicals and also the newspaper reports of Chatto's interrogation in Berlin. I read to her from a memorandum sent by the U.S. acting secretary of state on May 27, 1916, to the U.S. attorney general (*with reference to the so-called Indian Revolutionary Movement in the United States*) while reclining on her couch. I felt her toe on my feet and, since she didn't move it away, I slid my foot along the length of her shin. Then I put my hand there.

—Shin, I said. Is that the only part of the body that sounds Chinese?

—There's also *chin,* she said.

I kissed her chin.

—Tung, I said.

And sucked her mouth.

That was the first time we fucked.

October 8. Maya made pakoras using green chilies and invited Cai to her apartment. She told Cai that I was welcome too. Her apartment was on the next street and we took a bottle of wine with us. Peter wasn't there. Maya said that he had bought a new translation of *The Brothers Karamazov* and had told her before leaving for a café in the morning that he wouldn't come back till he had finished reading the remaining four hundred and fifty pages. Cai told me later that Maya had confided in her that Peter was depressed and advised to take "a ton of medication." Maya had spoken to Peter's mom in Germany. The mom simply said that she was dealing with the same problem. Peter's father, she said, "only liked his black dog." When I came back to my apartment with Cai that night, I saw that there was a letter for me from Patna. The handwriting on the blue aerogram looked vaguely familiar. It was a cousin on my mother's side called Pappu writing to inform me about Lotan Mamaji's death. Written in Hindi, the letter began: *It is with great sorrow that I'm writing to inform you* . . . The third line said that *it had been a matter of great hurt in the family that Lotan Mamaji had died under most unfortunate circumstances.* What the hell did Pappu mean? By the time I reached the end of the letter I had concluded that Mamaji hadn't died alone. Along with him, because of whatever circumstances Pappu had hinted at, Lotan Mamaji's adopted son, Mahesh, had also passed away. Several months would go by before I learned the truth: Lotan Mamaji had been murdered by Mahesh.

Mahesh was in his teens when Mamaji adopted him. He was the son of the woman who was Mamaji's mistress in Dhanbad. This is what Pappu had meant in his letter when he described the "twofold loss": Mamaji was dead and Mahesh was in prison. My sister told me when I was on a visit to Patna that Mahesh had tied Mamaji in a chair and then tortured him, asking him to sign over some property. Mamaji had signed the legal forms readily enough, but Mahesh wasn't satisfied. He wanted to avenge the humiliations of his past. How much more does certainty seem to lie at the tip of a steel knife than it does in rumors about your parentage!

But when I had first received news of Lotan Mamaji's death, the letter, which I also translated for Cai, was a puzzle. There was no way of unlocking the mystery of the death that night. So long ago, it seemed, I had told Jennifer about the monkeys on Lotan Mamaji's balcony. The story of the monkey's suicide. It was a story from my infancy in Ara. In later years, of course, I had spun that personal story into a broader narrative. Monkeys as metaphors for migration. The poor monkeys found electrocuted near the Hanuman Mandir in Connaught Place had lost their natural habitat. The modern-day menace of marauding monkeys, reported by Indian newspapers fond of alliteration, had to do with urban expansion and destruction of forests.

That's what I had originally thought. Then came the discovery that another important reason was the massive annual export of young male monkeys right up to the 1980s. The monkeys from Indian forests were living and dying in American labs. This story rescued the monkeys of my childhood from where they were stranded in nostalgia; they were now swinging from branch to branch on the tree of history.

One newspaper reported the request made in March 1955 by India's finance minister that senior officials in the United States please explain why the monkeys were needed from India. The Indian government had earlier been told that the monkeys were needed for scientific research on infantile paralysis and for the production of polio vaccines. Was there any reason to doubt this claim? The report doesn't say. Another account mentions that the Indian Prime Minister Morarji Desai banned the export of monkeys in 1978 because the Americans had violated their promise that the monkeys would be used only for medical research. Desai had cause to suspect that they were being put to military use to test defense systems and new weaponry. NASA's public records indicate that on June 11, 1948, a V-2 Blossom launched into space from White Sands, New Mexico, carried Albert I, a rhesus monkey. On June 14, 1949, Albert II was sent into space, gaining an altitude of eighty-three miles. Upon return, the monkey died on impact. On December 8, 1949, the last V-2 monkey flight was launched at White Sands. On this occasion the passenger was Albert IV. "It was a successful flight, with no ill effects on the monkey until impact, when it died." In

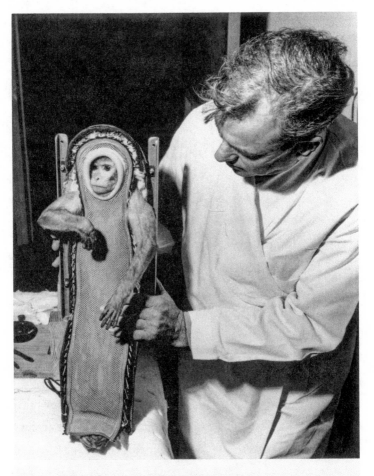

Figure 22.- The Rhesus monkey, Sam, after his ride
in the LJ-2 spacecraft.

September 1951, a monkey named Yorick was sent into space
and survived.

While reading about them I told myself that if I had at all
been using the monkeys for autobiographical purposes I needed

to stop and take note of the fact that they went further than I ever did. An adult monkey has the intelligence of a two-year-old human, and when zipped into its suit, locked in a metal case, its confusion and, if I can use this word, its courage must have been extraordinary. The NASA site notes that without the use of these animals in the early days of space testing in both the USA and USSR, there could have been great loss of human life. *These animals performed a service to their respective countries that no human could or would have performed.*

Was there a link between Indians and monkeys? The Republicans think so. In 2006 a Virginia senator named George Allen called an Indian-American youth a macaca. Allen was on the campaign trail and the teen he called macaca was working for his Democratic opponent. At his rally, Allen drew his supporters' attention to the young man, "Let's give a welcome to Macaca here. Welcome to America and the real world . . ."

Then he began to talk about the war on terror.

I was only nine months old at the time of the monkey's suicide, and when I returned to Lotan Mamaji's house a few years later the monkeys were still there, removing and eating what my young cousin said were lice from each other's hair. Beneath the tamarind tree's branches the mohalla's pigs rested like sacks of rotting wheat. They were actually black in color but were often coated with the dry brown mud of my birthplace. That summer I was quite taken with the pigs because they appeared in their loose packs, incessantly grunting, beneath the hole in the toilet, a wooden board placed a few feet above the ground, pushing their snouts inside the buckets under us.

I was already fifteen when, lying drunk on a mattress where I would find him the next morning sleeping in his own shit, Mamaji laughed at the old memory of my surprise at the sudden appearance of the pigs. The tears from his small eyes mixed with the red juice of the paan that bled from his mouth. We had come as members of the baraat party of the bridegroom for a marriage in a village called Garhi. It was about four hours' drive from Ara. Our hosts had made available the one large hall that was all there was to the village high school; sixty men were to eat and sleep and while away our time for the next two days in that room, surrounded on three sides by the monsoon rains, which had filled the village with water and the unrelenting croaking of bullfrogs.

Earlier that evening, I had watched Lotan Mamaji take out the moist bundle of hundred-rupee notes from under his sweat-drenched kurta and offer them, one at a time, to the dancer who had been brought from Calcutta for twenty thousand rupees. The elderly men from the district's landowning families had at last been able to watch live the dances first performed by Meena Kumari in *Pakeezah* a few months before she died of alcohol overdose. The village had no electricity, but a loud fuel-powered generator had been hired and brought from Ara. It lit three large bulbs, which attracted millions of moths and more than two hundred villagers. The dancer didn't seem mindful of the rivulets of sweat flowing down her front and back. Mamaji was lying on a thin mattress, leaning on his left elbow, his back propped by a pillow. In his right hand, he held a glass of Ambassador whiskey, which he would repeatedly refill. Whenever the dancer came close, he would set the glass down and grasp at her bangle-laden arm. If she lingered within reach or sat down in front of him, he would put a hand on her waist or push money down her blouse. Every time that she bowed and salaamed, he smiled at her and touched his mustache like a villain in a Hindi film.

During one performance, Mamaji allowed the woman to put in his mouth a paan that she had herself folded in front of him, placing a clove and a cardamom on the betel leaf with a show of delicacy. When she sat that close, she looked different. I saw the paint on her face and how sweat streaked the makeup on her cheeks. She had a hairy mole above her upper lip.

When the dance was over, a heavyset young man who had sat close to us through the whole evening helped carry Lotan Mamaji to the high school hall. The room was still bare even an hour after midnight except for an old man coughing in his sleep in the corner. Mamaji opened his eyes when I had settled his head on a pillow. He looked at the young man who was still standing next to me and then asked me if everything was okay. Then he drew out his .38 and pushed its barrel into my palm.

—To be or not to be, he said, quite meaninglessly. He said the words in English, a language that wasn't very familiar to him. His voice was lucid and unnaturally soft. A memory roused him momentarily and he laughed, the paan juice bubbling out of his mouth. He had just remembered something from my childhood. He said that when I was four or five, I had told him that I was going to drink more milk. Why? My young self had explained to him that my pee was yellow and I wanted it to be a normal color again.

My father's contempt for Lotan Mamaji, his brother-in-law, if described by means of a pie chart, would show 30 percent colored black for the lack of education beyond middle school. On that chart, another 30 percent would be shaded differently for addiction to alcohol, while the last 30 percent would be marked for adultery and lust. The 10 percent of the circle that remained would be a dappled slice attributable to other, unexplained sins. When I was growing up, the conversation between my parents made it clear that there were many flaws in Lotan Mamaji's character, but I was not very conscious of them. As a boy, I had watched him at sunset feeding the fish in his pond. He stood at the water's edge. His right fist moving in the air as if he were drawing in a kite that was the only one left flying gloriously in the sky, he threw puffed rice on the water, whose surface was broken by the dark mouths of many fish. When Lotan Mamaji cast his line and drew out a rohu whose scales glinted silver and black, I was moved by his love for me.

I was telling Cai all this, everything I could remember, all my devotion and my disappointment. If I wanted I could perhaps have used terms we bandied about in our seminars: about the unfulfilled lives or futile deaths of people—because of their class or upbringing—caught between an older feudal order and an emergent capitalist society. There was some pathos but it was better to be clear-eyed about the harsh judgment of history. As grad students we showed ourselves eager to understand contemporary life, but in reality, we were proclaiming our place in the future. I felt this most strongly when our friend Pushkin spoke of how the lives of the many anonymous others had been exceeded by the demands of hectic modernity. They were history's victims, the poor fucks, while we were not. I hated that brand of all-knowing academic talk. So, it is possible I mourned Lotan Mamaji's death, and my own childhood, in my conversation with Cai that night like a scene from a movie about a small town. There is a crumbling mansion in the background at the edge of a field. A large man with a mustache is sitting under a tamarind tree smoking a hookah. That morning the man sold to an antiques dealer a portrait with an elaborate frame that had hung on his wall; the portrait was of his father, who had been a minor landowning functionary under the British, and the man got a price that he knew was low but he wasn't prepared to bargain. Money is scarce, it is needed for food or maybe even medicines, and yet there are also other uses. After he has had a drink, or maybe several, the man is going to lift his body, which feels more and more tired these days, and take a rickshaw to the bar near the movie hall.

———

By the time the spring semester arrived, our course work was almost done; each of us would now have to write a thesis. While Ehsaan gave Cai books on insurgency in India, he also had a gift for me. Midway through the semester he called me into his office and said that he was going to recommend me for a Ford Foundation Fellowship for summer research. The fellowship earned me a ticket to Delhi. Ehsaan wanted me to push further with my reading of Agnes Smedley and the Indian radicals in America. Late one night in early June, in 1993, I landed in Delhi and the next morning took a train to Patna. I stayed with my parents for three days before returning to Delhi for my research. A taxi from Paharganj station brought me to Sutlej Hostel in JNU, where I had made a paying guest arrangement with a sociology student from Bihar. In the National Archives one morning, I found what I could start with. I had come across the letters of the Indian nationalist leader Har Dayal—whom

Smedley had met in Berkeley. Har Dayal was the founder of the Hindustan Ghadar Party. The organization's newspaper was published from San Francisco, but the letters in the file I found in the archives had been written from Algiers in 1910. These letters were addressed mostly to an older mentor, Mr. Rana, and his wife, whom Har Dayal called Madame Rana. In one letter, he had written to Madame Rana: *I shall write more later on. It has been raining all day today. I shall begin to learn your German in two or three months. Next year, I shall write to you in German. Then perhaps you will reply sooner!* Who was this woman, perhaps older, but also foreign, to whom this young revolutionary was pouring out his heart?

That morning, from outside the Reading Room, I could hear voices shouting in Hindi. Perhaps a wall was being painted. The librarian, a short woman with full, surprisingly pink lips, had been on the phone all morning. She would listen to the person at the other end, she would talk desultorily about work, and every few minutes begin to giggle, straighten her sari, and say lightheartedly, *Nahin, nahin.* I read the letters in the library and copied them in my notebook. The librarian went out for lunch to the canteen. I was alone in the Reading Room, sitting at my usual place. A painted sign to my right said PLEASE MAINTAIN SILENCE and, on the left, outside the door, on an iron frame, hung two red buckets with the word FIRE stenciled on them in white. I would pass those buckets each day of the fortnight I spent in Delhi: there was sand in them, presumably to be used to douse a fire, but there were also cigarette butts, crumpled paper, torn bus tickets, and clumps of dried paan juice.

I read more of the letters that Har Dayal had written. He was only twenty-six and already a prominent leader. But behind his discussion of politics, there stretched a vast solitude. *(I am doing well, though I feel awfully lonely. Several days pass without my speaking to anyone.)* There was a great deal of self-pity also. And moral sentiment, including advice on celibacy. It appeared that Madame Rana had a son called Ranji. Har Dayal wrote in a letter to her: *Never let him waste time on arranging his hair beautifully with care. Spartan simplicity should be enforced in youth, so that the character should be manly and not* [the last word was illegible]. *Further, when he is a little older, don't take him into society where he should meet girls—parties etc. For between the ages of seventeen and twenty-two, much intercourse with girls should be avoided. It makes a man frivolous and produces the feeling of love precociously, and distracts his attention from studies and moral ideas.*

Har Dayal had been involved in what he called in one of his letters the "bomb affair." His studies at Oxford had been interrupted. But the rupture in his life was broader: *The suppression of the natural filial, fraternal, conjugal, and paternal feelings, the total estrangement from all early friends, whom I loved as the light of my life* ... And the struggle was not only political. His disturbance was clearly more profound. Consider document number 2388 (11), serial number 11. From the Hotel de la Californie, Algiers, on June 13, 1910. A Monday. Har Dayal had written a fourteen-page letter to Mr. Rana. It passed from the seemingly personal—*I often find relief in crying*—to the plainly political—*I read in the papers that thirty-three confessions have been made in Nasik Trial! That is terrible.* Then, apparently only an hour later, he sat down to write another letter to the same address. He declared in this letter that he would take a vow not to ever again do two things: *1. Moneymaking. 2. Sexual intercourse, even with my wife.* And then this despairing admission: *I have stooped to meat eating, wine drinking, frivolity, sightseeing, gossip, reading tales and novels, and indolence in order to soothe my heart pain and relieve my nerves and get good sleep and appetite.*

I wanted to stop reading when, over and over again, I came across such lines. The tone of self-pity was wearying, yes, but what also depressed me was that the litany of regrets reminded me of my journals.

What was this freedom that they were fighting for?

===

When I returned to New York at the end of the summer, Cai was getting ready to leave for India. Her stay was going to be longer, perhaps up to a year. I was going to miss Cai; I already missed her when I was in India. I remembered what Nina had said about finding someone and loving her. I was in love with Cai, I think. But love wasn't something I equated with a person's life goals. At that time a part of me considered such a preoccupation selfish or immature or plainly reactionary.

On a rainy evening Cai and I were walking through the park to Ehsaan's apartment on Riverside Drive when she stopped to pick up a large magnolia blossom that had fallen from the tree. The white petals were heavy with water, but Cai just took the whole flower and pressed it against her cheek. The expression on her face was one of surpassing sadness. Had she shed a tear? Or was it just the rain? I didn't ask. Cai was very open and loving, but I always felt that there was an inner knot of sadness that never loosened in her heart, and this melancholy made her real to me. I wanted to surrender all my sympathy to someone. To her. Embrace of sadness was okay, I said to myself. It wasn't reactionary.

Ehsaan welcomed us, kissing Cai on both cheeks. She worshipped him, and so did I, but I could see how much she was learning from him. I was failing as a scholar. My research was always too scattered. Perhaps because I wanted to be a writer, my academic questions kept getting entangled in some personal inquiry I wanted to conduct into the complexities of the human soul. Cai had a clearer agenda and a much stronger focus. When Mahasweta Devi came from India for a week's visit to a seminar where her writings were being taught in translation, Cai met with her to discuss her thesis. With Ehsaan's help, Cai was reading thick tomes on peasant insurgency in India; she read books on history, literature, and even sociology and religion. Also memoir and journalism, all the books arranged in neat piles on her dining table. Of all the books I had seen in her hands, I had read only one, a memoir by a young British woman who had been jailed in Hazaribagh after her arrest in the company of Maoists. That evening at Ehsaan's house, Cai was seated next to Ehsaan on the couch and was asking him questions about the writings of an Oxford political scientist on militancy in eastern India.

Unwilling to join the conversation, I fussed with the bottles of wine and salted peanuts. But Ehsaan wouldn't let me do that for long; he asked me to sit and listen while he told Cai a story.

—As a young man in Lahore, I must have been eighteen or nineteen, I considered myself a communist.

One evening I and my other communist friends were sitting in a room in our hostel drinking tea. We lived in different rooms but we shared what was called a ward servant. This would be a male of any age, between maybe seventeen and seventy, who would be responsible for anything from cooking to washing clothes to buying newspapers. Yes, even though we were communists we had a ward servant. He was a man around forty years in age. His name was Qamroo.

Now, this particular evening, Qamroo had made us tea and egg omelets with green chilies in them. We were all feeling very grateful and kind toward Qamroo. Then I said to my friends, This is all fine and good. But we are after all communists. We have to show Qamroo more respect.

One of my comrades said that we ought to call our servant Uncle. We should call him Qamroo Chacha. But this didn't seem radical at all. So, I suggested that we would now share Qamroo's chores. Whenever we could, we would step into the tiny kitchen with its black walls and ask if we could be of assistance to Qamroo.

Now, I could immediately see that the response to this proposal was less than enthusiastic. My friends said that they were required to attend classes, they needed to go to political meetings, organize rallies. One of them, the son of a feudal landowner in Punjab who had pledged to fight for an egalitarian society, said that he didn't even have time to post a letter sometimes and had to ask Qamroo to do it for him. Another one pointed out that labor was not degrading; we only needed to make sure that Qamroo felt he got fair wages.

But how to find this out? That was the question. Well, we must ask Qamroo himself. We called for Qamroo. The loudest of us shouted for Qamroo Chacha, and the man appeared with a grin on his face. He hadn't heard this name before. But there was an air of solemnity in the room. He was told that he was no longer our servant. He was our comrade. We would all treat each other equally.

Qamroo was not grinning anymore. In fact, he looked a bit puzzled. He was not saying anything. So the boys explained that they were going to help him with his work whenever they could. Next I asked him if he thought his wages were fair. Qamroo looked a bit afraid, maybe because he thought that with this offer of help we were going to cut his wages.

I understood this. I said to him that the reason why we were asking such questions was because we wanted to show him respect. In fact, I said, I don't know why you are standing. Please sit down on that chair.

More than one chair was suddenly offered to Qamroo, who had never before sat down in our company. We were all well-to-do people. He was our ward servant. During Eid, we would embrace him and say *Eid Mubarak* and give him money, but how many times in a year do you have Eid?

He cooked for us every day; he washed our shirts, our trousers, and our dirty underwear. He swept the three rooms where we slept. We didn't even know the names of his two children, who lived with their mother in the village. But we were now calling him Chacha and asking him about his needs. He had gastric ailments and his teeth chattered at night.

We were stronger than he was. We held his arms and asked him to sit in the wooden chair we had put in the center of the room. Please sit, we said, please sit with us. Against his resistance, we pulled him down and released his arms only after he had seated himself. But once we loosened our grip on him, he found himself propelled out of the chair. He just couldn't sit there and since we wouldn't let him stand in the room he left at once despite our cries.

Ehsaan paused. He kept looking at Cai.

—Do you understand what I'm trying to do here? I want you to remember this story and when you go and talk to the Maoist leaders who have spent their lives in villages, relate to them my story and ask them, *Why didn't Qamroo sit on his chair?* Let them hear my story and answer you. You will then have your book.

I remember that evening very clearly. I remember Ehsaan's story and what I also remember, as if it were a scene in a film, is the way in which Cai and Ehsaan sat together discussing historical change. Many years would pass before I was able to give meaning to that scene. Ehsaan and Cai were able to see the future, while I was either blind or simply too perverse to draw a straight line between my love for Cai and the society they were describing. Cai took Ehsaan's advice and wrote the book that he wanted her to write. About ten years ago I found her on YouTube discussing her new book. She was sitting onstage under a white-and-red tent at a literary festival in Delhi. The man interviewing her was a BBC journalist and Cai was telling him about living in a village in Chhattisgarh and she then invoked her teacher who would have been pleased to see this book.

In that same video, you can see Cai reading, interrupted only by laughter from the BBC man, a letter to Edward Said that Ehsaan wrote shortly before he died. Cai wanted the audience to appreciate Ehsaan's exaggerated and mordant style, the pleasure and flattery with which he offered his criticism on an op-ed by his comrade Said:

> Son of Palestine, Friend and Ally to the Wretched of
> the Earth, Keeper of the Flame in the World, the Text,
> and the Critic,
>
> I made a brave attempt to attend your talk yesterday but the press of bodies at the door was deeper and denser than even experienced in the tinbox buses on the crowded, sticky streets of Lahore or Accra. I saw the brief dazzle of your features and admired, from a distance, the elegant shine on your Savile Row suit. Then you began to speak! Such flowing oratory! Has anyone else ever been more eloquent on the narrow and constricted semantic field through which Islam is interpreted in the West? But I wanted to hear you and

discuss these things in person, and not from behind a wall of perspiring bodies! When will you provide this timid and undeserving soul the benefit of your attention? I published the attached in *Dawn* last week—it was already in production, alas, by the time your own words on the subject fell like rain on my parched soul at your public address last afternoon—and I hope you will read it. I have tried in my own weak way to say something meaningful about Islam not only by saying that the Western construction of Islam is a fiction, a purely ideological construct, but by insisting on presenting the concrete, not to mention divided, struggles under way in polities that happen to be Islamic.

As always, with a sense of devotion that is your due and tender regards, I remain,

Ehsaan of no consequence

Part VII

Peter and Maya

I am interested in wisdom. I am interested in walls. China famous for both.

—SUSAN SONTAG, "Project for a Trip to China"

I used to think marriage was a plate-glass window just begging for a brick.

—JEANETTE WINTERSON, *Written on the Body*

Cai and I stopped by Maya's apartment because she was coming with us to the Guggenheim Museum. We were going to see the exhibition of the works of the Chinese artist Liu Huong. In the *Times,* we had read that Huong's installations were "quietly devastating."

Maya had great affection for Cai and they got together often, but I felt that Maya didn't like me very much. Even though she was always polite, I feared she saw me as unsophisticated and a bit of a lout. How did she form this judgment? Once there were five or six of us at her place wondering if we would have class the next day — the professor had gone to Paris earlier that week. I volunteered to go down to the pay phone at the corner and call the professor at home — if she answered, I'd hang up. When I suggested this, Maya looked at me and said, Kailash, you're such a creep. This was said with some conviction, and it affected my behavior with Maya. I became nervous. The next time we saw each other, it was again at her apartment. She hugged and kissed Cai. Then I stepped into her doorway, but I didn't know whether I should kiss her or not. We hugged and I thought she was about to kiss me on my right cheek. Or was it the left? In my confusion, I ended up brushing her lips with mine. I didn't know then whether I would make it worse if I apologized and so I kept silent.

We took the 1 train down to Eighty-sixth Street and then the M86 bus to the other side of the park. On the bus, I let Cai and Maya sit together. I sat down next to a big sweaty man in a suit. He held a huge bouquet of flowers wrapped in tissue paper; water from the bouquet trickled toward the bus driver. After a short wait in the line at the Guggenheim, we produced our IDs for the student discount and then we were inside.

Liu Huong had been born in Beijing in 1950, and unlike Cai, he had lived through the Cultural Revolution. His parents were doctors who had been sent to the villages to work. Huong's portraits of his parents in Mao uniforms were austere and utterly devoid of emotion. There was no overt judgment, but the blankness of their expression was haunting. The artist had also painted huge portraits of party officials, and here the intent was less disguised: you saw the men, and one woman (probably Mao's wife), as scheming and complacent. They were painted, perhaps a bit ostentatiously, with complexions that made them resemble pigs.

After the portraits, we entered the next room, which was dominated by two giant paintings that looked like posters. The caption for the first poster read HAVE FEWER CHILDREN, RAISE MORE PIGS and showed a man and a woman with a small child. On the opposite wall was the other poster, with the caption LONG LIVE OUR BRIGADE LEADER. This latter picture, as gigantic as the first one, showed a group of villagers sitting together in a room watching a woman on TV, who was addressing them. Once again, the figures were so emptied of genuine feeling they appeared as automatons, creatures driven by a controlling ideology.

This was absorbing but not deeply affecting. I was just forming this thought when we entered the third room, and what I now saw made me change my mind. We were looking at an installation titled *Hunan School*. The whole of the long room had taken on the appearance of an abandoned, decrepit classroom. Benches were broken or overturned, pictures had slid out of frames, maps appeared bleached, and Mao's posters were stained with rainwater. Dust and a visible air of decline touched everything in sight. In dirty glass closets on the side there were on display old trophies, but they too appeared lost to history: the triumphs they celebrated had faded forever. Huong had painted the walls red up to waist level, but the red paint, just like the white paint above it, was peeling. In a few discarded boxes on the floor there were test tubes, funnels, and some disintegrating books. Every object was evocative and, at the same time, represented decay and death. At the far end were three showcases: desk-like structures with glass tops under which were displayed objects and brief accounts in Mandarin script. These were children's stories about ordinary items they had picked up or otherwise come across in their daily lives. There was a story about the painting of the benches. Another one about a fly a kid had caught. Cai translated a third account written in a child's hand: *With this rope Li Chen tied the dog Hei Bao to the fence near the school and he didn't untie him until the next morning. Hei Bao could have died and Li Chen was expelled from school for a week.*

We left the museum half an hour later; we were headed to Chinatown for a very late lunch. I was full of praise for *Hunan School*. The installation showed how the students were doomed. I loved it. But Cai wasn't so thrilled.

—How many visitors today were made to think of the students killed in Tiananmen?

Maya and Cai talked heatedly, each supporting the other, just as they used to do in Ehsaan's classes. I knew better than to challenge them, but I could see absolutely nothing wrong with what Huong had done. In fact, he had evoked an entire world for me. I stayed silent. We got to Mott Street, and when we were waiting for the food, I heard Cai and Maya talking about Peter. Their low tones suggested that I ought not to eavesdrop. I hadn't seen Peter for a long time. I tried to imagine how he would have responded to Huong's art. It would take me a long time, at least months, to reach a simple understanding of what Cai and I had experienced differently when looking at *Hunan School*. For me, the richness of the experience had been about conjuring the mundane details of a point in time. Art as an attempt to capture a mood, a feeling, which reflected what it meant to be alive in that place at that time. It wasn't the same for Cai. The politics of equality and radical change that she cherished had been sullied in China. That was the meaning of the massacre in Tiananmen Square. She had been in school then, and there was no mention in the news, but her uncle, her father's younger brother, had come back from college in Beijing with a gunshot wound in his arm. I didn't realize this at once, but what I came to see later was that Cai went to India to find among the peasants and the tribals in places like Chhattisgarh a purer idea of politics. It was her quest, different from, and yet similar to, the hippies going to India in the sixties. It was a tableau full of innocence and that is why the disappointment I later caused her was even more devastating.

=====

Late one night in Lehman Library, I watched an old Hindi film about China, *Dr. Kotnis Ki Amar Kahani*. The film had probably been made even before Independence. A young Indian doctor from Kolhapur decides that because of the assaults of the Japanese army the poor people in China need medical help. The film was set in the late 1930s. Five doctors from India went on this humanitarian mission, and the film was the story of the one who didn't come back. Young Dr. Kotnis falls in love with a Chinese peasant girl, played by an Indian woman who speaks in a high, singsong falsetto. Their marriage is seen as a bond between the two nations; the next day the Japanese bombing begins. Amidst widespread death and destruction, the doctor cures diseases and then succumbs to them. The drama of return, et cetera.

The thought came to me: I could perhaps go to China if I could find a connection with the work I had already done. I

went to talk to Ehsaan about it. Characteristically, he asked me if I had eaten. He was looking at me with his wide-apart eyes.

—How are you? I get the feeling you are a bit adrift.

I shrugged.

Ehsaan said that it was useless to ask me about the future, I first needed to sort out the issues that were facing me in the present.

—There's a famous ghazal of Javed Qureshi's that begins *Dil jalaane ki baat karte ho* . . . The relevant lines for you are *Hum ko apni khabar nahin yaaron / Tum zamaane ki baat karte ho*.

He recited the Urdu couplet and smiled.

I knew the song. Farida Khanum's rich voice came back to me, a golden length of rough silk: I have no news of myself, my friends / You are demanding a report on the world.

Ehsaan was wearing a pale blue kurta over a black turtleneck. While he cooked, we talked. He was stirring the pot in front of him, not saying too much. He had leftover zucchini in the fridge and was making a chicken curry for us to eat with rice.

I said something about the men whose letters I had read, their strange relationship to sex and to loneliness.

After a pause he addressed the chicken in the pot.

—And Agnes Smedley?

I sensed an opportunity.

—What was she looking for when she fell in with the Indians? Was it the same impulse that took her to China?

More silence from Ehsaan. He was still looking away from me when he spoke again.

—Talking of the same impulse . . . Cai will be going to India in a month. You are going to China. What am I to make of this?

—In the last couple of years, India and China are being talked about in the same breath. India is familiar to me. I want to go to China to look at India in a new way, to find—

I stopped, suddenly uncertain. But Ehsaan was nodding.

—It's not just the opium that went from India to China, he said. There was a flow of nationalist ideas. This flow, at different times, was in both directions. As you know, Cai is working on Maoism in India . . .

I came back to my apartment well fed and slightly drunk. I let the phone ring in Cai's apartment for a long time and debated whether I should leave a message. I began speaking into the machine, but then she picked up.

—Hi.

—How was your dinner?

—I want to have a drink with you. You want to come over?

—I can't. I'm putting these highlights in my hair. Can't you come here?

I was happy to walk over. Cai had silver foil wrapped in her short hair. There was a half-finished bottle of Chardonnay in her fridge that she took out, and I poured the wine in two glasses. She didn't touch hers. Instead, she took off her flip-flops and stepped into the bathtub. I put down the cover of the toilet seat and sat on it. Dark color flowed from Cai's hair when she bent her head and poured water over herself.

I took the mug from her hand. The water was warm. My fingers touched the back of Cai's neck. I lowered my face and kissed her wet neck.

—More water, more water, please. Kailash!

After she was done, Cai sat on her couch, a towel draped around her head. I took a seat on the easy chair. I told her that Ehsaan had encouraged me to look into Agnes Smedley's friendship with the writer Lu Xun. He had said that I could go to China for a semester. Cai was on her way to India, but the thought of me going to her country excited her.

—Will you go to Shanghai? You can visit Lu Xun Park.

—I don't know yet.

—You can take a train and visit my parents. It will take just half a day to reach there from Shanghai.

Her parents!

I had never met Nina's parents. She hadn't asked me to visit

Maine that summer. But here was Cai proposing that I visit her parents. What would she tell them about me? I kissed her and then hurried back to my apartment because both of us had to take care of our TA work for the next morning. I felt very tender toward Cai. A circle was closing. I was happy that I was going to China. I felt confident that I would do good work there.*

On the walk back, I thought about a day in autumn the previous year. It was the closest we had ever been, both of us settled into the routine of studying and, yes, loving each other. The day was gorgeously sunny and warmer than the rest of the week had been. Some of the students chose to wear shorts and T-shirts at least while the sun was out. Cai said that we should get ice cream. We walked past a bookstore that had taken advantage of the weather to roll out bookshelves with used books piled on them. A pink-covered book caught my eye because of the name on it. Ismat Chughtai. *The Quilt and Other Stories*. The book had been published by a feminist press in Britain. Two dollars for a used copy. During the afternoon I had planned to grade papers,

---

* If you were settled in love, you could get your work done. This piece of writing advice had come from Ernest Hemingway.

INTERVIEWER: Is emotional stability necessary to write well? You told me once that you could only write well when you were in love. Could you expound on that a bit more?

HEMINGWAY: What a question. But full marks for trying. You can write any time people will leave you alone and not interrupt you. Or rather you can if you will be ruthless enough about it. But the best writing is certainly when you are in love. If it is all the same to you I would rather not expound on it.

but I set that aside and turned first to the short story that had inspired the film *Garam Hawa*. One after another, I read more stories in the book. Ten years earlier, I had read some of those stories in Patna, and now for the first time I was reading them in English. I tried to remember, but the original words would not come back. I had bought the book because it seemed it had been waiting for me there among other books that spoke another language. We shared something, this book and I, we belonged with each other. But where had this obstacle come from? I passed my hand through the pages. *The reflection from the red twill lit up her bluish-yellow face like sunrise.* What would those words have been in the original Urdu? What had Chughtai got in mind when she described the face as "bluish-yellow"? Was that what she had even written? At least I remembered the original title of the story. I remembered also the summer afternoon in Delhi when I had gone to watch the film for the first time, and how the sorrow had struck home. But here I felt stranded in language. I had become a translated man, no longer able to connect with my own past. What else had I forgotten? The sorrow of the world, but sorrow also for myself, gripped my throat. Without warning, I began to cry.

Till then, Cai and I had been reading in bed. We were lying at an angle to each other, our heads together but our legs pointing in different directions, so that our bodies formed a V. The first sob that was wrenched out of me provided such release that, with a small yelp, I turned and touched Cai. She turned to me with alarm.

—What happened?

But I was like a child, hiding my tears by pressing into her cotton shirt. It was an expensive shirt: she had worn it because in her mind it was summer that day. She realized after a minute that I was actually crying.

—Oh, Kailash, she said, and cradled my head in her arm.

I let the tears come; the sorrow I had felt was abating, and in its place a feeling of exhilaration was taking wing. After a few minutes, I felt empty, and free.

Cai was looking at me, with a slightly worried expression, and I explained to her that I had been moved by what I was reading. It reminded me of what one poet had called *the gentle poverty of my homeland.*

I wiped my nose.

Without looking at her, I unbuttoned her shirt, which was already wet with my tears. She began to laugh, a short, amused laugh. Wordlessly, I took her breast in my mouth and began to suck as I would a mango when I was a boy. I had been reading about an unmarried girl in Chughtai's story; youth was passing her by, she would never know a man's touch. But here was Cai, already panting from the effort of assisting me as I stripped her clothes. I felt my soul had been cleansed by sorrow: I was able to savor what I possessed. She slipped her body under mine, and delicately drew my cock inside her. We were good when we were together. Everything fitted around a memory of what we had always done. She didn't have the passivity of the sad and helpless girl I had been reading about in the story. When I started pushing into her, she unwrapped her legs and held them up in the air. Cai was one of the quietest people I knew, in public and in private, but she always made noise when we fucked. Her moans came suddenly and resembled the rhythmic fugue-like grunting of geese as they flew overhead when you were lying in the grass beside a river.

Cai flew to Bombay. She published a brief piece in *The Village Voice,* and Ehsaan pasted the cutting on his door. The story was about the mauling of a child in a town called Akola in central India. A dog had attacked a two-year-old boy and gouged his eyes. The child's parents were daily-wage laborers. They had been working nearby, mixing clay at a brick kiln, rags tied around their heads. Cai had expertly linked the savagery of the attack, which read like a parable, to the relentless depredations of a system that had ruined farmers. The child's parents had lost their meager farm and become migrant workers. The much-vaunted liberalization of the Indian market hadn't brought wealth to the poor; on the contrary, it had made them more vulnerable and left them helpless and alone.

Her next piece was a long interview with a young widow whose husband, a cotton farmer, had killed himself by drinking the pesticide that was to be used on his land. The farmer was in debt to a village moneylender who charged 5 percent monthly interest. The dead man also owed money to a bank. The expensive seeds he had bought had all gone to waste because the rains

had failed. The widow had told Cai that the liter bottle of pesticide her husband had ingested had also been bought by taking a loan of three hundred rupees from a neighbor. The huge subsidies given by the United States to its farmers lowered the price of cotton worldwide while the new laws in India meant that the small farmers there had to contend with reduced earnings and higher rates of interest. I saw Cai's article and the photograph of the widow, which had been taken by someone called Sebastian D'Souza. The photograph showed the widow holding a portrait of her husband: he was sitting on a chair in the studio, dressed formally in trousers and a shirt. On his feet he wore a pair of oversize slippers. The image, with its quiet pathos, held my attention. I would look at the plastic flowers placed by the photographer to the farmer's right, and then my eyes would be drawn to the young widow's sad and beautiful face.

Cai sent me a postcard and then nothing for a while. The postcard showed Salman Khan flexing his biceps. Cai had written that she had been busy and was looking for change; she was going to move to Bhopal and work with an NGO. But that probably didn't happen because three months later, when we were still dealing with snow on our streets, Cai published a long report. This one was about her travel in the nearby forests of Chhattisgarh with the Naxals who were fighting for land rights. This report, nearly five thousand words long, was published in *Mother Jones*. It was less an analysis of a skewed economic system, though it was that too, than a record of terrible violence against the protesting tribals. Police executions at the edge of the forest or sometimes even in homes; torture and killings in police stations; army combing operations that included rape and the burning of huts. The report described appalling acts, but the emotion that I felt most strongly was perhaps envy. Cai was living in India and reporting on the changes that had come since I left. I lay sleepless in bed thinking about the thesis I first needed to write. I would have to do this soon. One night I woke up from a dream in which I had walked into the ocean with a book that I had been reading. Cai was standing on the beach. She was saying that we should be leaving now. But before I could get out, a wave washed over me and it swept the book away into the deep waters.

I had sent a brief missive to a journalist I knew, one of the most beautiful women I had ever laid eyes upon. She lived in Park Slope. *You wrote last week that you would write a longer note "in a minute." You didn't. I haven't moved since then. I haven't eaten, or slept, or made love.* Such longing.* Until that note got sent to Cai by mistake, accidentally mailed to India along with the detailed letter I had written for her about my work, a mistake that resulted in the abrupt end of our relationship, I received her reports from Delhi or towns in Bihar or Madhya Pradesh, where she was doing research.† She was studying Hindi while living for six months in a town called Amarkantak. It delighted her that she had learned all the names of the local trees. The town's inhabitants were fond of her—a Chinese girl in Indian clothes. A nun had been raped in a village an hour away but the person

---

* *If you ask me what I want, I'll tell you. I want everything.* —Kathy Acker, *Pussy, King of the Pirates*

† After we became lovers, one of the things we did was share a notebook where we wrote down the new words we had come across. Both of us were immigrants and wanted to know the names for all kinds of objects and emotions. Cai's first entry was *dormer: a window that projects vertically from a sloping roof.* Her second entry was *bunion: a painful swelling on the first joint of the big toe.* I remember my first entry in that notebook. *Pyriform breast: pear-shaped breast.* Years after I had made the stupid mistake of sending Cai the wrong letter, I found a word from Congo in an article in *Time* magazine that I think would have helped me with my appeal: *ilunga: a person who will forgive anything the first time, tolerate it the second time, but never a third time.*

who gave her this news said that Cai was safe because she wasn't a Catholic. In her letter to me, Cai wrote that she was going to interview the nun. I reached the end of her note, and when I turned the page I saw my own handwriting. For a moment, I was confused. Without a word of commentary or a question, Cai had returned to me the letter I had stupidly sent her. *You wrote last week that you would write a longer note "in a minute." You didn't* . . . I didn't write to Cai to apologize. What was the point of saying sorry? Oh, I was contrite, of course, but I knew I had done irreparable damage. I didn't receive another letter from her.

I thought of Cai constantly and read her earlier letters over and over again. During her first weeks in Delhi she had watched a play called *Netua*. A netua is a man who puts on women's clothes and dances during weddings and festivals in the villages of Bihar. The play was about a netua called Jhamna, who gets married and brings his bride back to his village. During Holi celebrations, the drunken, upper-caste youth in his village watch him dance and then they come for his bride. Jhamna lets go of his inhibition and hits out at the oppressors, but when they flee he falls upon his wife. The writer had skillfully transferred all the violence of the ruling class onto poor Jhamna and his rage. Cai said that, inspired by what she had seen our friend Pushkin do long ago in his translation work, she was going to collaborate on the translation of the Hindi short story on which the Jhamna play had been based. The writer was Ratan Verma from Muzaffarpur, and she was going to meet him in a fortnight.

This information had startled me. Muzaffarpur was where my father had gone to college when he left his village and I still had distant cousins living there. One of them owned two buses and another ran a timber business. I used to visit them when I was in Patna. If my cousins saw Cai Yan, a Chinese woman in a salwar-kameez, in a crowded street near their home, would they ever guess that she was my lover? No one there could imagine how hard she had worked to journey to a place where her present met my past. I also had other worries about Cai wandering around alone in a town like that. When I was a boy, maybe seven or eight years old, I was on a visit to Deoghar, walking on a street near a hill with my sister. Our parents had gone to the temple for which the town is famous. The guesthouse where we had found a room was a little distance away from the center of the town. It was a pleasant evening, small green trees, red earth, a winding road leading to the rocky hill maybe half a mile away. A motorcycle passed us, and then after it had gone a few hundred yards down the road it turned around and approached us. There were three young men sitting on it. They parked the bike and came to us. One of them asked my sister if she needed a ride. She didn't answer them. The fellow who had asked the question took out a small plastic comb from his pocket and started passing it through his hair. The youth ignored their bike and fell in step with us. My sister jerked my hand to make me walk faster. One of the young men, a fellow in a tight blue shirt, stepped close to my sister and just pulled her dupatta off. Neither my sister nor I said anything. We kept walking, but I was conscious that my sister was breathing hard. Then I realized that she was crying. We walked like this for about ten or fifteen minutes, I'm not sure.

The boys trailed us. They sang songs and passed lewd comments, never letting us hope that they'd fallen far behind. Had one gone back to fetch the bike? I didn't look back. My sister didn't let go of my hand. Beyond a tree on our left, a path appeared leading down to a small cottage. I could now see an old couple sitting on cane chairs. My sister turned on the path. She went to the old man, who was easily seventy or eighty, and wearing a dhoti and a vest.

—Those boys are following me, she said.

That was the word, *follow*. A simple word whose meaning for a long time held a specific threat in my mind. The old man and his wife both looked toward the road. The woman remained silent, but after a while the man told us that we were welcome to go inside. The young men disappeared in the direction they had been originally going. While we were in the old couple's home, my sister had an asthma attack, the first of her life, and this added to her helplessness. Later in college, asthma would cripple her, and she was prone to anxiety attacks for many years, but that evening in Deoghar the old couple were calm and helpful, as if they were quite used to young women rushing into their garden and collapsing breathless on the ground. They suggested that my sister lie down on their bed and then gave her honey and ginger tea. My sister became calm, her breathing returning to normal, in about half an hour. It was still light out when we left their house. The old man accompanied us to the road. He carried a large flashlight in his hand.

Now when I thought of Cai at the bus station in Muzaffarpur or standing in the marketplace in Barauni, she took my sister's place in my mind and for a moment I was a boy again filled with fear. The problem, of course, was that I was older now and therefore closer in age to the young man I still remembered from the road in Deoghar, the one in the blue shirt who had snatched away my sister's dupatta.

=====

The only time that Cai called me from India was to tell me that Peter had died. I had just woken up and was confused by the news. Cai was telling me that I should go and look after Maya till Peter's parents got there from Hamburg. The phone connection was poor. I asked Cai where in India she was at that moment, but she didn't hear me. I went to the building where Peter and Maya had been living for the past six months; their apartment was larger because they had been given married students' housing. As I hurried along to the apartment, rushing past people who were headed for classes or for work, I wondered how Cai had heard the news of Peter's death. The answer presented itself when I arrived at the apartment. Ehsaan was sitting on Maya's couch with her. At my entrance, Maya got up and said that perhaps I could make tea for Ehsaan and myself. She said she was going to lie down for a bit. Ehsaan said to her, Yes, you go but know that we are here if you need us.

I stayed silent as I made strong tea, with ginger, cardamom, and cloves also thrown in. After the milk came to a boil, I let the mixture simmer. Ehsaan stepped into the tiny kitchen.

—This smells good. You know, make a bit extra. Let's try to get Maya to drink some tea.

He spoke in a very low voice, as if Maya were really trying to sleep in the bedroom. Naturally, I too fell into a whisper.

—Where is he?

—The police have the body.

—How?

—Hanged himself.

—In here?

—No. In the basement.

Ehsaan went out of the kitchen, perhaps to check if Maya's door was still shut. When he came back he told me that another resident had found Peter in the basement early in the morning and called 911. There was no medical intervention because a fire department squad arrived almost as quickly as the police and declared him dead. The belt that Peter had used was looped from one of the metal pipes that crisscrossed the basement ceiling. He had wrapped duct tape around his wrists so that his hands were tied together. He must have done this last before kicking away the stool. Ehsaan arrived at four in the morning after Maya phoned him. The police were in the apartment. They found a suicide note in Peter's pocket but Maya had put it away. When the police left with the body for the autopsy, Ehsaan urged Maya to call Peter's parents. She also called her own parents in Delhi and asked them to tell Cai.

The tea was ready. Ehsaan walked back to Maya's room and spoke her name. He said that she should perhaps have a cup of tea. Surprisingly, she stepped out.

We drank the tea without talking. Maya's eyes, or maybe more the area around them, had become dark. She seemed miles away from us, sunk into a silence that also had a madness in it.

Ehsaan said softly, The boy was in a lot of pain.

Maya pressed her lips together.

In a burst she was soon telling Ehsaan that just the following week the doctors were going to start ECT, electroconvulsive therapy. Peter ought to have waited. He would have been put under anesthesia and the doctors would have passed small electric currents through his brain. The delay had been because Peter had withheld consent; perhaps irrationally, he feared memory loss. But it was the only hope. Neither the Nardil nor the Restoril was working, Maya said, as if we knew what those names meant.

—You can't blame him, Ehsaan said gently. He was sick. He was in a terrible place.

Maya allowed herself a single sob that was like a spasm.

—The drugs confused him. I suspect he was flushing them down the toilet or something, and pretending to me that he was taking them.

I remembered Maya sharing this fear with Cai. I didn't say anything.

—I don't know what—

Ehsaan said, You can't blame yourself. We should keep our best thoughts of Peter in our hearts and pray for him.

Tears sprang into my eyes. I sat down next to Maya and touched her shoulder for a few moments before taking the empty cup from her. I think she thanked me for the tea.

When Maya went back to her room, I learned from Ehsaan that Peter's parents would arrive by evening. I asked him if he had seen Peter's corpse and he said that when he arrived they had him on a stretcher downstairs with a sheet covering his body.

—I removed the sheet from his face and then spread my hands and recited the Fatiha.

I had never known Ehsaan to be religious. Did I look surprised?

He said, Let me tell you a story about prayer.

He began telling me about the time he was in Beirut. He had gone to the Hizbullah headquarters in south Beirut with a French journalist who later became the ambassador there. Ehsaan interviewed the Hizbullah leader Sheikh Nasrallah. The piece he wrote was published under the title "Encounter with an Islamist." There was so much irony in that title because the man he had met was unexpectedly practical and not terribly weighed down by ideology. There were very few armed men in sight at the headquarters, and to Ehsaan, this suggested intelligence and efficient security arrangements. The women were moving around freely, dressed modestly, of course, but not wearing the hijab. And then there was the sheikh, quite free of doctrinal armor, a man unwilling to defend the eternal or universal nature of the Shariat.

But the main reason Ehsaan had wanted to meet Sheikh Nasrallah was that he was interested in him as a person. He had wanted to interview him ever since he had watched news foot-

age of him on television. This is what he had seen: seven coffins had been placed in a village school in south Lebanon, close to the border with Israel. A convoy of cars drove up before the burial. Sheikh Nasrallah came out of one of the cars and proceeded inside accompanied by his son Jawad. The bodies in the coffins were of Hizbullah fighters returned by Israel in exchange for the remains of an Israeli soldier. Nasrallah stopped in front of each coffin and offered the Fatiha. When he reached the coffin marked 13, he stopped and whispered in the ear of an aide.

The aide summoned two workers of the Islamic Health Association, which is a Hizbullah outfit. They opened the coffin, exposing a body wrapped in a white shroud. Sheikh Nasrallah's eyes closed, and his lips trembled as he recited the Fatiha. The body was that of Sheikh Nasrallah's firstborn, his son Hadi, killed in battle with the Israelis. Slowly, Sheikh Nasrallah bent down and stroked the head of his dead son. Jawad, the dead boy's younger sibling, remained quiet and pale behind his father. Sheikh Nasrallah stood with his hand resting on the chest of the body in the coffin. A deep silence had fallen in the room.

—Ehsaan said to me, I was unsure whether death had granted these people a grandeur that was denied them all their lives. But I felt that through his prayer Sheikh Nasrallah was giving their suffering and his own suffering some dignity. You understand?

══

The playbill said Pushkin Krishnagrahi's *Satish Sadachar in His Heavenly Abode*. Pushkin's play was about a man on his deathbed telling the story of his family. In the darkened theater I immediately thought of Peter, but Pushkin's character was an old Indian man. The bed was empty, the lights shining bright on a white sheet, while the man's disembodied voice filled the auditorium. Then the action started with all the other characters, his family members, in different corners of the stage. Sadachar, the play's main character, was dead and we only heard his voice. Whatever was new wasn't really better, but there was no reason to remain nostalgic about the old. This was the play's uncompromising message, its alert skepticism. I was sitting with Ehsaan's old student Prakash Mathan and a girl from NYU whom he had started dating. Ehsaan was there by himself, but he readily agreed to come to a bar with us. After we had got our drinks, he asked me quietly whether I had heard recently from Cai. I told him of our breakup.

—Your decision or hers?

—Hers, I said. I didn't have the courage to tell him what lay behind the split.

—Is this what you want?

—I don't know. My head says I should write to her. My heart knows she won't have me back.

He gave me a half smile.

—Thomas Jefferson wrote a letter to a woman in the form of a dialogue between his head and heart. Do you know it?

I shook my head.

The love letter was addressed to a married woman named Maria Cosway, an artist. He wrote the letter after meeting her in 1786. Jefferson was the U.S. ambassador to France at that time. He had been out on a stroll with Cosway and he leapt over a fountain. He fell and hurt his hand.

—The letter was written slowly with his left hand because he had broken his right wrist when he fell at the fountain.

Maybe I ought to write a letter to Cai with my left hand, I thought. But it was Jefferson's leap that I identified with. And the fall.

—The letter was several thousand words long, Ehsaan said.

This was the same man who had composed, ten years earlier, the Declaration of Independence. Which, incidentally, was much shorter than the letter.

Ehsaan wanted me to visit the library and read the letter.

Then he told me that Maria Cosway had remained with her husband till his death, and later moved to Italy to start a convent school.

Ehsaan looked at me. His eyes had a half-mischievous glint.

—Her husband was said to resemble a monkey. Jefferson became president around 1800.

Prakash and his girlfriend, Maeve, were drinking cocktails.

I turned my back to them and, summoning some feeling of urgency, told Ehsaan that I shouldn't wait any longer.

—I must go ahead and do the work I need to do in China.

Ehsaan could deliver a lucid lecture at any place and at any time.

—You must remember three points . . .

Deng Xiaoping was going to die soon but he was the model that the Indians were perhaps following. Deng had said that he wasn't interested in a socialism of shared poverty; he wanted capitalist growth. How were literature and art going to respond to these vast changes? Ehsaan said that I could go ahead and write a bit about Lu Xun, and Agnes Smedley, and maybe Saadat Hasan Manto on the subcontinent, considering the role of writers during a time of great upheaval, but I had to remain mindful of the present moment. This third point he felt was the most important.

He stopped and asked, So, what is your position? Where do you stand vis-à-vis the unfolding present?

My present position was that I was standing in a bar drinking a bottle of Sam Adams.

A good thing about Ehsaan was that he would often answer his own questions.

—You must travel from Beijing to Shanghai and then to places like Guangzhou and Shenzhen. The new zones wouldn't exist except for Deng. What is life like there? Take a look for yourself and let your perception frame how you write about the past in which Lu Xun lived. You know enough about India and Pakistan to write a commentary on Manto. Let's see how quickly you can do this so that you can then look for a job.

=====

For four months, at 10:15 in the morning on each weekday, I was to be found on the twelfth floor, in the class right next to the men's room, of the Beijing Language Institute. The institute was in the Haidian District. For an hour and a half, my official task was "to share and advance the bilingual/bicultural competence, extralinguistic/encyclopedic knowledge, and translation strategies/techniques" of about thirty students. The work was uninteresting because I learned nothing about the lives of the people I met. From time to time, a sentence would be read out to me in English and I would nod my head or try to reframe it. Simple sentences: You can't be too careful. Is that correct?

Or I would be asked questions that I didn't have any answers for: Why does English have such extensive use of passive voice? Don't you think English has more impersonal structures than other languages? *Impersonal structures! What were they?*

I always arrived on time and Professor Ning would welcome me with a smile. After that, I was ignored. I didn't know any Chinese and my real responsibilities were close to nil. Professor Ning would write sentences on the board in English and answer all questions in Mandarin. When the bell rang, I was expected to leave and I did. My presence was simply proof of a business relationship between two educational institutions; but it was of help to me because it got me a dorm room, where I slept peacefully, my white bedcover tinged red by the neon sign outside that said RESEARCH INSTITUTE OF PETROLEUM EXPLORATION AND DEVELOPMENT.

During weekends, I visited monuments and parks, but on weekdays, in the afternoons, after my lunch in the dorm, I would read about Lu Xun and also Manto. In the Lu Xun Museum, I saw pictures of Agnes Smedley. On the cover of the German edition of *Daughter of Earth* she had written: *Presented to Lu Hsün in admiration of his life and work for a new society*. She had signed the book on February 2, 1930. She would go on to spend much of the decade in China, often reporting from the warfront for newspapers like *The Manchester Guardian*. When she applied for membership in the Chinese Communist Party she was rejected for what was seen as her lack of discipline. One account said that her activities in China included racing horses, cross-dressing, and providing instruction to women—on birth control, Western dance, and romantic love.

In contrast to Smedley's activities in China, my life was dull; I was poor and often cold. I went to the library and read the stories in Edgar Snow's *Living China;* then I read Manto's *Kingdom's End and Other Stories*. Sitting in my room, an electric heater in the corner, I sipped pots of Da Hong Pao tea and began writing a comparative study of Manto's "Toba Tek Singh" and Lu Xun's "A Madman's Diary."* This solitude in an alien land, as well as the work I was doing, helped me; it made me think more deeply about what I wanted to say about literature. But it was not what I had wanted to do. My starting point had been different. A man like Har Dayal, who had embraced revolutionary ideals, writ-

---

* Pushkin provided me a letter of introduction to a Chinese writer in Beijing, Yu Hua, who had written extensively about Lu Xun. I took a translator with me for our meeting at a cultural center. Yu Hua turned out to be in his late thirties. He had a fine sense of irony, and a casual, relaxed manner that was not diminished but only enhanced by the fact that he continuously chain-smoked while we talked. Pointing to his watch, he sketched a circle and told the translator that Lu Xun's career had come full circle in China. At first, he was an author and his writings created controversy. Then he became a catchphrase during the Cultural Revolution, more of an empty slogan. When the Cultural Revolution ended, he was again an author and his name was caught up in controversies. But now, with the rise of rampant capitalism in China, Lu Xun was once again a slogan, a name to be included in ads. On a piece of paper, Yu Hua drew Chinese characters, a long list that my translator transcribed for me thus: *The characters and places in Lu Xun's stories have been put to work as names for snack foods and alcoholic beverages and tourist destinations; they serve to designate private rooms in nightclubs and karaoke joints, where officials and businessmen, their arms wrapped around young hostesses, sing and dance to their hearts' content.*

ing letters to women about desire and loneliness. That was an image in my mind. Or Smedley's marriage to Chatto, their long embrace and falling-out, the strain of being outsiders engaged in subversive activities. I wanted to write about love and, although I was blind to this at first, I wanted to be in love.

=

After I arrived in Beijing, everything reminded me of Cai. I tried to suppress my longing. I knew that she wasn't wasting time thinking about me; instead, she was filing away reports that would become part of her thesis. She was on her way.

I husbanded my energy. I seldom went out on weekdays. When I ventured out in the city, as I did sometimes in the evenings, to look for a drink called Pingo Sou, I carried a red English-Mandarin phrase book. Using that book in Beijing during those months reminded me of the time I was a fresh immigrant in the United States and everything was new. I drank my tea and was content to eat noodles and tofu, and sometimes, as a treat, shredded pork. Two blocks away was the Garden Restaurant, a shabby place with three tables covered with plastic tablecloths. It served my needs admirably. I ate at the same time every day. The owner expected me and brought my food soon after I sat down. His daughter, a cute toddler named Mei Ling, would come and sit near me. She would babble in Chinese and I understood not a word but I was filled with happiness. Back in my room, I read more stories by Lu Xun and Manto, and I

shaped chapters on subjects like truth and self-deception, sat-
ires against the powerful, the bodies of women and the body
of the nation. The conceit that I had smuggled into the thesis
was that it wasn't me but Agnes Smedley who was reading these
writers: her passions, her prejudices, even her biography, shaped
my reading of Lu Xun and Manto. The work was speculative,
even imaginative, but it was also systematic, and when my time
in Beijing came to an end, I had much of my thesis finished.

As Ehsaan had instructed, I made the trip to Shanghai and
went to Lu Xun's home, now preserved as a museum. I had the
phone number for Cai's parents but I didn't call. Only once,
late one night, when I was lost near a library I was visiting, and
unable to find anyone who spoke English, the thought came
to me that I should perhaps call Cai's parents. But then a cab
appeared in the drizzle and I showed the driver the card from
the hotel where I was staying.

I had a good two days there. At the museum, I took photographs of Lu Xun's statue and of the cover of his book of stories translated into Hindi. At another museum I found wooden
crates with PATNA OPIUM painted on them, and the mannequins of Sikh policemen in uniform on the streets. Dioramas of
Parsi businessmen and male Chinese customers with their hair
braided and hanging at the back. *Museums evoke a specific feeling
in me, Your Honor. This is the feeling of time being out of joint. And
why only time? Bodies out of joint. A displacement in time and place.
Not belonging. A few years ago, a white American writer described
another writer, one whose ancestors had migrated from India to the*

Caribbean, as looking less like a Nobel Prize candidate than a shopkeeper. *A malicious remark, but capturing a fear I have long held in my heart, about being a prisoner in the museum of someone else's imagination. The future Nobel laureate was likely to be mistaken for* a newsagent hurrying from the bank back to his shop, where he hawked cigarettes, chewing gum, and the daily newspapers, keeping the tit-and-bum magazines on the top shelf. *Was there any escape from this museum? I know people who will throw numbers at you to prove we belong here. So many doctors! So many engineers! But where's the museum to show the aching feet of the shopkeepers? Or, for that matter, the fate of the woman from India who was the first to acquire a doctor's degree in the United States? Your Honor, in a cemetery in upstate New York lie the ashes of a young Indian woman who was born only a few years after the 1857 rebellion in which my distant ancestor Kunwar Singh cut off his arm.* ANANDABAI JOSHEE, M.D., 1865–1887 FIRST BRAHMIN WOMAN TO LEAVE INDIA TO OBTAIN AN EDUCATION, *reads the inscription on the tombstone. Joshee was aged nine when she was married to a twenty-nine-year-old postal clerk in Maharashtra, and twenty-one when she received a doctor's degree in Pennsylvania. A few months later, following her return to India, she died of tuberculosis at the age of twenty-two. Her ashes were sent to the woman who had been her benefactor in the United States, and that is how Joshee's remains are now buried in a plot overlooking the Hudson. All the craters on Venus are named after women and I read in an Indian newspaper that one of the craters now bears Joshee's name.*

I was a tourist in Shanghai and did the things that tourists do. For instance, I ate spicy chanzui frog at a restaurant where they also had live crocodiles with thick rubber bands on their snouts. Before I left, amidst the lights of the evening, beside a river full of glittering cruise boats, I took a walk on the Bund.

From Shanghai, I went by train to Guangzhou. I saw the factories and then the new construction sites covered in a green mesh and the familiar grid work of bamboo scaffolding. That evening, at a bar on Xiao Bei Road, I met an Indian banker named Zutshi, who told me that no building in China can be more than seventy years old. When it turns that age, it is pulled down. I don't know why I was taking notes.

— India has great scope, Zutshi said. We are good in IT. And then he added, But we will never overtake China. The Chinese have the habit of work and they are obedient citizens.

On the train back to Beijing I put down my impressions of the journey. Ehsaan had suggested I use my travel in China to write the preface to my critical study of Lu Xun and Saadat Hasan Manto. Was industrial development going to solve our social problems? Would the powerful and the very rich become more charitable if they had made enough profit? What was a writer to do as a witness in a changing world? What was the writer who was a traveler, an outsider as well as a woman, to do as an activist? I took notes in a brown notebook that said TIAN GE BEN, and back in Beijing, while I waited two more days before my flight back to New York, I typed up my preface on the computer. My master's thesis was done. On the British Airways flight back, after having eaten and drunk the complimentary red wine, I felt relaxed and took out a fresh Tian Ge Ben notebook. I wanted very badly to go back to what I had ignored in my thesis. I wanted to write about love. Not just the story of one love, its beginning or its end, but the story of love and how it is haunted by loss. I thought of the time I had first gone to pick apples. On the sound system on the plane, I listened to Jimmy Cliff singing "You Can Get It If You Really Want." With my earphones on, I played the song over and over again.

Epilogue

The preceding picture is in my notebook for this novel. I must have torn it from a magazine, maybe *Outlook,* during a visit home. A reproduction of some of Satyajit Ray's sketches when he was making his first film, *Pather Panchali.* This is the storyboard for the scene in which Apu and his sister Durga catch sight of a train for the first time. It is a scene celebrated in the history of cinema. As in all of Ray's work, simple scenes, elegantly framed, producing a cumulative emotional effect that is shattering. Nothing in my notebook to indicate why I have cut this out from a magazine. It is possible I was thinking of collage. I suspect I was thinking more of ordinary life being transformed into art. Not just in the final film, but in these sketches too. These drawings are like calligraphy, awash with movement, as if a subtle suggestion was blowing through them like an invisible breeze.

It is June. This is what I've decided to do with my life just now. Here I am in middle age, taking a break from the demands of teaching and family life, writing about youth and love and politics. (Mixing the aesthetic and naked desire, this line stolen from the review of a photography book: *Nearly every composition rides that fine line between hand-to-hand combat and cunnilingus, as all art must*.) I have been looking at old letters and my journals. How important these pages, written long ago, because, after a while, everything fades, and even the body, maybe especially the body, doesn't remember anything.

═══

I became a U.S. citizen last year. The ceremony was held at noon on a Saturday in the high school in a town nearby. A table was set with twenty miniature American flags on it. And a stack of certificates. The ceremony got under way with three pudgy Boy Scouts bringing onto the stage a large U.S. flag. They held their fingers up in a salute, hands close to their temples as if they were in pain. We were informed that together we represented citizens of Somalia, Mexico, El Salvador, Jamaica, and India. The

Somalis were one large family, dressed in shiny clothes. The judge, a man of Filipino origin, asked us to repeat the oath. Like everyone else, I held my right hand up. Once that was done, the judge said, Congratulations, you are now citizens of the United States. You have forsaken the country of your birth in exchange for the rights and privileges of this country. He repeated the word *privilege,* saying, You are not *entitled* to be in the United States. Instead, it is a privilege. There is no better country in the world.

But I only felt like a man without a country and tears came to my eyes. I was crying perhaps only because the judge, in a poor, inaccurate choice of words, had used the word *forsaken.* The man next to me, a native of Guadalajara, thought these were tears of happiness and began to congratulate me.

The judge said that he was now going to ask a man "who embodied the American experience and was a hero" to speak to us for a few minutes. A large black man with bad knees climbed to the stage: he had played for the Denver Broncos in the 1999 Super Bowl. I don't remember his name. The speaker said, It's been a long journey for you, you have endured pain and tribulation . . . I wondered whether this was true of any one of us. The speaker wiped his brow with a handkerchief, and the cloth, maybe because it was new, stuck to his forehead. He said that he appreciated diversity and was glad to welcome us to this country. Then a young girl named Rachel with drooping eyelids and a melancholic smile walked to the microphone and sang the national anthem rather beautifully. I was surprised that the Mexican gentleman to my right seemed to know the words to the song. When the ceremony was over, people were taking pictures.

In the car, certificate in hand, I wished I had eaten lunch before coming. I hadn't driven farther than two miles on I-84 when I saw the flashing lights of a police cruiser behind me. The cop was an elderly man with a thin mustache. When he asked for my license and registration, I picked up the U.S. flag and the certificate and showed them to him.

—Officer, I've just become a citizen. Only ten minutes ago. I was rushing home to tell my wife.

—Did you also get your license today?

—No sir, I've been driving—no, I didn't get it today.

—Then I won't be needing these. Your license and registration, please.

The ticket he wrote was for $165. I thought he had behaved fairly and hadn't questioned the lie about my having a wife— but I was also suspicious that I had been punished for having become a citizen.

As I proceeded to my house, driving under the speed limit now, I thought of Jennifer with gratitude. She had taken me to the DMV in Harlem in her old blue Volvo. I had been living in the United States for maybe two or three months by then. I drove her car for the test. The man who was the examiner turned out to be a Pakistani. I was afraid he was going to fail me. As I followed his instructions (Please change lane, turn left, park on the right, et cetera) the thought came that I should get on friendly terms with him. I tried to make small talk.

—Where are you from in Pakistan, Mr. Alvi?

—Do not talk, he said, his eyes fixed on the road ahead. Please drive.

When the test was over, he said I had made one mistake but I had successfully passed the test. I said *adaab* to him. We shook hands. Jennifer said that she was quite sure, even when she had picked me up that morning, that I was going to get the license. Then she laughed and said, I became certain when I saw that you were going to be judged by your brother.

That far-off autumn day came back to me in the car when I was given the ticket after the citizenship ceremony. More than two decades ago. Might have been a day in early October. To celebrate the fact that I now had a license we had gone for lunch to an Indian restaurant on Amsterdam Avenue. I was talking in Hindi to the Punjabi woman who was the owner, and Jennifer joked that after I had had my fill of white women I would return to India to live there and enter an arranged marriage. She imitated a head wobble and began to laugh loudly. She shut her eyes and her mouth formed a rictus. Her face had turned red. I had no idea where this sudden bitterness was coming from—her behavior was unusual but it probably made me think that this was the real Jennifer. It is possible that *that* was the moment when I began to move away.

So, Jennifer, I don't have an Indian wife. And actually I'm a citizen now. This is not to say that you were wrong and I was right but simply that nothing turns out the way we imagine. (It certainly hasn't for me.) But thank you for taking me to the DMV.

Your Honor, this is not a parable. I have narrated this auto story, ha ha, because I was in the car yesterday driving into Saratoga Springs to buy wine. On the car radio there was a report on children learning about death at a grief support center. The children were being encouraged to process the death of a family member. So many kids whose fathers had committed suicide, in some cases with a gun to the head. Today is Father's Day and I can't stop thinking of the voices of the children I heard yesterday. One little girl, the reporter said, had watched her mother have a heart attack. In the playroom at the grief support center, this girl picked up the toy phone and spent the entire session dialing 911. "Hi, 911, my mom's dying. Hurry. Come quick." "Hi, 911, my grandma's dying. Hurry. Come quick." And listening to the show I thought of Jennifer. I said nothing, wrote nothing, to her after she asked me to leave her house. We never talked frankly about anything. The story I'm telling here of the trip to the DMV and to the restaurant is my first step in that direction.

And what of Ehsaan! Ehsaan, beloved by his students—and also the FBI. When he died, Ehsaan was struggling to establish in Pakistan a university that would teach the humanities. The university was never built; according to *The Economist*'s obituary of Ehsaan, he *died before a rupee was raised for it*. If he came close to finding a sudden, unexpected visibility after his death, it happened after the September 11 attacks, when Ehsaan's 1998 speech on terrorism found a new life on the Internet. In that speech, Ehsaan wanted terrorism by disaffected groups to be seen in relation to the much wider, more destructive use of state terrorism. In a characteristic move, he began by pointing out that President Reagan had welcomed the bearded mujahideen from Afghanistan to the White House and called them "the moral equivalent of our Founding Fathers." Then, once the Soviet Union had pulled out from Afghanistan, the same people became terrorists in the eyes of the United States. A host of op-eds quoted Ehsaan in the months after the attacks, calling him "prescient" and "the face of progressive, secular Islam." All this praise compelled me to look on YouTube for footage of Ehsaan in the years before I knew him. There were several clips of him, not just years but decades before the September 11 attacks, warning the United States that the support of covert operations worldwide would one day come back to haunt America. If the U.S. was going to be undemocratic elsewhere, peace was also unlikely at home. In one video of a teach-in from the late seventies, you can see Ehsaan explaining this contradiction by telling his audience: A man cannot be violent and sadistic to his mistress and be gentle to his wife.

Ehsaan had introduced me to the work of Agnes Smedley, and my thesis project had taken me to China. Smedley was tormented by the FBI, and even when she was dead the House Un-American Activities Committee held a posthumous hearing about her. Smedley's biographer has written that it wasn't till the 1970s that, after years of obscurity and historical neglect, *Smedley emerged as an unblemished heroine of the modern women's movement and* Daughter of Earth *was reissued to critical acclaim.* While reading about Smedley's resurrection, I asked myself whether Ehsaan's reputation would enjoy a similar rebirth. Will Ehsaan find fame? When a critic called the writer Richard Stern *almost famous for being not famous* I thought of my old professor.* This book is a token of my fond remembrance. I have seen

---

* Later, I read in Stern's obituary in the *Times* the following comment from Philip Roth, but this reminded me not of what I admired about Ehsaan but about Roth himself: *One of the reasons he never became famous — he was most famous among famous writers — was that his tone was hard to grasp, and some readers didn't feel morally settled,* Mr. Roth said, *not because he was difficult or abstruse but because he was generous to all his characters. And that befuddled them.* (On second thought, these words apply to Ehsaan too. His generosity to all parties baffled the righteous guardians on both the left and the right.)

the declassified FBI files on Ehsaan's activities in this country. There is no element of doubt in those files, or much of ambivalence; certainly there is no feeling; the masked writer of those reports, name redacted, the anonymous hack of the state, isn't required to risk vulnerability. All of which is understandable, of course, but my purpose here is to engage in magical thinking.

I'm back on a plane that has now reached New York City. I'm returning from a research trip to China. The young woman I'm in love with is neither from my country nor from the country where I'm now living. Our countries have in the past fought wars, and our meeting here in New York City is the result of border crossings. We are working with a mentor we adore. My lover is in her university apartment and when I look out of the plane's window I do so with the certain knowledge that of the millions of glittering lights beneath me there is one light that is hers. This naïve thought might be the result of my long travel, this sense of exhaustion that I've endured during my research. It's also possible that, just a generation removed from rural life, I am dazzled by the trappings of urban civilization. In our mentor's class, a line from Trotsky: Yet every time a peasant's horse shies in terror before the blinding lights of an automobile on the Russian road at night, a conflict of two cultures is reflected in the episode. I am and I am *not* the peasant; I am *never* not the horse. I marvel at the fact that there is one phone number, the right numbers in the right combination given to the phone operator, which will make the phone ring in the room of the one person in the world who is waiting for me. All of that is true. But there's more that I want in that moment. I want to present my best self to my lover, and tired as I am, I want to sleep with my limbs entangled in hers. As I look out of the plane window into the night, I can taste her in my mouth.

=====

But first a question: aren't we condemned to repeat our stories and write the same book over and over again? Or, to put it differently, don't we fall in love every time with the same person and make the same mistakes? I sometimes feel that all my life I've been faithful only to the fact of this experience — so that all my nostalgia is for my familiar struggles and my all-too-familiar failings. An account of what is familiar becomes the story of one's life. *It is life*. I have always wanted to be in love; all I have managed to do is tell a story. That is not entirely accurate. I'm like the monkey who, crouching in front of a mirror, tries on a hat. He is only imitating his master. But the monkey has plans for this summer night. Although it is difficult to think clearly, or to remember previous nights, not least because his idea of who he is *or was* is mixed up with what he thinks he must become, he would like to step out precisely at 7:00. He will pause to sniff the open air. Then he will sally forth. Hat on his head, arm in arm with someone who knows about his journey, who will turn her head and smile when he starts humming his song.

Author's Note

Immigrant, Montana, doesn't exist. Although I visited the town of Emigrant, Montana, in August 2008, immediately after Barack Obama accepted the Democratic nomination in Denver, I wish to state that the map presented here is faulty. Even the historical account accords only with what is remembered. Memory is real but it is not accurate. It is arguable that history is not accurate either; however, this novel isn't the place to stage that particular debate.

After Barack Obama was elected president I read about his courting Michelle. She was his boss, assigned to advise him during a summer job, but Obama began to ask her if she would go on a date. Before the end of the summer, she agreed to go out for a movie—Spike Lee's *Do the Right Thing*—and an ice-cream cone at Baskin-Robbins. The clipping in my notebook includes these lines: *Vacationing on Martha's Vineyard in 2004, Barack met Spike Lee at a reception. As Michelle has recalled, he told Lee, "I owe you a lot," because, during the movie, Michelle had allowed him to touch her knee.*

Here is a partial list of those to whom I owe a lot:

for providing conditions to write, the Lannan Foundation, the Guggenheim Foundation, United States Artists, the Norman Mailer Center, the Corporation of Yaddo;

for help on sections of an early draft, Jeffrey Renard Allen, Scott Dahlie, Sheba Karim, Siddhartha Chowdhury;

for reading the final manuscript, Karan Mahajan, Kiran Desai;

for their various acts of encouragement and friendship over the years, my thanks to Rob Nixon, David Means, Ken Chen, Amit Chaudhuri, Teju Cole;

also, for their support, Ian Jack, Rick Simonson, Suketu Mehta, Erin Edmison;

for early conversations about Eqbal Ahmad, Zia Mian, Dohra Ahmed, Robin Varghese, Julie Diamond, Anthony Arnove;

for bringing out the Indian edition, Shruti Debi, David Davidar (again), Aienla Ozukum, Simar Puneet, and Bena Sareen;

at Faber, the singular Lee Brackstone, and at Knopf, the inestimable pair of Sonny Mehta and Timothy O'Connell, and also the wonderful Anna Kaufman, no simple thank-you will suffice;

and, for making all this happen, David Godwin, Susanna Lea, and Lisette Verhagen at DGA.

This novel is about love, and since love comes at a price, I acknowledge my enormous and unpayable debt to my loving family, particularly Mona, Ila, and Rahul.

Most quotations are accompanied by attributions in the body of the text. Where the source isn't provided, as with clippings from notebooks, a simple Google search will do the job.

In addition to the titles mentioned in the novel, I have used the following books: Grace Paley, *Just As I Thought;* Elmore Leonard, *Rum Punch;* David Omissi, ed., *Indian Voices of the Great War: Soldiers' Letters, 1914–18;* Harold A. Gould, *Sikhs, Swamis, Students, and Spies;* William O'Rourke, *The Harrisburg 7 and the New Catholic Left.* The reference in a footnote to a Pico Iyer quote comes from *The Global Soul: Jet Lag, Shopping Malls, and the Search for Home,* and the response to it is taken from a review essay by Kai Friese, "Globetrotter's Nama," *Outlook,* August 28, 2000; the art installation *Hunan School* is very much inspired by Ilya Kabakov's remarkable *School No. 6* at the Chinati Foundation in Marfa, Texas; I had enjoyed my exchange with Yu Hua at the Asia Society and I have quoted from his essay on Lu Xun; a malicious but accurate remark is borrowed from Paul Theroux's entertaining book *Sir Vidia's Shadow.* Ehsaan Ali is a fictional character, but parts of him are based on my interviews with family, friends, and former students of Eqbal Ahmad; I have relied upon Eqbal Ahmad, *Confronting Empire: Interviews with David Barsamian;* I also interviewed Stuart Schaar, who is the author of *Eqbal Ahmad: Critical Outsider in a Turbulent Age;* my thanks to the staff at the Hampshire College archives for showing me the letter written by John Berger. I have drawn upon Ruth Price's excellent *The Lives of Agnes Smedley* while recasting details of Smedley's loves. Unless otherwise indicated, use has been made here of found images and I will make grateful acknowledgment if any further debts are owed.

"'Don't mess with Mr. In-Between,' my father would often advise me, but it seems to me that Mr. In-Between is precisely where we all live now." So writes David Shields in *Reality Hunger*. This is a work of fiction as well as nonfiction, an in-between novel by an in-between writer.

Illustration Credits

with HarperCollins Publishers India Private Limited
from the book *The Pather Panchali Sketchbook,* edited by
Sandip Ray and first published by them in association
with Society for Preservation of Satyajit Ray Archives
© Sandip Ray, 2016

A Note About the Author

Amitava Kumar is a writer and journalist. He was born in Ara and grew up in the nearby town of Patna, famous for its corruption, crushing poverty, and delicious mangoes. Kumar is the author of several books of nonfiction and a novel. He lives in Poughkeepsie, in upstate New York, where he is Helen D. Lockwood Professor of English at Vassar College. In 2016 Amitava Kumar was awarded a Guggenheim Fellowship (General Nonfiction) as well as a Ford Fellowship in Literature from United States Artists.

A Note on the Type

This book was set in Hoefler Text, a family of fonts designed by Jonathan Hoefler, who was born in 1970. First designed in 1991, Hoefler Text was intended as an advancement on existing desktop computer typography, including as it does an exponentially larger number of glyphs than previous fonts. In form, Hoefler Text looks to the old-style fonts of the seventeenth century, but it is wholly of its time, employing a precision and sophistication only available to the late twentieth century.

Composed by North Market Street Graphics, Lancaster, Pennsylvania

Printed and bound by Berryville Graphics, Berryville, Virginia

Designed by Anna B. Knighton